Cassie watched as he walked through the mall, in, but not of, the holiday traffic. He stood perfectly still as he rode the escalator down one level, the escalator depositing him just on the fringe of Santa's Workshop. Without appearing to muscle anyone out of his way, Little Mack glided through the crowd and suddenly was standing at Santa's side, patting the slight bulge in his suit jacket (right where Cassie imagined a shoulder holster would be located) and whispering in his ear.

Looking down on the scene from her spot at the railing, Cassie could see the alarm in Santa's eyes. She watched as Santa put up the rope at the front of the line, the one with the sign that said, "back in fifteen minutes." She saw the elves start to argue with Santa. An elf even tried to unhook the rope, but Little Mack reached out with one hand and the argument stopped. Little Mack put an arm around Santa and maneuvered through the crowd.

No one dared to tell Little Mack that Santa wasn't scheduled for a break yet. Then one clear voice spoke up for the children. "Hold it right there!"

The crowd of children waiting to see Santa moved aside. In his brown mall of New Jersey security guard uniform, Oliver Berryhill stood at the edge of Santa's Workshop. He screwed up his courage and locked eyes with Little Mack. "Santa's not going anywhere just now."

Cassie looked at her watch. It was noon. High noon.

I0545584

I'd like to thank the many authors and editors, booksellers and librarians, readers, bloggers and friends who have helped to make me a better writer. I'd especially like to thank my wife, Carol, who read the earliest version of the manuscript and told me which parts worked and which parts didn't. Hopefully I was paying attention.

It's Beginning to Look a Lot Like Murder
A Cassie O'Malley Mystery

by JEFF MARKOWITZ

GORDIAN KNOT BOOKS

Dedication

To my son Josh, who reads Ovid and Cicero, Dickens and Dostoyevsky, but who still finds time to enjoy the Cassie O'Malley Mysteries.

Turkey and Gravy Soda

Thursday morning, Tommy awoke alone in his studio apartment and listened to his telephone ring. He was dreaming that the phone was ringing and then gradually he realized that it really was ringing. It was a cheap phone, with a cheap ring, more buzz than ring, and it was persistent. He swatted at the phone and cursed, knowing that she would not give up. It would not be his girlfriend on the line (thank God for that). His girlfriend, Bobbie, was angry and no longer talking to him. Tommy had no doubt who was on the line. Weary, after too few hours of sleep, Tommy picked up the receiver.

"What do you want Greta?"

"How do you know it's me?" Greta growled in his ear.

"Am I wrong?" Tommy sighed. "What do you want?"

Greta's laugh was throaty and phlegmatic, too many cigarettes, too many meds. "What do I—grr—want? What I want is—grr—a vacation in Maui, a Lexus, a . . ."

Tommy interrupted Greta's wish list. "My bad, Greta. I shouldn't have asked. We both know I don't give a damn what you want. But that's not why you called. Right?"

"No, that's—grr—not why I called."

"So why did you call me at . . ." Tommy looked at his alarm clock and groaned, "Seven-thirty? Surely not to wish me a Happy Thanksgiving."

Greta got to the point. "You're way behind in your damn child support payments."

"I'm doing the best I . . ."

Greta was not in the mood. "Grr—you're not doing shit and you know it."

"Okay Greta. Let's say you're right. I'm a deadbeat dad. I'm not gonna argue the point. So what do you say we skip over the general bullshit and you tell me why you've chosen this particular morning to bust my balls, okay?"

"Tommy Junior is marching in the parade today," Greta said. "I called—grr—to remind you to turn on your television."

"Shit, Greta. I know that. I'll be watching." Looking for a piece of paper, Tommy scribbled a reminder on the palm of his right hand.

"And if they get a shot of his feet on TV, I want you to notice he's the only kid in the band wearing sneakers. You got that Tommy? Your son needs band shoes. Send me a damn check." Greta slammed the receiver back in its cradle.

Tommy hung up the phone just in time to hear the knocking at his front door. Neither especially loud nor insistent, Tommy recognized the deliberate style of the Macks. He opened the door slowly, and found two men just outside the door, crowding out Tommy's view of the world beyond. The men were big. Huge. Refrigerators in blue pinstripes and Italian sunglasses. Tommy had fallen behind in his payments.

The Macks were a family business, father and son loan sharks and freelance enforcers. Big Mack was approaching sixty from the wrong side. Part Irishman, part Choctaw Indian, at six foot tall, two eighty, he was built like the proverbial brick shithouse and, even now, approaching retirement, remained the muscle of the team. Big Mack loved to hit.

Little Mack was his youngest, and only living, son. The three older boys all died in combat—Ernie in Nam, Billy in Iraq and Eddie in a hooker's bed in the Ironbound section of Newark. Little Mack had outgrown his father by the time he was fifteen. In his early thirties, he was six-six and weighed three forty-five. Despite his size, Little Mack's role, until his father retired, was to be the mouthpiece.

Tommy understood why the Macks were at his door early on a Thanksgiving morning. Without waiting, Tommy rolled into action.

"Heh, heh, it's the Macks. My two favorite all-beef Paddies. Long time no see boys. How the hell are ya? Still hittin' the special sauce?"

Little Mack stepped inside and grunted a terse, "Fuck you, Tommy." Big Mack merely nodded and rubbed his knuckles.

"Look, boys," Tommy said, "it's great to see ya, and I'd love to shoot the shit with a coupla sparkling wits like yourselves, but it's Thanksgiving. I ain't got time for a Mack attack today."

"Hold your water, Tommy. This ain't gonna take long." Little Mack spoke softly, his voice a hoarse whisper. His father, standing in the doorway, filling the doorway, rubbed his hands impatiently.

"My dad ain't real happy with you, Tommy. You let him down. You let us down. You were supposed to make a payment last week. Here it is Thursday, and you still ain't made good on the debt."

Tommy was ready with an answer. He only hoped the Macks were in a Thanksgiving sort of mood. "Here's the thing, boys. I got a job." Big Mack barely moved, but Tommy saw, in the tilt of his head, that Big Mack was impressed.

"Yeah, I start work tomorrow."

Little Mack asked, "Who's the numbnuts what hired you Tommy?"

And Tommy said, "I got a job at the mall." When Little Mack made no comment, Tommy explained. "Startin' next week, I can make a payment every week. Every week," he repeated for emphasis.

Little Mack barely moved his lips. "We'll be in touch." Big Mack nodded, and with that, the Macks were gone.

Tommy closed the door.

Tommy mentally made a list of the things he was thankful for this year.

His ex-wife was hassling him for money he did not have, but she would just have to wait her turn. Tommy owed money all over town. Greta was annoying, but she wasn't especially dangerous. On the other hand, Tommy's bookie was less annoying than Greta, but capable of causing him real pain. And as bad as the Macks could be, neither measured up to the danger that was his current girlfriend. Bobbie was withholding sex until he completed anger management class. *And how does that make you feel?*, they asked him that first night in class. *Like hittin' something*, he told them. His health was bad in indeterminate ways and his medical coverage had been cancelled. His bank account was a joke. Tommy was six months behind in child support. The state of New Jersey had suspended his driver's license. At least he had a job at the mall, now that the holiday was here.

Tommy looked at the bottle of turkey and gravy soda in the fridge and shuddered at the possibilities. He put a Swanson Hungry Man turkey dinner in the microwave and turned on the television, flipping back and forth between the parade and ESPN. He tried to put a bet down on the Detroit Lions game, but his bookie had cut him off. Happy Thanksgiving.

His boy, Tommy Junior, fifteen and a sophomore in high school, was somewhere in the long line of marching bands in the Macy's parade. Tommy had forgotten about the parade until his ex-wife called. A trombone should be easy to spot, he told himself, but Tommy could not find Tommy Junior on TV that morning. He did, however, see a couple of decent marching bands and all the really good balloons . . . Kermit the Frog, SpongeBob SquarePants, Garfield, Al Roker.

And, of course, at the end of the parade, Tommy watched Santa Claus arrive at Herald Square. Santa's arrival marked the official start of the Christmas season, a month of peace, of brotherhood, of good will, and, for Tommy, a month to show his girlfriend he could manage his anger, to show the Macks he could pay his debts thanks to a month working as a department store Santa at the Mall of New Jersey.

Tommy watched the football games. With no action on the games, he found that football did not hold his interest anymore. He re-considered the bottle of turkey and gravy soda, mixing it, one part soda and two parts Jack Daniels. Tommy lit a Newport and fell asleep in front of the television.

Big-Ass Cigar

"**Y**ou missed another meeting, O'Malley." Everything the new owner-slash-editor of the recently re-titled *Jersey Knews Magazine* knew about publishing he learned at the movies. In the movies, the editor always called his writers by their last name. Cassie O'Malley pictured Jack Cambrian on the other end of the phone . . . his rumpled white shirt, the top button unbuttoned, tie loose at the neck, suspenders, wide-brimmed fedora, and Arturo Fuente maduro. Jack Cambrian was never without his big-ass cigar.

Cassie cupped her hand over the telephone receiver to muffle the sound. "Asshole."

"What was that O'Malley? I can't hear you."

Cassie removed her hand and sighed. "Do we really have to do this again? Can't we just agree to disagree? You know I don't come to staff meetings."

Jack Cambrian snorted. "Listen to me, O'Malley," he said, not unkindly, "it's been a year already since I bought the *Knews,* and I'm getting pretty tired of you telling me how Morris used to do things. Morris is gone. It's time for you to accept that O'Malley."

Cassie bit her tongue. She couldn't accept that Morris had sold her magazine. To Cassie, never mind who owned the *Jersey Knews*, it was her magazine. Morris, at least, had been good at the job. Cassie waited for the inevitable question. Jack Cambrian didn't disappoint. "Do you want to write for my magazine?"

Cassie had been asking herself that very question. It had been a full year, and Cassie still couldn't find common ground with her new boss. "Yes, Mr. Cambrian."

"So you'll start coming to the meetings?"

"Yes, boss."

She could see Jack Cambrian smile through the receiver. "You don't like me very much, do you, O'Malley?" he asked.

Cassie considered the question carefully before responding. Until Morris sold the magazine, there were two things Cassie could count on. One, that her personal life was a disaster. Two, that her job was a refuge from that disaster. Now that Jack Cambrian owned the magazine, there was only one thing on which Cassie could count. She poured an inch of Tullamore Dew into her coffee cup before responding. "To be honest, I don't know you well enough to like you or dislike you, sir. Maybe, if you took the time to explain what you're trying to do with the magazine, I would be more enthusiastic."

"Maybe if you came to the damn meetings . . ." Jack Cambrian immediately regretted his answer. Once upon a time, Cassie O'Malley had brought readers to the magazine. She could do it again. "I'll have to give that some thought, O'Malley."

Jack Cambrian debated how much more he wanted to say. "When I bought the magazine, Morris asked me to be patient with you . . . he told me you'd just come through a bad time. Well, O'Malley, it's been a year. You know what I think? I think we've both got some decisions to make. Me . . . I've gotta decide how much longer to carry you, waiting for you to produce. Your decisions, if you don't mind my telling you this, are a lot bigger. You're still a young woman. Do you really want to spend the rest of your life hiding in your condo, in an old pair of sweats, nursing a shot of Irish whiskey?"

Cassie wondered how Jack Cambrian knew. She put down her coffee cup of whiskey. There was an awkward moment of silence, the phone and other connections tenuous.

Cassie hated to have to ask. "So what's my story assignment?"

"The mall, O'Malley, the mall at Christmastime." Jack Cambrian paused, almost disappointed when Cassie voiced no objection to the crummy assignment. "Oh, and by the way," Jack Cambrian added by way of good-bye, "Happy Thanksgiving."

The Scarlet Letter

Mayor Harbrough peeked in the window of her stainless steel oven at the twenty-pound golden-brown butterball turkey resting comfortably inside. Turning to her guests, Cheyenne announced with thinly disguised pride, "It's almost done. Can I freshen anyone's drink?

Silently, Cassie handed Cheyenne her glass. Cheyenne dumped the melting ice cubes and poured Cassie a new Jameson's and rocks. Cheyenne noticed that the whiskey level inside the bottle of Jameson's was diminishing rapidly. She was not alarmed—Cheyenne had long known Cassie to be a heavy drinker—but she was disturbed that Cassie's drinking of late seemed to be so . . . Cheyenne searched for the right word . . . so unproductive. Cassie seemed no more drunk than when she had arrived for Thanksgiving dinner with the mayor. Neither drunker, nor happier, as though the Irish whiskey were simply a way to mark time. With a fresh drink in hand, Cassie wandered down the hall to check the score of the Cowboys game.

Cheyenne was grateful for the private moment with her dad. Cheyenne's dad, the Harbrough in Harbrough and Daughter Property Development Inc., was nursing a Ketel One martini, dry with a twist. He waited until Cassie left the kitchen. "Did you call your mother? Is she coming?"

"Mom should be here any minute now." Cheyenne didn't understand anything about her parents' separation. She didn't understand it when her mother had announced that her marriage of near forty years had been a mistake. And she certainly didn't understand why her father had insisted that Cheyenne invite them both for Thanksgiving.

Stephen Harbrough tried yet again to explain it to his daughter. "I have loved your mother for four decades, but I have not always honored that love. You have to tend to love or one day, you wake up and realize that your wife of forty years is a stranger. There's a difference between sharing a bed and sharing a life." He shook his head, saddened by his failure. "But we still share a daughter. And we can still share a turkey dinner."

Cheyenne hugged her father. She turned her attention back to the tur-key, surreptitiously wiping her eyes with the kitchen towel.

Cheyenne heard the front door open. That would be her Mother letting herself in. In another life, the well-endowed Cheyenne Harbrough could have modeled for the painter Rubens. In another life, Cheyenne's mother, Rae, thin as her daughter was plump, had modeled . . . for Andy Warhol.

"It's me," Rae said, announcing her arrival. "I hope you don't mind, but I brought a date." From behind her, a tall white-haired gentleman with thin lips and a carefully modulated smile introduced himself. "Hello. I'm Charles Meriwether, the third. You may call me Chas."

Cheyenne kissed her mother and greeted Mr. Meriwether. "Welcome. Please make yourself comfortable while I set another place at the table."

Cheyenne pushed her chair back from the table and surveyed the scene in her dining room. Twenty pounds of turkey were largely gone. There would be barely enough leftover to make a decent sandwich. The sweet potatoes cooked in cognac were gone, the stuffing gone, the crescent rolls gone, the green beans almandine gone. There was, however, an ample supply of uneaten cranberry. In a town dotted with cranberry bogs, the cranberry was critical to Doah's economy. It might cost her votes in the next election, but Mayor Cheyenne Harbrough was no fan of the cranberry.

Considering the guest list, Thanksgiving dinner had been remark-ably peaceful. At the far end of the table, her father picked absently at a turkey wing. On her left, Cassie refilled her wine glass with a modest merlot, laughing at a private joke. On her right, her mother, the former Mrs. Harbrough, and her date Charles Meriwether the third were arguing quietly.

"Is everything okay?" Cheyenne asked.

Mr. Meriwether came straight to the point. "I couldn't help but notice that you didn't say grace tonight."

Drawing on her considerable mayoral charm, Cheyenne did her best to sound pleasant when she responded. "No."

"Do you mind if I ask why?"

Cheyenne wondered what her mother saw in her dinner companion. "You are a guest in my home, Mr. Meriwether . . ." Cheyenne refrained from adding, *an uninvited guest.* "My reasons are my own and, I mean no disrespect, but they are none of your business."

Cheyenne's mother stood up suddenly. "Cheyenne! I will not . . . I believe you owe Chas an apology."

Cheyenne was ready for an argument. She had been ready from the moment her mother had walked in with Mr. Meriwether in tow. And she had been remarkably tolerant, she knew, of her mother's prissy dinner companion.

Mr. Harbrough watched the storm gathering force in his daughter's eyes. "Do you remember high school English, Cheyenne?"

Cheyenne smiled, knowing immediately what story her father was about to tell.

Mr. Harbrough continued. "Your class was reading *The Scarlet Letter.*" Mr. Harbrough turned to his ex-wife's dinner date. "In case you're not familiar with the book, Hester Prynne had to wear a scarlet 'A' around her neck, as punishment for committing the sin of adultery so that she might be ostracized by her community."

Mr. Meriwether bit down on his lower lip, saying nothing.

Mr. Harbrough looked straight at Mr. Meriwether. "Cheyenne's assign-ment was to identify a sin that she had committed, to design the letter and then to wear it all day in school."

Mr. Meriwether said, "How interesting," but it was clear that he found nothing of interest in the story.

Mr. Harbrough turned to his daughter smiling. "You left for school that morning wearing a giant letter 'H.' Do you remember what the 'H' stood for, Cheyenne?"

Cheyenne looked at her dad with a wicked grin. She remembered. "Heathen."

Mr. Harbrough sat back in his chair, the proud parent, beaming. "That's my girl!"

Mr. Meriwether nearly spat out his coffee. "Surely you believe in God, don't you, Mayor Harbrough? Especially on this day of thanks. Who else should we give our thanks to?"

Cheyenne's mother turned sharply on her companion. "Of course my daughter believes in God. Don't you dear?"

Cheyenne wasn't sure what she believed. Religion was not a powerful force in her life. She had not given much thought to the subject of God. "I guess I believe there is a 'that which is knowable' and a 'that which is unknowable.' If you want to call the unknowable God, I guess I'm okay with that." She paused, gathering her thoughts. "But if you want to attribute divine knowl-edge to that unknowable . . . special powers . . . intentionality . . . well, no, I guess I don't really believe in that God."

"Cheyenne!" Mother stared at daughter.

"Don't give me that, Mother. You never gave a rat's ass for religion. At least you didn't until you began dating this . . . this . . ." Cheyenne sputtered to a stop.

Mr. Meriwether's face turned crimson. "Rae?"

Cassie had been sitting at the dining room table, sipping merlot and quietly watching the argument blossom. "I wonder what's happening in the football game." She was halfway out of her chair, when it became obvious that no one was ready for some football.

Rae came to her dinner date's defense. "Cheyenne, I will not have you speak to my . . ." And Rae paused, looking for the right word to describe their relationship. ". . . my friend Chas in such a tone. I raised you better than that."

Chas stood. "Get the coats, Rae. We're leaving."

Rae made no move to leave.

"Now, Rae."

Stephen Harbrough did his best to look away, embarrassed for his ex-wife, for his daughter, for himself.

Finally Rae stood up from the table. "Dinner was lovely, Cheyenne."

Chas Meriwether walked quickly to the door. One hand on the doorknob, he turned to face his hostess. "I will pray for you, Madam Mayor."

Santa on the Shuttle Bus

Friday morning, Tommy awoke alone, hung over and, inexplicably, happy to be alive. He looked at the red suit hanging on his door. Tommy thought it unlikely he would be recognized at the mall, but he was inclined to be cautious. Tommy decided it would be smart to arrive at the mall white-whiskered and red-suited. Half an hour later, he was on his way to the Mall of New Jersey, Santa, AKA Tommy V. on a suspended license, behind the wheel of his 1996 Plymouth. He parked at the off-site employee lot, riding the employee shuttle to the mall itself, Santa on the shuttle bus, ho-ho-ho.

Santa's Workshop was overrun with children, eagerly awaiting his arrival, some climbing on the giant candy canes, some punching their little brothers and others hopping up and down in urinary distress. All the while, their parents, yelling at the elves, demanded Santa's immediate attention.

"Ho. Ho. Ho." Tommy settled into his special Santa chair, truly the king of all he surveyed. "Okay, who's first?"

One by one, the kids climbed on his lap, with their earnest innocence and their special requests.

"Play Station 2."

"Malibu Barbie."

"A red bicycle."

"An iPod."

"A puppy dog."

After a while, the kids all seemed to run together, an endless line of innocent desire.

"Harry Potter."

"Operation."

"Electronic battleship."

"My mommy says I'm supposed to ask for my grandpa to get well."

Santa looked at the young boy on his lap. "I'm sorry. What was that?"

The little boy with the blond buzz cut repeated his request. "My mommy says I'm supposed to ask for my grandpa to get well."

Santa looked more closely at the kid sitting on his lap. "What's your name, kid?"

"Tommy."

Santa almost blurted out, *me too*, until he remembered his name, for the moment, was Santa.

Santa spotted an older man with thinning hair, a caved-in chest and hacking cough. "Is that your grandfather?"

The boy shook his head vigorously from side to side. "No." He pointed to a man standing off to one side, a middle-aged man with a blond buzz cut, broad shoulders, rock hard, with just the traces of impending weight gain. "Him."

Santa examined the man with interest. "He looks okay to me."

Tommy fidgeted, suddenly shy sitting on Santa's lap. "Am I allowed to ask for two things?"

Santa asked, "Have you been a good boy this year?"

Tommy smiled sweetly, playing to his audience of one. "I've been double good."

Santa smiled. "Go for it, kid."

"A Dell dimension 4700 with a 3.2 gigahertz Pentium processor and a flat panel monitor."

In the first hour, Santa, aka Tommy V., estimated he must have had a hundred whining kids on his lap, a hundred demanding moms on his case. His eyes traveled along the nearly infinite line of kids waiting for Santa, scanning for MILFs. *I can't effing believe what I have to do to satisfy my girlfriend.* Santa signaled to the photographer.

Santa was on a break. It had been a difficult morning, the crowd larger and more demanding than he expected, even for Black Friday. It was as if a year of lingering disappointment had been unleashed on this first day of lap sitting and gift listing. Santa felt like he was the world's complaint department.

Santa was on a break, but it took no great intellect to realize, with his white beard and red suit, there was no break for Santa. Anywhere he might venture in the mall, Santa Claus was still on duty. Eating a slice of pizza in the food court, he was Santa. Reading magazines in the bookstore, Santa. Looking for blue jeans in the Gap, Santa. Shoplifting cigarettes in the drug store, Santa.

Tommy V. had barely finished the first morning of the first shift of the first official shopping day of the holiday season, and he was already rethinking his decision to spend a month at the mall.

Standing at the urinal, he was still Santa and he still drew attention. Tommy always had trouble pissing in public. He ducked into a stall, grateful for a precious few minutes of privacy. When the men's room emptied, Tommy considered lighting up a Newport, but the beard was too much trouble. He sat in the stall lost in thought, grateful for a seated moment without a child squirming on his lap.

Fully clothed he sat in the stall; inexplicably he started to sing. "You better watch out, you better not cry, you better not pout, I'm telling you why . . ."

From just outside the stall, someone picked up the tune.

"Santa Claus is coming to town."

Peering under the door, Tommy saw two pair of legs, tree trunks really, a small forest of legs, under the door.

"Get the fuck out here, Santa. Now." Tommy didn't immediately recognize the voice. He could handle this, he told himself.

When Tommy opened the door, he discovered that the voice was attached to the Big Mack and Big Mack was attached to a Smith & Wesson 686P.

"Get out here." The normally mute Big Mack was enjoying this way too much.

Tommy was genuinely confused. "What the fu—"

"Get out here," Big Mack repeated.

Tommy had not led an exemplary life. Still, he had never stared into the barrel of a handgun before. "C'mon. Put the gun away. Shit, what if someone walks in here?"

"Shut the fuck up." This time he pointed with the gun. "Now."

Little Mack looked at his dad. "It's okay, you can put the gun away. Tommy's not gonna be trouble." He turned to Tommy. "Are ya?"

Tommy vigorously shook his head. "Me? Trouble? Of course not."

Little Mack laughed. "Look at you. When you said you had a job at the mall . . . Santa-fucking-Claus. What's the world coming to?"

"So what can I do for you boys today?" asked Tommy, still standing inside the stall, the door propped open to talk with the Macks.

Little Mack explained. "My dad and I talked. We decided to make sure you were telling the trut' about a job." Little Mack laughed again, a rumble deep in his throat. "I love the way you look in red." Little Mack examined the Santa suit. "Come on out here and give us a show, Tommy."

Tommy reluctantly came out of the stall.

"Give us a look." And Little Mack motioned with his arm for Tommy to do a three-sixty. Slowly Tommy showed off his Santa suit, from all angles.

Little Mack grunted his approval. Big Mack nodded. "This'll be perfect Tommy. Here's the deal. We're prepared to take a payment every week until you're paid up."

Tommy tried to express his thanks, but Little Mack wasn't done yet. "But there's somethin' else you gotta do for us."

"What I gotta do?"

Little Mack said, "Here's the thing, Tommy. While you're in the mall, my dad wants you to do some Christmas shopping for him."

Tommy was confused. "Is that all?"

Little Mack grinned. "He's got a pretty long shopping list."

Tommy had a bad feeling, but he had to ask. "So what? I'm supposed to buy the stuff and then what? You gonna count it against my debt?"

The rumble started again in Little Mack's throat. "You're a pretty funny guy, Tommy. No . . . you're gonna pay up every dollar you owe us. And then, because of the inconvenience you caused, you're also gonna boost some stuff from the mall, electronics mostly and some jewelry."

Big Mack brought the meeting to a close with the slightest nod of his balding head and exited the men's room without waiting for Tommy's response.

Little Mack stared at Tommy. "We'll be in touch." Little Mack turned abruptly and heavy-stepped off after his dad.

Doing Thirty in the Fast Lane

When Cassie agreed to meet Cheyenne for breakfast at the Eggery, she did not intend to eat. Thanksgiving still sat heavy in her stomach. The waitress did her best to push the specials—"We have—grrr—turkey hash, turkey pancakes and egg 'n' turkey sandwiches"—but Cassie was not tempted.

"I'll just have coffee this morning, and lots of it." She looked across the table at Cheyenne who ordered a bran muffin with her coffee. "I was surprised you didn't invite a guy to Thanksgiving dinner."

Cheyenne frowned. "I had this pipe dream about getting my parents back together."

Cassie sipped her coffee. "I guess when your mom showed up with a date . . ." Cassie didn't bother to finish her thought.

"Yeah," Cheyenne frowned. "Think about it, Cassie. I'm not dating anyone right now. You're not dating anyone. But my mother's got a date. What the fuck's wrong with us, Cassie?"

Cassie knew there was no simple answer. If the answer was simple, there would have been two more men at the Thanksgiving table. "It's all gotten so damn hard."

Cheyenne nodded. "It wasn't always this hard."

To Cassie, it seemed a lifetime since dating was fun.

Suddenly the waitress was at her elbow with a fresh pot. "More—grrr—coffee?" And without waiting for an answer, she topped up their cups. Cassie sipped her coffee. The second pot was stronger than the first. She added a little sugar and milk.

"Your mom's date got on you pretty heavy. What was that all about?"

"It's the holidays, Cassie. A lot of people are pissed that the town's not setting up the manger again this year."

Cassie was surprised. "That decision was made more than a year ago . . . before you were even elected."

"But it was never really settled." Cheyenne thought back to the ugly arguments during the mayoral campaign. "There are some folks in town think it's not enough to celebrate Christmas in their home and church. They think they have a right to celebrate Christmas at the entrance to the municipal building."

"Is it gonna get nasty again this year?" Cassie wondered.

"I hope not," said Cheyenne.

Cassie took a sip of coffee and changed the subject. "Are things between your parents as bad as they look?"

A cloud crossed Cheyenne's face. "Forty years Cassie. How do you fall out of love after forty years? It doesn't make sense."

Cassie knew how hard the impending divorce would be for Cheyenne. They say divorce is hard on the kids. Even when the kid is nearly forty. "Maybe they just weren't happy, Chey. They deserve to be happy."

Cheyenne wouldn't hear it. "You know my parents for twenty years Cassie. Did they seem unhappy to you?"

Cassie was not in the mood to do this, but she owed her best friend an honest answer. "Maybe not unhappy, but lonely. Your mother seemed lonely, Chey."

Cheyenne had not expected Cassie's answer. "Lonely? Really? I guess I need to think on that."

Cheyenne sipped her coffee and nibbled on her bran muffin. "Maybe you're right, Cassie, but did she have to show up with Charles Meriwether, the third?"

Cassie said, "Sometimes lonely people do desperate things, Chey."

Chey wondered if Cassie was still talking about her mother. "Yeah, I guess."

Cheyenne signaled for the check and got ready to leave. "I'd love to spend the day with you, Cassie. You know, kick back like in the old days, maybe watch a movie, but I've got to make an appearance at the football game." It would not be smart for the mayor to miss the annual Thanksgiving game. Doah Township took its high school football seriously. "Why don't you come with me, Cassie?"

"I can't, Chey. I'm going to the mall."

"Today, of all days? You hate to shop."

Cassie shrugged. "I'm working on a story."

"It's about time." Cheyenne sat back down at the table. "How are things at the magazine?"

Cassie didn't have the energy to explain. "Same old."

"You know, Cass, you never did tell me why Morris sold the magazine."

"Morris said he was tired of the magazine business."

Cheyenne heard the doubt in Cassie's voice. "But?"

"But," Cassie continued, "Morris loved the magazine business."

"So you think it was something else?"

Cassie nodded. "Yeah."

Sitting in her Mustang, Cassie switched off the CD player, saying good-bye to Thelonius Monk. She circled the overcrowded parking lot in search of a spot. Up one row and down the next, a long line of cars, jockeying for position, blocking passage, bending fenders. *Does anyone over the age of fifteen really like coming to the mall?* Finally, a spot opened in a location so remote Cassie was reminded of economy parking at Newark airport. She began the very long walk to the mall entrance.

Cassie understood what Jack Cambrian wanted: a warm and fuzzy holiday tale about the Christmas shoppers, about peace on earth, good will toward men, with a special focus on stores that bought ads in his magazine. Cassie longed for the pre-Cambrian era at the magazine, when she got to write stories about more important subjects, things like space aliens and Siamese triplets. It's no wonder she wasn't going to the staff meetings.

Taking her time as she strolled in the mall, Cassie allowed herself to experience the full insanity that was Black Friday. She felt like an old lady doing thirty in the fast lane, shoppers with their strollers filled with boxes and bags, their toddlers toddling to keep up, shoppers on her tail, pushing her to accelerate, honking for her to pull over and let them get by.

Cassie was developing a feeling about the mall at Christmastime, about the shoppers making this holiday pilgrimage; she was feeling many things, but none of those feelings could honestly be described as warm and fuzzy.

Cassie located an empty seat at the edge of the food court, a seat near the railing, overlooking Santa's Workshop in the lower vestibule, and sat down to make a few notes. From her seat up above the workshop, she watched the line of children snaking its way around the North Pole, boys and girls waiting for their turn with Santa Claus. Happy children, nervous children, eager children, terrified children, boys and girls waiting for the chance to share their secret gift wish with Santa, the meeting to be commemorated with an eight-by-ten digital photo costing their parents a mere $9.95. It was yet one more example of the cheesy commercialization of Christmas, but for just a brief moment, Cassie allowed herself to remember what it felt like to be a girl of ten, dressed in her best party frock, sitting on Santa's lap, asking for a Beatles album and a Cabbage Patch doll. Cassie spent the better part of an hour watching the children meet Santa. She watched Santa, the center of attention in his workshop, and then she watched him on a break, as he tried without success to blend in, to be just another overweight shopper in a red suit and white beard, but children followed wherever he might go, even to the very door of the men's room.

The Mall of New Jersey, Director's Cut

Oliver Berryhill loved his job as security at the Mall of New Jersey, loved strolling amongst the shoppers dressed in his neatly pressed brown Mall of New Jersey security uniform, carrying his official Mall of New Jersey walkie-talkie, munching on his Mall of New Jersey waffle fries and drinking Mall of New Jersey coffee. Mall security was a great job, even on Black Friday. Nothing ever happened, and Oliver liked it that way. It gave him plenty of time to think about his screenplay. Oliver was going to make movies. The security job was merely a way to pay the rent. Nothing ever happened other than the occasional shoplifter and even that, Oliver knew, was handled by store security. He was mall security.

Oliver viewed the mall through an imaginary camera lens, using his job to practice framing his shots: *The Mall of New Jersey, Director's Cut*. The movie always started early in the morning, before the stores opened with senior citizen mall walkers making the circuit. Oliver liked to start with a tight shot of the walkers, typically two elderly women in their lavender Liz Claibornes, and then he would pull back on the shot, revealing the awakening mall around them, panning across the broad open space that would later be filled with shoppers.

And then there were the scenes of morning managers preparing to open their shops, checking the inventory, fixing the displays, sipping their morning cups of coffee.

Oliver Berryhill framed dozens of shots every day and remembered each and every shot.

On Black Friday, Oliver's camera lens moved effortlessly from wide shots of Santa's Workshop to tight shots of the children's faces as they climbed up on Santa's lap. He filmed Santa on his break, eating pizza in the food court, browsing through magazines in the bookstore, shopping for blue jeans at the Gap. Oliver Berryhill's camera lens followed Santa to the door of the men's room, but not inside. Oliver Berryhill didn't make that kind of movie.

Oliver loved picking out a shopper and filming her day at the mall, but Oliver had no interest in documenting the life of yet another frustrated south Jersey housewife. While she picked out shoes or flatware or panties, Oliver filled in the most extraordinary back-story. Seen through his eyes, the typical mall shopper had a secret life as a supermodel or a CIA operative or a porn star.

Back at the food court, through his camera lens, Oliver spied a good-looking woman with dirty-blond hair. Oliver pegged her for her late thirties. She was thin enough for real life, but a couple of pounds too heavy for the movies. In the midst of the Black Friday bustle, this woman was detached, like Oliver, a spectator to the mall madness. Oliver tried, without success, to imagine her back-story.

An older man approached the lady in the food court. In Oliver's movie, he was a film noir private eye, or a racketeer, waving his cigar like a piece. The Mall of New Jersey was a no-smoking mall, but the cigar didn't appear to Oliver to be lit. He made no move to intervene, allowing the imaginary film to roll.

"I was hoping to find you here, O'Malley."

Cassie looked up from her note pad. "Mr. Cambrian." She nodded her head in greeting. "I must say I'm surprised to find you at the mall."

Mr. Cambrian smiled and reached for an empty chair. "May I join you?"

"Of course." Cassie pushed her note papers to one side, clearing a spot at the table.

They sat at the edge of the food court in silence, watching the holiday traffic swirling below, forming eddies around Santa's Workshop. Finally, Jack Cambrian spoke up.

"I think that's the story," he said pointing to the children waiting to meet Santa.

"I guess." Cassie was unconvinced.

"No, really. Christmas as seen through the eyes of a child." Mr. Cambrian paused. "Maybe it's not the most original idea. But I'd like you to give it a try. Spend a couple of weeks observing Santa's Workshop. Somewhere on that line of children, there's a story. Okay O'Malley?"

"Okay, Mr. Cambrian. Maybe I'll find a space alien."

Jack Cambrian laughed. "Maybe you will, O'Malley. Maybe you will."

White Gold

Cassie spent the next week at the Mall of New Jersey, and she saw many things. Or more to the point, she saw one thing many times, as one by one each little boy or girl climbed on Santa's lap and revealed a young heart's desires, but she did not find a space alien and she did not find a story. Gradually as she watched, Cassie's focus shifted from the endless boys and girls to the ever-patient Santa. The first few kids were probably fun, Cassie decided, maybe even the first few hundred. But in that one week, Cassie estimated that thousands of children had sat on Santa's lap, some giggling, some arguing, some crying, a few, in the excitement of the moment, wetting themselves and Santa. The job can't possibly pay enough, she told herself. What would bring a man to seek employment as a department store Santa? Cassie studied Santa's routine.

Each morning, Santa would arrive at the mall in full costume. Cassie would catch him at the entrance, before the customers began to arrive, puffing quietly on a Newport, adjusting his padded stomach, talking to himself.

"Mornin', Santa," she would say as she approached him at the entrance. The first morning, Santa turned away, like a taxicab flashing its off-duty sign. The second morning, Santa grunted a terse "hello." Cassie lit a cigarette and stood alongside Santa in the chill morning air.

On the third morning, Cassie could tell as she approached the mall entrance that Santa eagerly awaited her arrival. "Can I bum a cig?" asked Santa.

Cassie took out a pack of Salems, lit one for Santa and one for herself. "I'm Cassie," she said and she handed him the cigarette.

"I'm Tommy," he replied. "Thanks for the cigarette."

"So what's it like being Santa Claus?" Cassie wondered aloud.

"It's a job," explained Tommy, and he went inside to start his shift. "A pretty crappy job."

Cassie found "her" table at the edge of the food court and studied the routine in Santa's Workshop. From his raised platform in the center of the workshop, Santa greeted the children, while elves in tights directed traffic. The photographer snapped pictures, and the photographer's assistant slipped each digital photo into its cardboard picture frame and collected the cash. Cassie watched, impressed by the elvish choreography. Each child received a precious moment to speak with Santa, and then another moment for the photo. As soon as the photo was snapped, an elf helped the child climb down while Mom paid the bill. Meanwhile, a second elf prepared the next child for the encounter with Santa, and a third elf directed the rest of the line to be ready. In such fashion, every minute brought another child onto Santa's lap. Cassie did some quick arithmetic. At a child a minute, Santa saw sixty children an hour. Taking Santa's breaks into account, Cassie figured he saw some five hundred kids each day. In a five-day work week, Cassie estimated he saw two thousand kids. In the four weeks between Thanksgiving and Christmas, Cassie figured some eight thousand children climbed up on Santa's lap.

"What's it like being Santa?" Cassie understood Tommy's answer.

Perhaps the worst parts of the job were the breaks—children waiting on line for their encounter with Santa, nearing the head of the line, only to find their wait indefinitely extended when an elf hooked a velveteen rope across the entrance to Santa's Workshop and hung a sign from the rope. The sign read *Santa will return in fifteen minutes.*

Children who were too young to read understood what the sign meant. It meant that their Moms were about to start yelling at Santa's elves. Meanwhile another line of children snaked along behind Santa, following his every move as Santa tried unsuccessfully to slip away quietly for a well-deserved break.

On break, surrounded by the little children, Santa stared in the window of the jewelry store, admiring the gold and diamond bracelets, trying out excuses for the Macks. He was not exactly opposed to petty thievery to square his debt, but Tommy could not imagine how he was supposed to move around surreptitiously, unnoticed in his red Santa suit. When a cute salesgirl waved to him from inside the shop, Tommy wanted to sneak off and hide, but Santa went inside to say hello. "Ho! Ho! Ho!"

"And a ho, ho, ho to you too, Santa." The salesgirl smiled at Santa. "Does

Santa need to do a little Christmas shopping? Can I show you anything?"

Tommy stared at the salesgirl's chest. He knew exactly what the salesgirl could show him and nearly said so, but Santa was discreet. "I'm looking for a bracelet."

"For Mrs. Claus?"

"Huh?" Tommy was distracted. "Yes, of course . . . Mrs. Claus."

The salesgirl unlocked the display case and began picking out bracelets. "White gold is very popular this year."

Like many a Christmas shopper, Santa was ambivalent. The salesgirl patiently pulled one bracelet after another from the display case, offering Santa a short course on bracelets. "This one is called a bangle bracelet," she said, picking up a simple gold bracelet. "This one is called twisted rope," she explained pointing to the interwoven strands of gold. "And this one is what we call Venetian link." Santa hardly listened as he cased the shop, looking for a weakness in the security.

"If you're on a tight budget, we have some very fine fourteen-carat pieces, but Mrs. Claus will be happier with an eighteen-carat bracelet. For beauty and durability, you can't do better than eighteen carat."

Santa immediately recognized an important difference between the eighteen-carat and the fourteen-carat pieces. Only the eighteen-carat pieces were kept in a locked display case. Santa thanked the salesgirl for her assistance and promised to think it over.

"I hope you'll come back when you're ready to buy. Ask for Judy. I'm here Tuesday, Thursday, Friday, and Saturday." Judy handed him her card.

Tommy took the card and smiled. "I'm Santa. I'm here every day until Christmas."

An Elderly Gentleman
Adjusting his Sansabelts

Cassie popped a CD in the player and drove home from the mall on back roads through the Pine Barrens, the smell of pine mixing with the sounds of McCoy Tyner on piano. When she pulled into the condo lot, the parking spots were all taken, even her reserved space. Cassie created a spot along the edge of the property, careful to leave enough room for cars to get by. Party sounds drifted over from the adjoining unit. Cassie let herself into her empty condo and poured herself a Tullamore Dew.

She logged onto the computer and stared at the blank screen. Cassie tried to remember the last good story she'd written. It was, she realized, the last story she'd written for Morris before he sold the magazine. She told Jack Cambrian it was writer's block. She told him it was normal, that every writer went through these dry spells, but they both knew otherwise. Cassie logged off the computer and turned on the television.

Flipping through the channels, Cassie stumbled on the town council meeting, which was carried on local access cable. Before Cheyenne was elected, back when "Big Jim" had been Mayor of Doah, nothing was more entertaining than a meeting of the town council. Cassie was proud of Cheyenne's performance as mayor, but she missed the fistfights that had been the hallmark of Big Jim's administration.

"My friends," Cheyenne Harbrough was saying, "I am pleased to report to you on the progress at the old Norris Farms site."

"Point of order, Mayor Harbrough." Councilwoman Becht interrupted, in the clipped tones of one who believed that the wrong woman was sitting in the mayor's chair. "I may be foolish to raise this issue again, but I am distressed that, for the second year in a row, the town will not be setting up a display here at the municipal building."

Cheyenne Harbrough looked to the township attorney for help. "That issue is not on the council's agenda, Madam Mayor," he said.

Watching at home, Cassie was disappointed that there would not be any vitriol at the council meeting. It might be bad for the town, but it made for riveting television.

"If I may continue," said Cheyenne, "the clean-up is currently ahead of schedule and under budget. I believe that we can . . ." But before Cassie could learn more about the mayor's plans for the restored property at the south end of town, she was pulled away from the television by her telephone.

"Hi Cassie."

"Morris! How are you?" It had been months since Cassie and Morris last spoke. "Where are you?"

"I'm good," he said, but he didn't sound good. Cassie thought Morris sounded nervous.

"Really, Morris? Is everything okay?"

The telephone line went quiet for a moment before Morris responded. "I need to talk to you about something."

"Sure, Morris. Go ahead."

"No, Cassie. Not on the telephone." It was not like Morris to be so mysterious. "Can we meet?"

"What's going on, Morris? Are you okay?"

"Do you know the rest stop on the parkway?" asked Morris. "The one just outside of Atlantic City?"

"Yeah."

"Can you be there in an hour?"

Cassie looked at her watch. It was ten-of-eight. "I'll be there by nine," she said.

At nine o'clock, Cassie was sitting in her Mustang in a stopped line of traffic on the Garden State Parkway, several miles from her destination. She tried calling Morris on his cell, but he wasn't picking up. She waited ten minutes and tried again.

"Dammit Morris. Pick up."

It was nine-thirty when Cassie finally pulled her Mustang into a parking space at the Atlantic City rest stop. She hurried inside, searching for Morris. There was the usual assortment of parkway travelers, businessmen heading home after a very long day, salesmen returning from their last sales call, families on vacation, moms and dads stretching their legs, kids grateful to be out of the car, and senior citizens by the dozens stepping carefully off tour busses, stopping to use the restrooms before descending on the casinos.

Morris, however, was nowhere to be found. He was not at Burger King. He was not at Starbucks. He was not in the gift shop. Cassie startled an elderly gentleman adjusting his sansabelts as he exited the men's room and sent him back inside to look for Morris. He was not in the men's room.

Cassie bought a diet soda and sat down to wait. She checked her watch. It was nine forty-five. At ten-fifteen, she tried Morris on his cell, but there was still no answer. At ten-thirty she had a cup of coffee and dialed Morris's number one more time. At eleven-fifteen, she walked to her car. It was nearly midnight when she let herself back into her condo. Her answering machine was beeping, but when she tried to retrieve the message, the tape was blank.

Two Large Feet in Fine Italian Shoes

Cassie slept poorly, Morris slipping in and out of her dreams, always on the edge, just beyond explanation. In the morning, she drove to his four-bedroom home in the quiet residential town just north of the Pine Barrens proper. Cassie had known Morris for nearly two decades, considered him a close friend, but had never in all those years, even one time, been to his home. Even with her handy internet directions, she had trouble locating the housing development. She passed the turn three times before identifying the right turn with the missing street sign. Once she made the turn, she had no trouble finding the four-bedroom center hall colonial with cedar shingles. It was much too large for a single man to call home, but Morris's name was clearly marked on the mailbox.

Cassie slowly drove past the house. Yesterday's newspaper sat in the otherwise empty driveway. She had the impression that the house was empty. Cassie continued past the house, parking her Mustang around the corner and walking back to 3386 Peachtree Drive. Cassie rang the doorbell. She did not expect, and was therefore not surprised, when no one answered the door. She jiggled the doorknob, but the door was locked. She walked around the house, but the sliding glass door in back was also locked. She noticed a window cracked open on the second floor, and for a moment, Cassie remembered what is was like to be fifteen and grounded, sneaking in and out of her second floor bedroom window. But Cassie was not fifteen, and the second floor window was not a viable option.

She noticed the keypad by the garage. It should not be difficult to guess the code, Cassie realized. Morris's computer password, after all, was "password." Cassie tried 1-2-3-4, but the garage door did not open. She tried his house number 3-3-8-6, but the garage door did not budge. She stared at the keypad. A small piece of masking tape was stuck to the inside cover. On the masking tape, 1-4-4-8. Cassie punched in the numbers and laughed. The garage door opened. Cassie let herself in.

The first floor of Morris's home included a sitting room, formal dining room, eat-in kitchen with large center island, and two guest bathrooms. Cassie went through the rooms seeking clues to Morris's sudden disappearance. But walking through the house, she felt as though she were touring a "model home" with its faux domesticity. Even in the kitchen, Cassie had the odd sensation that the groceries were merely props. It would be difficult to say whether Morris had recently disappeared in a house that bore little evidence that it had ever actually been inhabited.

Cassie climbed the stairs to the second floor. Halfway up the stairs, she stumbled over a pile of magazines. Catching herself, she climbed to the landing at the top of the stairs. The sterile atmosphere of the first floor was quickly forgotten in the jumbled mess of stuff that was the second floor of Morris's home. There were piles of newspapers and magazines, CDs and books, videos, photos and correspondence. There were clothes draped on chairs and candy bar wrappers on the bed. Cassie picked her way carefully through the master bedroom.

There was a small pile of magazines on the nightstand next to the bed, a couple of recent issues of the *Jersey Knews*, Jack Cambrian's name splashed loudly on the masthead, but mostly older issues, from before Morris sold, back when the magazine was fun, Cassie thought. Cassie leafed through the pile, stopping to read one of her own stories, one of her favorites, about the Siamese triplets.

Cassie forgot about Morris, her thoughts turning to the summer of 1905 and the amazing Ederle sisters. So she was not really paying attention when she first heard the door being pushed open down below. But when she heard a footfall on the stairs, Cassie was fully, scarily, in the moment. Instinctively she understood it was not Morris. She glanced around the room, looking for a place to hide. She had few choices . . . the closet, the master bath, the bed. Cassie looked again at the open window, wishing she were fifteen, and then she got down on the floor, shimmying under the bed, counting on the bed skirt to keep her hidden.

From under the bed, Cassie listened as the visitor made slow progress on the stairs. Halfway up the stairs, the footsteps stopped; she heard a man's voice cursing before the footsteps resumed climbing. Peeking under the bed skirt, Cassie glimpsed two large feet in fine Italian shoes shuffling into the bedroom. Her heart was pounding. Cassie pulled back farther under the bed, sure that the intruder could hear her. He shuffled around the room, grunting and cursing. He sat down suddenly, the bed creaking under the weight, the box spring banging down on Cassie. Cassie held her breath and listened as the intruder gasped for air, trying to catch his breath.

Cassie heard a second set of footsteps coming up the stairs. She saw the second pair of Italian loafers. She heard him ask, "Did you find anything?"

The man on the bed cursed. "No."

"So whaddya think?" asked the second pair of loafers.

The man on the bed cursed again. "I think I'm getting too old for this."

The second pair of loafers was already leaving the bedroom. "We oughta be getting out of here."

"Gimme a minute to catch my breath."

Possession of the Sugar Cookie

Santa stood in the main pedestrian walkway on the second floor at the Mall of New Jersey peering into the jewelry store. The mall was crowded with shoppers, women loaded down with gift bags holding onto children, teenagers looking for inexpensive Christmas presents for their girlfriends or boyfriends. Inside the store, Judy was showing watches to a balding businessman in a blue sport coat. She looked up and waved to Santa, smiling. He felt his cheeks grow red, matching the Santa suit. When Judy finished with the watches, she stepped out from behind the counter and joined Santa in front of the store.

"Hi, Santa."

"Hi, Judy."

It pleased Judy that Santa remembered her name. "Have you decided yet on a gift for Mrs. Claus?"

"Not yet."

Judy smiled at him. "When you do, remember to come back and ask for me." Judy gave Santa a quick peck on the cheek and went back inside the jewelry store.

He wondered how he was going to steal enough inventory to satisfy the Macks. Hell, he wondered how he would boost even a single piece of jewelry.

Santa failed to notice the commotion until it was upon him, a young woman with two children and three large bags full of Christmas presents, the two children, a boy of perhaps six and his sister of eight, fighting over a sugar cookie, screaming at each other and at their mother.

When children got out of control at Santa's Workshop, it was the elves who were paid to deal with the commotion. Here in the middle of the mall, Santa stood scant feet from the screaming children, embarrassed and unsure what to do. Finally, Mother put her packages down and took possession of the sugar cookie. Dragging her children behind her, she marched to the nearest trash receptacle, disposing of the cookie, all the while lecturing her children about the consequences of fighting. As Santa watched the mother approach the trash receptacle across the pedestrian walkway, he realized that her shopping bags were left unattended. He was about to yell to the woman, alerting her to the danger of leaving her bags in the mall like that, and then it hit him. She had left her bags unattended in the mall. Santa quickly looked around for witnesses, but everyone's eyes were following the procession to the trash can. Santa pulled one small box from the top of the bag and slid the fancy package under his red Santa jacket. Moving quickly, Santa made his way through the mall. He was well down the hallway, home free, when he felt the box slip out from under his jacket and hit the floor.

Someone approached rapidly from his rear. "Santa, wait up." Santa turned in time to see a mall security guard hustling to catch up. "You dropped something, Santa." The security bent down to retrieve the small package and handed it to Santa. "Merry Christmas, Santa."

"Merry Christmas . . ." Santa looked at the nametag on the guard's uniform. ". . . Oliver."

South of Trenton
and West of the Atlantic Ocean

Where am I? wondered Morris, sitting behind the wheel of his Buick, lost someplace south of Trenton and west of the Atlantic Ocean. He had spent twenty years pursuing stories for the magazine and knew his way around Jersey better than most natives. But in his panicked escape from the rest stop, Morris had driven blindly, heading ever deeper into the Pine Barrens, first on the parkway, then on the county roads, on local paved roads, dirt roads and gravel paths, until even these ancient trails had petered out. The digital clock on his dashboard was blinking nearly midnight. His fuel gauge was blinking nearly empty. Orion was blinking in the southern sky. Morris thought he might be somewhere near Batsto. Damn.

It had seemed like a good idea to disappear for a few days in Atlantic City. He wasn't trying to skip out, he told himself, just to play a few hands of poker and give himself a little time to figure things out. If he were lucky enough to win a big pot, he might even be in a position to pay off his debt. Meanwhile, he hoped that Cassie could help him by checking some information about the two men who were looking for him. The Macks had not as yet confronted him directly, but Morris had seen them nosing around the neighborhood. It would not be long before these two rough-hewn gentlemen in custom-tailored suits would come knocking at his door. So he arranged to meet Cassie at the rest stop, where he would be one more anonymous traveler stopping to use the toilet and grab a bite to eat.

Morris arrived at the rest area at 8:45; he bought a grande cup of coffee and found a seat where he could keep an eye on the entrance. Cassie was prompt about her appointments, rarely early, but never late. When Cassie didn't arrive at 9:05, Morris allowed that she was probably sitting in traffic. At 9:15, he told himself he was letting his paranoia get the better of him. At 9:25, when he saw two large men standing at the northbound entrance to the rest area, it didn't matter to Morris that they bore only a slight resemblance to the Macks. It's not paranoia, he told himself, when someone's really out to get you.

While the double-wide gentlemen clogged the northbound doorway, Morris slipped out the southbound exit and made his way quickly to his Buick. He pulled onto the parkway heading south, his eyes fixed on the rear-view mirror. He saw no evidence that he was being followed and interpreted that lack of evidence as proof of the stealth of his pursuers. At the next exit, Morris jumped off the parkway. No one followed him, but Morris could feel their presence. *Damn. Those guys are good.*

Morris realized he should call Cassie. Without slowing down, he reached across the seat, opened the glove compartment and rummaged around for his cell phone, swerving dangerously onto the shoulder. With his left hand, he steered the Buick back onto the county road, while with his right hand he began pulling objects from the glove compartment. He found maps and credit card slips. He found a missing pair of sunglasses and several unpaid parking tickets. He found a bag of stale Halloween candies and a flyer for Chinese take-out. But he didn't find his cell phone. *Damn.*

Morris continued his flight, focused on what he was driving from, not what he was driving toward, until he discovered that what he was driving toward was an abandoned path deep in the Pine Barrens, too overgrown to go forward, too narrow to turn the car around. Annoyed at his own stupidity, he put the Buick in reverse, gunning the engine. For a moment, the wheels spun madly and then the car lurched backwards.

Morris felt the wheel hit the spike, and then he heard the sickening pop. The right rear tire went flat. Morris thought he was going to hurl. He opened his window, filling his lungs with fresh piney air, forcing himself to take deep, even breaths. Morris sat in the Buick trying to make sense of his predicament.

He wondered if it would be safe trying to change the flat tire in the dark. He was no longer worried about the Macks. As soon as he heard the pop of the tire, he understood that the Macks were still at the Atlantic City rest stop—if it even had been the Macks he spotted in the doorway—or, by now, at Caesar's shooting craps. The only place the chase happened was in his imagination. So he was not worried, for the moment, about the Macks.

And he was not worried about the Jersey Devil. Despite the numerous articles that Cassie had written and he had published, despite the photographs and the eye-witness accounts, despite the magazine's loyal fan base, Morris understood that there was no such thing as the Jersey Devil.

No, what Morris was worried about were the nasty, creepy, slimy creatures that would get on and get under his clothes. Morris shuddered at the thought of the bugs that made their home in the Pine Barrens. He rolled up his window and tried not to think about the bugs.

And there was a practical consideration as well. Morris lacked confidence in his ability to change the flat tire in the dark Pine Barrens at night. If he tried, he understood that he might lose the lug nuts in the underbrush; he might damage the car's underbody, or worse yet, the donut spare. And he would surely cause himself bodily injury in the attempt.

He had begun the evening hoping to find a place to hide out temporarily. Looking around him at the pygmy pines crowding in around him, Morris had to admit he had found a pretty good hiding place. He would spend the night (what was left of it) napping in his Buick at the tail end of an abandoned trail, somewhere south of Trenton and west of the Atlantic Ocean.

A Good Place

Morris counted the minutes until . . . sleep . . . morning . . . insanity? He was beyond caring, sitting in the Buick, trying to make himself sleep, and every time he nodded off, hitting his head on the steering wheel. At some point that night Morris knew he must have fallen asleep; otherwise how explain the dream teeming with bugs? As the eastern sky revealed the first traces of morning, Morris congratulated himself for surviving. He pulled the owner's manual from the glove compartment and identified the storage location for the donut spare and the jack. Morris popped the trunk and walked around to the back of the car. He pulled up on the dirty gray "floor" of the trunk. In the wheel well that was revealed, Morris found, as promised, the Buick's spare tire. He lifted the donut spare from the trunk. *I can do this*, Morris told himself.

I can't do this. Morris stared into the trunk of the car. He studied the diagram in the owner's manual. He re-checked the contents of the trunk. The donut spare would do him no good. The jack was missing.

And so it was, in the faint pre-dawn light, Morris put the engine in reverse and began ever-so-slowly backing up, the Buick limping along on three tires and a rim, retracing his steps, backwards along the abandoned trail, until he found a small dirt road. It was not easy, but he jockeyed the Buick and, after several attempts, managed to turn the car, the Buick finally facing forward on this very small dirt road. He was still lost, somewhere deep in the woods, still riding on a badly damaged rim, still tired and hungry and cold, and as he turned the car around he was momentarily discomfited by the dead deer, but he was, for the first time that morning, facing forward and, after a long night of failure, he lifted an imaginary glass to his lips to toast this small success.

Two hours later, when the ground turned from dirt and rock to pavement, he lifted a second imaginary glass in triumph. This place, which had seemed so strange in the dark of night, in the adrenaline rush of flight, was, at mid-morning, peaceful and vaguely familiar. Morris was not far from town. What town he was not certain, but he was certain that it was near. His thoughts turned to hot coffee and an even hotter shower.

He passed a fish pond on his right, deserted on this chilly day at the end of November and imagined summertime, the pond rimmed with young men and boys, their poles dangling in the pond. And then, just ahead on his left, he spotted a small motel on the outskirts of Woodbine. He pulled his car to a stop, on three tires and one very badly damaged rim, in the parking lot just beyond the small motel sign. Morris dragged his tired body from the Buick and walked into the lobby where he was greeted by the manager, Beejit Bhait.

"You will be needing a room, good sir?"

"Yes." Morris nodded. "I will be needing a room. Do you have a vacancy?"

"I have twelve very nice cabins. I have twelve vacancies." Beejit Bhait frowned. "We are too far from the parkway."

Morris looked at the small Hindu shrine behind the reception desk. "You're not from around here, are you?"

"No, good sir. I am not originally from here." He paused. "But I am very happy here in this place. It is a good place."

Morris hoped he wasn't prying, but he was curious about this Hindu gentleman who had settled in Woodbine. "Did you come here by yourself?"

"Oh, no, sir," Mr. Beejit Bhait explained. "I came here with my mother."

On the wall behind the reception desk, twelve keys hung from a small corkboard. Beejit Bhait reached for the key to number three before reconsidering and handing Morris the key to cabin one.

Morris went outside to retrieve an overnight bag from the Buick and let himself into cabin one.

It was a small cabin, smelling of wood paneling and cardamom seeds. There was a bed, a bureau, a chair, and a television. At the front of the cabin, a window looked out onto the parking lot. Morris peered through the window at his wounded Buick. There was a bathroom at the rear of the cabin . . . a toilet, a wash basin and a tub. There was a small window in the bathroom, which opened onto an endless field of wildflowers and weeds.

Morris turned on the shower. The water pressure met with his approval. He climbed out of his rumpled clothes and into the cascading shower. Pulling the shower curtain closed, the universe narrowed to this small white tub, this chrome shower head, this torrent of steaming hot water. For the moment Morris forgot about the rest stop, the pine forest, the flat tire, the . . . Morris let his mind go blank, let the hot water beat down on him, and then . . .

Bam! A sickening thud sent shudders through Morris's still shaken spirit. *What the fu* . . . Cautiously Morris peeked around the shower curtain, seeing nothing. Cautiously he stepped out of the shower, alarmed and confused. He noticed the enormous mark on the window, the avian-shaped mark. A shore bird apparently had slammed into the bathroom window. Morris exhaled. Then Morris looked out the window. Where before he had seen a field of wildflowers, now he could see only shore birds, thousands of shore birds, filling every inch of the field. Morris quickly toweled off, got dressed, and placed a telephone call.

"Hi, Cassie. It's me."

"Morris!" Cassie was relieved to hear his voice. "Where are you?"

"I'm in Woodbine."

"Are you okay, Morris?"

"I'm tired. I'm hungry. My car's messed up. I'm in Woodbine. For God's sake, do I sound okay?" Morris realized his voice was getting way too loud. "I'm sorry, Cassie. Look, can you just give me a ride? I'll explain everything when you get here."

"I'll be there in an hour. Where in hell . . . ? I'm sorry Morris, where in Woodbine are you?"

"Bhait's Motel." Morris hung up the phone and went looking for Beejit Bhait.

"Can you recommend someplace nearby where I can get lunch?" Morris asked the manager.

"My cousin Gupta has a very fine restaurant just up the street." Mr. Bhait pointed past the shore birds a few hundred yards to the north. "Please to tell him that you are my guest."

"Thank you." Morris paused. "Sure are a lot of birds out there."

Beejit Bhait nodded. "Yes, good sir."

Morris walked up the street, finding it hard to breathe, his eyes focused only on the restaurant, birds watching his progress sitting on the telephone lines that ran along both sides of the street. He knew he was being foolish, but Morris felt a keen sense of relief upon reaching the restaurant.

He sat on a stool at the counter and ordered the blue plate special— lamb sagwaala, biryani rice and chapatis—and lingered over a cup of strong Indian coffee. It seemed hardly possible, but while Morris was at the luncheonette, even more birds had arrived. As he paid the bill, Morris pointed to the scene outside.

"Sure are a lot of birds out there."

Gupta smiled. "In my country, we say that the birds bring good fortune."

"I hope you're right," said Morris. His shirt was wet with perspiration, from curry or from anxiety, he could not be certain. Morris pushed open the door and exited the luncheonette.

Deep's Quick Lube

When Morris returned to the Bhait's Motel, Cassie was sitting in the parking lot, in her Mustang, staring at Morris's Buick and listening to Lightnin' Hopkins sing "Automobile Blues." She hopped from the car, running to meet Morris, giving him a big hug.

"Geez Morris. You're soaking wet."

Morris smiled. "Tell me about it." He unlocked cabin one, holding the door open for Cassie. "Thanks for coming."

Cassie looked around at the generic motel room. "What the hell is going on, Morris?"

What the hell is going on? Morris shared only as much as he knew for certain. "A couple of goons are looking for me."

"Goons?"

Morris nodded. "Yeah. Two big guys. Huge, really."

"What kind of shoes do they wear?"

Cassie's question took Morris by surprise. "Huh?"

"Shoes, Morris. What kind of shoes?"

"Shit, Cassie. I wasn't watching their feet." Morris thought for a minute. "Why do you ask?"

Cassie remembered her view from under the bed. "I saw them at your house this morning."

Morris couldn't figure out which question he wanted to ask first. "You were at my house this morning?"

Cassie nodded. "When you didn't meet me last night . . . well, to tell you the truth, Morris, I was worried about you."

Cassie was worried about him. Morris felt the blood rush to his cheeks. And despite his own worry and fatigue, despite all the craziness, he felt the blood rush to another place as well. "And you say you saw them at my house?"

"Yeah. They were looking for you."

Morris thought about the two men at his house. "When I asked you to come down here, I wanted you to give me a ride home. I can't go home now. What am I going to do Cassie?"

Cassie took a closer look at Morris's cabin. "I guess you better stay here for a couple of days."

Morris hated himself for what he was about to say, hated himself for being too weak to stop himself. "I've got an idea. Why don't you stay here with me, Cassie? Take a little vacation in Woodbine?"

She wanted to be angry with Morris. He had no right to ask, not after all they'd been through. "You know I can't do that, Morris." She kissed him lightly on the cheek. "But I guess I could spend the afternoon." And then, to make sure there was no misunderstanding, she added "Let's go see about getting your car fixed."

Morris and Cassie found Beejit in the motel office. Beejit looked up from his paperwork. "And how was lunch?"

Morris was pleased to tell Beejit that his cousin's lamb sagwaala was delicious. "I need to get my car repaired. Do you know someone?"

Beejit Bhait smiled broadly. "My sister's husband, Deep, is a most excellent mechanic." And he gave Morris directions to his brother-in-law's garage. "Remember to tell Deep that you are my guest."

Morris wanted to save the cost of a tow, so he nursed the crippled Buick through the quiet streets of Woodbine, Cassie following in her Mustang, until they located Deep's Quick Lube.

Deep examined the damaged rim. "You should not be driving on a flat tire. This is not a good thing you are doing."

Morris only nodded. "What's this gonna cost me?"

Deep understood that Americans only cared about money. "First I will need to see how much damage you have done to the Buick."

Morris was not about to be taken by some small town auto mechanic. "Look, it's just a flat tire, and a rim, right?"

Deep frowned. "I cannot tell until I put the car up on the lift, good sir, but I believe it is possible you have done more serious damage. I think that maybe this will not be such a little job."

Morris was ready to start yelling, but Cassie reached a hand out, touching him lightly on the arm. She looked at Deep. "How long will it take you to assess the damage?"

Deep smiled broadly. "I will be knowing the damage tomorrow."

"Tomorrow then," Cassie said, and she started to walk back to the Mustang.

"Thank you, gentle lady," Deep said, bowing slightly.

Cassie was already approaching her Mustang. Morris, running to catch up, stumbled, banging his leg on the fender before climbing into the passenger side. They rode back to the motel in silence. Cassie didn't even bother to turn on a CD.

Back at the motel, Cassie said good-bye without even bothering to get out of the car. "Perhaps I can find something out when I get home."

"What about me?" Morris hated himself for sounding so pitiful.

"You need to wait here," Cassie suggested, "at least until Deep can fix your car."

Cassie popped Sunnyland Slim into the CD player and pulled her car out of the parking lot. "The Devil is a Busy Man" was playing on the CD. *Yes, he is*, Cassie thought. *Yes indeed*.

The birds seemed to be watching as the Mustang made its way out of Woodbine.

For Old Time's Sake

Tommy V. rolled over in bed and opened his eyes; the sun coming through the window was already high in the sky. Even Santa gets an occasional day off. He hopped out of bed and took another look at the watch he'd boosted at the mall. It was a Tag Heuer Men's Steel Watch and according to the tag in the box it had a retail value of nearly $700. Tommy knew a fence in Woodbine. He was going to enjoy his day off.

He looked in his refrigerator, hoping for a couple of eggs and a glass of OJ, but all he could find was some ancient grape jelly and an empty bottle of ketchup. He smiled, thinking about the meal he would purchase after his trip to Woodbine.

Tommy placed a call to his girlfriend, Bobbie. This was shaping up to be a great day.

"Hey, babe. It's me. Whaddya say I take you out to dinner tonight?"

Bobbie was surprised to hear from Tommy in the middle of the day. "Aren't you supposed to be working, Tommy?"

"It's my day off, babe. So whaddya say? You can pick the place. Italian. Chink. Whatever you want."

"You know the deal, Tommy," Bobbie reminded him. "I'm not going out with you until you graduate from anger-management. Are you still going to class, Tommy?"

In class they talked all the time about triggers. Tommy recognized Bobbie's question as a trigger. He took a deep breath. *Maybe the class is helping*, he thought.

"Dammit, Bobbie. You wanna go to dinner or not?"

"Call me when you finish the class, Tommy." Bobbie hung up the phone.

Tommy stared at the receiver. He counted to ten. Gently he put the receiver back on its cradle. He took another deep breath. Then he punched the wall.

"Dammit!"

Tommy was not about to let his girlfriend ruin a great day. Within the hour, he was behind the wheel of his Plymouth. He had ten dollars in his wallet and nothing at all in the bank, but he had a seven hundred dollar Tag Heuer watch and a scheme. Unfortunately he also had a fuel gauge pointing to "E." Halfway to Woodbine, he stopped to buy one gallon of gas and a pack of cigarettes.

Ten miles after his stop at the gas station, a light rain began to fall. Twenty miles and he was approaching Woodbine when Tommy's Plymouth ran out of gas. Using the car's momentum, he steered the Plymouth off the road into a small motel parking lot. Tommy put the Tag Heuer in his pocket, and began to walk the remaining mile or so to Louie's. He noticed that the rain was coming down harder. Still, he had a seven hundred dollar watch in his pocket. Tommy was having a great day. He was soaking wet by the time he found Louie's pawnshop.

It is said that every man has a doppelganger, an identical twin as it were, who inhabits another corner of the universe. He may live on a remote island somewhere in the south Pacific or just on the other side of town, but most men have no evidence of their double. Louis Feldman, however, was not like most men and the evidence of his double, unimpeachable. With his slight stature and his perpetual shrug, his thinning red hair and thick black glasses, even down to his New York Jewish whine, Louis Feldman was a perfect genetic double for Woody Allen. He had, in fact, once worked as Mr. Allen's stunt double in an early movie.

When Tommy walked into the pawnshop, he was surprised to find Louie pacing nervously behind the counter, muttering sotto voce about an appointment with his psychiatrist. Louie looked up over the glasses that had slipped down the sweaty slope of his nose. "Tommy V. As I live and breathe." Louie moved farther back behind the counter, creating more space between the two men.

Tommy held out his hand in peace. "I'm into anger-management these days."

A nervous laugh escaped from Louie's throat. "I'm glad to hear it." Louie took a handkerchief from his pocket and wiped his brow. "What can I do for you, Tommy?"

Tommy pulled the small box from his coat pocket. "I got merchandise." And he showed Louie the watch. "How much?"

Louie examined the Tag Heuer closely. "Nice, Tommy. Very nice." He made a few quick notes on a pad that was sitting on the counter. "One eighty-five."

"One eighty-five!" Tommy struggled to control his temper. "This gets nine hundred at the Mall of New Jersey."

Louie looked around the pawnshop. "Does this look like the Mall of New Jersey to you, Tommy? C'mon, you know how this works."

Tommy knew exactly how it worked. "Listen, Louie, I'm gonna have lots of stuff to move in a couple of days. Watches, jewelry, electronics, all kinds of shit. And I want you to move it for me. For old time's sake. But not at those prices."

Louie made a few more notes on the pad. "As it is, I'm gonna take a loss on the watch." He looked at Tommy closely. "What the hell, Tommy. Two twenty-five. For old time's sake."

Tommy pocketed the two hundred twenty-five dollars and said goodbye to Louie. "I'll see ya in a coupla three days." A light rain was falling on the peaceful town of Woodbine. Tommy spotted a gas station. He bought a container and filled it with two gallons of unleaded and walked back to his car with the gas can and nearly two hundred twenty-five dollars in his pocket. Tommy was having a great day.

When he came to within fifty yards of the motel parking lot, Tommy spotted a man examining his Plymouth. Tommy slowed his pace, checking out the stranger as he approached his car.

Kings over Aces

At first glance, the man appeared to Tommy to be remarkably average, but on closer inspection, Tommy decided he was actually not quite average in remarkably average ways. He was of average height, only shorter. He was of average weight, only heavier. He wore a black suit and gray t-shirt, and he couldn't quite manage the look. His hair mostly matched the suit. The gray at his temples matched the t-shirt. He looked up as Tommy approached.

"Hey, cool. I was feeling kinda weird being the only guest. Which cabin are you in?"

Tommy uncapped the gas can. "Not stayin' here."

Morris watched him transfer the gas to his tank. "You ran out of gas?"

Tommy busied himself with the gas can. "Yeah."

"So where you heading?" When Tommy didn't answer, Morris tried the more direct approach. "Can you give me a ride to Atlantic City?"

Atlantic City, Tommy thought. *Not a bad idea.* "Sorry, fella, I can't help ya."

Tommy threw the empty gas can in the trunk of the Plymouth, climbed behind the wheel and pulled out of the parking lot, leaving Morris standing alone in the motel lot, his hands on his hips, shaking his head.

Tommy was heading home with nearly two hundred twenty-five dollars in his pocket. Maybe it was the cash that had him feeling so good or maybe it was the Christmas spirit, but Tommy decided to call his ex-wife.

"Greta, it's me."

"What—grr—do you want now, Tommy?"

"Can I stop by the house today? I wanna see you and Tommy Junior, maybe take you and the kid out to dinner."

"What's this—grr—all about?"

"Does it have to be about something?"

"I don't know, Tommy."

"C'mon, Greta. I'm tryin' to get my shit together. Gimme a chance here, okay?"

There was silence on the line. Tommy tried again. "Okay, Greta?"

Greta sighed. "Okay, Tommy. Come on by the house around six and we'll—grr—see."

"Later." Tommy hung up the phone and looked at his watch, not a Tag Heuer, a Timex. He had a couple of hours to kill and nearly two hundred twenty-five dollars in his pocket. He took the turn for Atlantic City. Half an hour later, Tommy was sitting at a three-six table in the poker room at Caesar's, a hundred dollars in poker chips stacked in front of him and plenty of cash in reserve.

With the recent popularity of Texas Hold 'Em, novices were flocking to the poker room, senior citizens and young kids alike, with their dark glasses and their nicknames, used to playing on line, ready to try their luck at a "real" game. Tommy looked around the table, anticipating future earnings.

Tommy ordered a scotch on the rocks and folded his first hand, nine-four, unsuited. He complimented himself on his tight play and watched with interest as the hand was won by an older woman with a dye job, a facelift, a lucky troll, and three queens. Tommy sipped his scotch and smiled. He took a small pot with pocket nines and another with two pair, his stack of chips waxing and waning, playing tight, picking his spots, waiting to strike.

With pocket kings, he raised before the flop. When a king came up on the flop (along with an ace-four), Tommy raised again, forcing most everyone to fold. But the old lady with the lucky troll wanted to play. A second four came up on the turn. He raised again. Tommy was surprised when the old lady called the raise. The river card was an ace. Tommy pushed the action. The old lady re-raised and Tommy called. He leaned back in his chair and smiled, revealing pocket kings, a boat, kings over aces. The old lady showed an ace, her boat, aces over fours. Tommy looked on in disbelief. The old lady drew her boat on the river. His stack of chips was dangerously low, but most of his cash, Tommy reminded himself, was still in his pocket. He cashed the few chips that remained and exited the poker room.

Once upon a time, before anger management, Tommy would have been pissed about the poker hand. He would have been pissed, and he would have responded by lashing out at someone he loved. Thanks to his class, Tommy understood it was okay to feel the anger, but not okay to act on it. Tommy felt the anger lodged inside him like a kidney stone. He didn't want to show up at Greta's angry. He needed to deal with his feelings (that's what they told him in class). He needed a beer.

There were plenty of bars in Atlantic City. Tommy's favorite bar offered Heineken on tap and two-for-one lap dances. Tommy had three Heinekens and two lap dances and felt the anger pass.

Tommy checked his watch. It was nearly six. He exited the bar and jumped in his Plymouth. He would be late getting to Greta's. Still, he was having a great day. And he had nearly two hundred twenty-five dollars in his pocket.

Veal Piccata

"You're—grrr—late." Greta smiled. "C'mon in, Tommy."

After the divorce, it bothered Tommy to be invited into "his" home, but this time it didn't make him angry. *Maybe the anger management is working*, he thought.

"Thanks, Greta." Tommy looked around. "Where's the kid?"

"I told Tommy Junior to be home by six, but he said you were gonna be late." Greta laughed. "He's with his girlfriend."

"The kid's got a girlfriend?" Tommy puffed up with pride. "Is she cute?"

"Shit, Tommy. Does it always have to be about looks?"

Tommy didn't need to think about Greta's question. "Abso-fuckin-lutely." He smiled. "Hell, Greta. That's why I asked you out. And that's why I asked you to marry me."

Greta remembered it differently. "You asked me out—grrr—'cause I had a reputation, and you married me 'cause I got pregnant."

Tommy looked at Greta, at her tired eyes and her prematurely gray hair, at the exhaustion that was etched deep into her face, and he remembered the cute teenage girl with the tics. "Maybe, but you still were the prettiest girl in high school."

"What has—grrr—gotten into you Tommy? Do you feel all right?"

"Nuthin'. I don't know. It's just . . . nuthin'." Tommy wasn't sure what was happening, but it had been a long time since he'd talked to Greta without getting into a fight. Not fighting felt good. "So how about dinner?"

"I don't know, Tommy."

But Tommy did know. "Veal piccata. Fettuccini. A bottle of red. C'mon, it'll be fun."

Greta was wavering. "Dinner, Tommy. Just dinner. You understand?"

"I got it, Greta. No dessert."

Greta surrendered to the veal piccata. "Give me a minute to freshen up."

Alfonso's was a cozy neighborhood restaurant, casual and moderately priced. Still, as Greta looked at the menu, she had second thoughts. "Are you sure you can afford this Tommy?"

Tommy patted his pocket. "I can afford it, Greta."

Greta wanted to yell at him about child support, wanted to ask him how he could afford to pay for dinner but not buy shoes for his son. But more than wanting to yell, what Greta wanted was veal piccata.

After two glasses of red wine, Tommy looked at Greta, her growling quieted by the wine. "Why'd we split up Greta?"

Dinner had been friendly, verging on intimate. She considered Tommy's question. Greta almost allowed herself to start believing again. Then she remembered what her marriage had been like. "Why, Tommy? Because you were a jerk. That's why."

Greta saw the hurt in Tommy's eyes. "I'm sorry, Tommy. But you're not being a jerk tonight."

They ordered two espresso and a tartuffo. The bill came to sixty-two dollars. Since fencing the Tag Heuer earlier in the day, Tommy had spent some of his cash, but he knew he still had nearly two hundred twenty-five dollars. He made a big show of pulling cash out of his pocket. Eight dollars and forty-seven cents.

"I don't know what happened, Greta. I should have nearly two hundred-twenty five dollars here."

Greta reached into her purse and found just enough cash to pay the bill. "Leave the tip, okay, Tommy?"

Tommy put six bucks on the table. Greta looked at him and said nothing. He could feel himself beginning to get angry. "It's plenty," he said.

A Remarkably Jolly Afternoon

"**O**'Malley!" Jack Cambrian barked into the telephone. "You weren't at the mall yesterday."

Cassie cupped her hand over the receiver and looked across the table at Cheyenne. "It's my boss."

"What's that, O'Malley? I can't hear you."

Cassie turned her attention to the telephone. "I skipped a day." She turned away from the phone and whispered to Cheyenne. "It's not like one day at the mall is any different than the others."

"Listen to me, O'Malley. I want you back at the mall today."

Cassie imagined she heard something in Jack Cambrian's tone. "Okay, but why don't you tell me what this is about? What's your interest in the mall?"

Jack Cambrian considered telling her the truth. "How many people you figure will go to the mall today?"

Cassie thought about the mass of Christmas shoppers. "Thousands, I guess."

"That's right, O'Malley. And a lot of them read magazines. So get me a good story about Christmas at the damn mall." Jack Cambrian hung up the phone.

Cassie sipped her coffee and signaled the waitress for a refill.

"Are things any better with your boss?" asked Cheyenne.

"Not really. How are things with your parents?"

"I was telling my mother about the last council meeting, and you know what she said? She said, you're not going to believe this, she said, 'It's nice you found a hobby.' A hobby." Cheyenne shook her head in resignation. "Moms."

"I saw a few minutes of your hobby on TV this week. It seems like you've got things pretty much under control."

"Yeah, mostly. The town's in good shape. My family . . . that's another thing entirely. I'm taking my mother shopping today." Cheyenne chuckled. "I must be crazy."

"The mall?" Cassie asked.

Cheyenne nodded.

"That's it!" Cassie laughed. "I'll do a feature about the mayor going Christmas shopping."

When Tommy V. returned to the Mall of New Jersey following his day off, he arrived early and parked right up by the door. He was supposed to park in the offsite employee lot, but he was a Santa with a plan. He retrieved a large bag from the back seat of the car and entered the mall. During his first break of the day, Santa strolled around the first floor of the mall, choosing his marks with care and deliberation. When an elderly lady asked him if he knew where the bathrooms were, Santa boosted a small ceramic vase even as he gave her directions. She thanked him for his help and hurried down the hall to find the toilet. Santa stashed the vase in his bag. Ho! Ho! Ho! He swiped an MP3 player from a teenage girl talking on her cell phone and a tennis bracelet from a young mom arguing with her toddler. He grabbed a couple of DVDs from a middle-aged gentleman in a business suit and a pair of earrings from the businessman's assistant. Each item made its way into Santa's bag of gifts, and each time the owner failed to take note of the loss.

During his lunch break, Santa cruised the second floor. He spotted the security guard eating lunch and was tempted to boost the man's walkie-talkie. Instead, he swiped a digital radio and a pair of sneakers, dropping them into his bag of Christmas gifts. Just for the hell of it, he took one kid's happy meal and another kid's soda.

Before returning to Santa's Workshop, Tommy stashed the bag of stolen goods in the trunk of his car. He wondered if everyone had this much fun playing Santa Claus.

The line of children moved easily that afternoon in Santa's Workshop. Parents seemed more patient, while their kids enjoyed a visit with Santa Claus. Mrs. Claus was feeling frisky. Elves were feeling especially elvish. Even the assembly-line photographer seemed to be in unusually good spirits. It was a remarkably jolly afternoon. Cassie watched Santa's Workshop from her spot at the edge of the food court. She wished she could give Jack Cambrian a warm Christmas tale about the Mall of New Jersey. *There's no story here*, she told herself yet again.

"Cassie!"

Cassie looked up in time to see Cheyenne and her mother, Rae, hurrying over, loaded down with shopping bags. "Welcome to my home away from home. You ladies having a successful shopping trip?"

Rae dropped the shopping bags and sat down next to Cassie. "Here. Let me show you what we bought."

Cheyenne rolled her eyes. Her mother began pulling boxes out of the bags. There was a gift box of white musk bath bubbles, a set of four champagne flutes. There was a string of pearls and a pair of pearl earrings. There was a box from Victoria's Secret that Rae Harbrough was embarrassed to open. "It's a red teddy." There was a beautiful black cashmere sweater. Rae Harbrough rummaged through her shopping bags. "Where's the matching scarf? " She turned to her daughter. "Cheyenne, do you have the matching scarf?"

Cheyenne did not have her mother's matching scarf. "Look again, Mother. It's probably in the bottom of the bag."

Rae Harbrough took another look in her bags. "It's not there." Turning to Cassie she added, "Someone stole my black cashmere scarf."

Cassie started to say something, but Cheyenne interrupted. "No one stole your scarf, Mother. Here. Let me look." And she began rummaging through her mother's shopping bags.

"It's not in here," Cheyenne said.

Rae Harbrough was already standing up. "We have to go report this to security."

"Slow down, Mother. Maybe we ought to retrace our steps. You probably left it somewhere."

Rae turned to Cassie. "What do you think, Cassie?"

Cassie tried for noncommittal. "I guess it's possible."

Rae's mind was made up. "I'm going to the security office. Are you coming with me, Cheyenne?"

Cheyenne made a show of standing up. "I'm coming, Mother." She turned to Cassie. "Care to join us?"

Cassie was tired of staring down at the line of children waiting their turn with Santa Claus. "Yeah, I guess."

The three ladies went in search of the mall security office to report Rae Harbrough's missing—"stolen dear, not missing"—scarf.

Oliver Berryhill looked up as the three women marched into the security office—the older woman actually marching, trailing the two younger women behind her. He smiled. "How can I help you ladies?"

Santa's Helpers

The line waiting for Santa was mostly little children, pre-schoolers and toddlers overflowing with excitement. Occasionally an older boy or girl would risk embarrassment for the chance to give Santa a gift list. But never had Santa's elves seen two such as got on line that afternoon at the Mall of New Jersey. Two large men in custom-tailored suits and fine Italian leather shoes. Either of the men, alone, towered over Santa. Together, the Macks dwarfed his workshop. Little Mack wanted to jump to the head of the line, but Big Mack counseled patience. Finally, it was their turn to sit on Santa's lap.

"We need to talk," said Little Mack.

"Ho! Ho! Ho! Gimme a break, guys. Can't you see I'm working here?"

"You're on a break Santa." Little Mack reached for the velvet rope and the sign that read,

Back in fifteen minutes.

"I can't take a break now. I'll get in trouble."

Big Mack broke his customary silence. "What part of, 'You're on a break,' don't you understand?" Big Mack took the rope from his son and hooked it in front of the line. He turned to the children waiting behind him. "Santa's on a break."

Little Mack focused on Santa. "Let's go for a walk."

Santa began walking, flanked by two of the unlikeliest helpers in the history of Santa's helpers.

"Where can we talk that's private?" asked Little Mack.

"There's no place really private," Santa explained. "Believe me, I've looked."

But Little Mack had an idea. "Follow me." And he led them to a little used loading dock in the back of the mall. "Time to make a payment Santa."

"I don't carry cash in my frickin' Santa suit."

"We've been patient with you. Real patient. But you need to get with the program, Tommy." While Little Mack talked, Big Mack rubbed his hands, getting ready, warming up. "Or we'll do it Big's way." Big Mack nodded his head and smiled at Tommy.

Little Mack continued. "You got paid today, Tommy. Lemme see your paycheck."

Tommy wanted to tell the Macks that he didn't carry his check with him, but he realized he was just postponing the inevitable. He reached into his Santa suit, pulled out the paycheck and turned it over.

Little Mack took one look at the number on the check and doubled over in laughter. "That's all you get paid?" He pointed to the number on the check. "That's all?"

Tommy tried to hide inside the Santa suit.

Little Mack folded the check in half and placed it in the inside pocket of his suit jacket.

Tommy spluttered at the sight of his disappearing paycheck. "Bu-bu-but I . . . look guys, I'm willing to make a payment, but I need to keep at least a hundred."

Little Mack roared. "You're a comedian Tommy, a regular Santa Dice Clay." The check stayed in Little Mack's pocket. "Now about that other matter."

Tommy was ready. "You know what I've learned since I started working? Santa can't sneak around. Anyplace I go in the mall, kids follow me and parents follow them. It doesn't give me a chance to swipe much of anything." Tommy was talking non-stop, not wanting to give Little Mack a chance to respond. He reached inside his Santa suit and pulled out a bracelet, earrings and a black cashmere scarf. "Sorry guys, it's the best I could do."

Little Mack examined the bracelet and earrings. "Well it's a start. You'll do better next week."

Big Mack was fingering the cashmere scarf. "Nice." He draped the scarf around his neck, liking the way it looked against his custom-tailored suit. "Very nice." Big Mack turned and walked off.

"See ya next week Tommy." Little Mack followed his father to the exit.

Rae Harbrough exited the security office, disgusted with the meager investigative resources of mall security. "They should have the authority to lock down the mall if they need to."

Cheyenne was still thinking about the scene her mother had made in the security office. "Mother, it's just a scarf."

"No Cheyenne," Rae Harbrough tried to explain to her daughter. "It's the principle. Right, Cassie?"

But Cassie was not about to be sucked back into the same argument. "Sorry, gotta run. Chey . . . Mrs. Harbrough . . . it's been a pleasure." And she made her way quickly down the hall.

Rae and Cheyenne, mother and daughter, made their way to the mall exit. Standing in the parking lot, scanning for their car, Cheyenne Harbrough noticed two enormous men in fine suits. "Look at them."

Rae looked at the Macks. "Cheyenne, look. The one on the right. He's wearing my scarf!"

Cheyenne drove her mother home from the mall in a silent automobile. Mother and daughter, unable to agree on anything else, had agreed to put their argument on hold. Cheyenne wished her mother could let the scarf go. Literally. When Rae Harbrough saw the black cashmere scarf in the parking lot, draped around a gentleman's neck, nothing was going to stop her from approaching this pair of exceedingly large gentleman.

"Excuse me, sir, but I believe you have my scarf."

Big Mack continued walking as though he hadn't heard.

Rae Harbrough was not going to be ignored. "You have my scarf, sir."

Big Mack stopped walking. He turned and stared at this skinny old lady in her designer sports suit, a suit designed for many things, but none of them sport, and then at her very well endowed, very embarrassed daughter. Big Mack smiled into Cheyenne's cleavage and said nothing.

Little Mack looked nearly as embarrassed as Cheyenne. "I am sorry, ma'am, but I believe you are mistaken. There must be thousands of scarves like the one my father is sporting. Why would you possibly believe this particular scarf belongs to you?"

Rae Harbrough smiled. "Because it does." And she reached up, grabbing one end of the scarf, refusing to be denied.

Big Mack had hit people for far less, but he would not hit a bony old lady over a scarf. Neither would he allow anyone, certainly not a bony old lady, to take anything off his person, and so he simply placed one very large hand on the other end of the scarf and waited.

They stood like that in the mall parking lot for the better part of half an hour, Big Mack and Rae Harbrough, bizarre Siamese twins, attached at the scarf, saying nothing because they had nothing to say, and Little Mack and Cheyenne attached by their embarrassment, saying nothing because they could think of nothing to say. Cheyenne was reminded of an endurance stunt on the TV show *Survivor* and nearly said so. After twenty silent minutes, Big Mack turned and walked away. Rae Harbrough had won the immunity challenge. She would not be voted off the island this week.

Rae looked at Big Mack. "I need the box and the receipt. In case I decide to return the scarf."

Cheyenne had no doubt how the Macks would vote next week.

One Bourbon, One Scotch and One Beer

Sitting in his room at the Bhait's Motel, Morris could hear an argument in the office, on the other side of the adjacent wall. Beejit Bhait and his mother were arguing, apparently about Morris. He could not hear any of the words clearly, but the tone strongly suggested that Mrs. Bhait did not approve of his taking up temporary residence at the motel. *Hell*, he thought, *I'm just waiting for my car to be repaired.*

Morris dialed the number for Deep's Quick Lube and spoke to Deep about the Buick. Deep had bad news to report.

"I put the car up on the lift today, good sir, and I found much damage. The tire, of course, and the rim, but also the brake lining has been damaged."

"Is that bad?" asked Morris.

"It is not good," explained Deep. "I will know more when I start the work."

Morris was growing agitated. "You haven't started yet?"

"Oh, no, sir. But I have scheduled the work for tomorrow. Please to call me again tomorrow afternoon. Excuse me, sir." Deep hung up the phone.

Morris stared at the receiver, as if Deep might yet return. He felt a tightness growing in his chest, felt his thoughts beginning to accelerate. He knew where this was heading, but was powerless to stop. He began gasping for air, even as he told himself to breathe deeply and slowly. He could feel the adrenaline rush. Morris paced inside the room, like a caged tiger, a slightly shorter than average, slightly heavier than average caged tiger on the verge of another panic attack.

He thought about calling Cassie, but he was too jumpy to dial the phone. He thought about taking a walk, but the great outdoors was more frightening than his motel cage. The argument, at least, had ended in the adjacent office. Unfortunately, it continued in his head. Morris sprawled on the bed, burying his head under the pillow. The argument continued. He curled up on the bed, waiting for the imagined disaster, or for the panic attack, to subside. It didn't really matter which; Morris just wanted it to be over.

Sometimes when he was like this a hot shower helped him relax. As he undressed, Morris had the uncanny feeling he was being watched. Standing under the torrent of water, he sensed that something horrific was about to happen. Panic stabbed at his chest like a knife. Suddenly he felt dizzy, grabbing at the shower curtain to steady himself.

As the dizziness passed and his balance returned, Morris could feel the panic leaving his body, washing itself down the shower drain. He turned off the water and toweled dry.

Morris dialed the office and asked Beejit Bhait for the name of the local bar.

"Ah, yes. A drink should help you to relax." Morris wondered how much Mr. Bhait knew. "My nephew Maha owns a very nice place in town. You can't miss it . . . the Maha Bhar and Grill. Please to tell him you are my guest."

"Thank you, Mr. Bhait."

"I am most pleased to be helping. You will be needing a ride I think."

Morris hated to ask. "Do you know a good taxi service?"

Fortunately Beejit Bhait had many nephews, and one of them just happened to drive a cab. Mr. Bhait placed a call to his sister's youngest son, Ajip, who arrived moments later in his pick-up truck.

"That's your cab?" asked Morris.

"Does it look like a friggin' cab, man?" Unlike the rest of Beejit's relations, Ajip was fiercely, proudly American. "My old lady's got the cab tonight." Ajip offered Morris his hand. "My friends call me Pete."

Pete opened the passenger door of the pick-up and Morris climbed in. When they pulled away from the motel, Pete turned briefly to face Morris. "The Maha Bhar sucks man. You don't want to go there."

"You got a suggestion?"

Pete nodded. "Maybe."

As they headed for the highway, Pete pointed out the Maha Bhar.

"It looks closed," Morris said.

"It always looks like that."

Twenty minutes later Pete pulled to a stop in front of Walt's.

Morris could hear blues coming from inside the busy club. "Sounds great."

Pete nodded. "Don't it though? And you gotta check out Walt's single malts."

Morris looked in his wallet at his dwindling cash. "I don't think I can afford single malt tonight."

Pete laughed. "Not a problem. I bring Walt a lot of business. Last night I brought in a wealthy developer . . . Harper, Harban, something like that. Anyway, the guy ran a tab. If I know Walt, the tab's still open." Pete climbed out of the pick-up. Morris followed him inside.

It was a small room, maybe twenty tables and a tiny stage in front. A lone musician was doing his best to sound like John Lee Hooker. Morris noted that the guy's best was pretty damn good. "Nice."

Pete nodded. "Yeah." They found a table. Pete asked for a bottle of Talisker and two glasses. He poured each man an inch of scotch. Morris loved the peaty aroma of the Talisker. He sipped. "Are we near the water?"

"What do you mean?" asked Pete.

"Seaweed," Morris said.

Pete nodded. "That's the Talisker."

On stage, the musician was singing, "One Bourbon, One Scotch, and One Beer."

At the table, Pete and Morris lapsed into silence, enjoying the music and more than one scotch. During a break in the music, Pete looked up from his scotch. "People leave Woodbine. No one comes to Woodbine. So what's your story? What are you doing at my uncle's motel?"

Morris frowned. "Car trouble."

Pete laughed. "Don't tell me, your car's at Deep's."

Morris nodded.

Pete laughed again. "Be careful. It could get expensive for you here in Woodbine."

"Yeah. Today he told me the repair is bigger than he first thought."

"That's Deep," said Pete. Morris shook his head in disgust. Pete explained. "No, it's not like that. Deep's honest. It's just, he doesn't get a lot of customers, so when he does, well, let's just say, he's thorough."

"What about Beejit?"

"Same thing. He'll do whatever he can to encourage you to stay as long as possible."

Morris remembered the argument. "What about Beejit's mother? She doesn't seem eager to have me stay."

Pete perked up at the mention of his grandmother, Beejit's mother. "Have you met my grandmother yet?"

"No," Morris admitted.

"I didn't think so."

A Complete Rotation

Morris dialed the local number.

"Thank you for calling Deep's Quick Lube. How may I be helping you?"

"Is my car done?"

"Who may I ask is calling, good sir?"

"How many cars are in for repairs?"

"Just one, sir." Deep paused. "Of course. How silly of me. I am most sorry, sir."

Morris was growing weary with Deep's polite non-answers. "My car, Deep. Is it ready."

"Oh, no, sir. Your car is being more damaged. You will be needing new tie rods and struts, sir."

"Enough already!" Morris was screaming into the phone. "What if I decide not to replace the tie rods and struts? What if I come over right now and get my car?"

"Certainly, sir. It is your decision." Deep was philosophical. "I understand how you feel. I do not have to be fixing the tie rods and struts. Unfortunately, sir, your car will not be driving without this repair. So your car will have to be sitting on my lot until you have it towed." Deep took a breath before adding. "Please to not be taking too long because I will be needing to charge you a daily storage fee as long as your car is parked at my lot."

Morris quickly ran the numbers in his head. "Go ahead and replace the tie rods and struts."

"You are a wise man, sir."

"Look, Deep. I just want my car back. When can I come get it?"

"Please to call me again tomorrow." Deep hung up the phone without waiting for an answer.

Morris debated finding something to do, but he was running out of desire and Beejit was running out of relatives. He sat in his motel room, the TV on in the background, killing time. He didn't bother eating. He barely slept. Somehow, he convinced the earth to make a complete rotation on its axis.

He picked up the telephone and dialed the familiar number.

"Thank you for calling Deep's Quick Lube. How may I be helping you?"

"It's Morris. What else is wrong with my car?"

"Ah, Mr. Morris, sir. Your car is ready. You will come this afternoon?"

"Yes, I will come this afternoon," said Morris.

"Please to ask for Deep."

Morris hung up the phone and placed a call to Pete. "Can you give me a ride to Deep's? My car is ready."

Pete chuckled. "Gimme a few minutes."

And just a few minutes later, Morris spotted the pick-up truck pulling into the parking lot. The truck had barely come to a complete stop when Morris was pulling open the door. "Thanks, Pete."

"No problem, man." Pete was still chuckling as they drove to Deep's.

Morris had never been so happy to see his aging Buick. "Thanks for the ride, Pete."

"Do you want me to wait?"

"Nah. Deep said the car is all set." Morris was grinning at the thought of getting behind the wheel of the Buick. He hopped out of the pick-up and went inside to find Deep.

Pete decided to stick around, just in case.

Inside, Deep was printing out a copy of the bill for Morris.

"I am hoping you will be satisfied with the quality of Deep's service."

"Yeah, sure. It's . . ." and Morris looked at the bill. ". . . Eight hundred and forty-two dollars! How the hell can it be eight hundred and forty-two dollars?"

"Please to be looking at the bill, good sir. There was much damage."

Morris wasn't interested in looking at the bill. "But I only came in here for a flat tire."

Deep seemed embarrassed by the bill. "I am most sorry. You are right, Mr. Morris. The tire. I forgot all about the tire." He took the bill from Morris, ran a few numbers on his calculator and printed out a new copy of the bill. "I am most sorry. The bill is nine hundred and eight dollars."

Morris was livid. "There's no way I'm going to pay nine hundred and eight bucks to fix a flat tire. The car's not worth nine hundred and eight dollars."

Deep had already checked the blue book value of the Buick. "You are right, sir. The car it is valuing at nine hundred dollars."

Morris got to the point. "I don't have nine hundred and eight dollars."

"This is most difficult, sir." Deep frowned. "Perhaps there is another way."

Morris waited to hear what Deep was going to propose.

"Perhaps you would be selling Deep the Buick?"

Morris realized that his options were limited. He couldn't afford to pay for the repair. And the longer he waited, the worse this was going to get. Eventually Deep would prevail. Morris signed over the car.

"Thank you, good sir. Now you will be owing Deep only eight dollars more."

When Morris walked outside, he saw that Pete had waited. He climbed into the pick-up truck. Pete was still chuckling.

"Don't say a word. Not a word."

They drove in silence back to the Bhait's Motel.

The Smell of Pine
and the Sound of Miles's Trumpet

Cassie stared at her computer screen. She couldn't pretend anymore. She had forgotten how to write. She poured another Tullamore Dew and stared at the screen. For fifteen years, she had written stories for the magazine, good stories, popular stories, stories that built the magazine's fan base and bottom line. But somehow, in the year since Morris sold the magazine, she had written nothing. Not a single story. Jack Cambrian was running out of patience and, at moments like these, Cassie had to admit he was correct. She was a writer who had forgotten how to write. Cassie sipped her Irish whiskey and stared at the computer screen.

Feeling sorry for herself, she pulled up old stories on the computer— sea monsters, psychic spies, space aliens, Soviet secrets, Siamese triplets. She was reduced now to writing warm and fuzzy stories for Jack Cambrian about a shopping mall. And she couldn't even manage that. It was pitiful. It was Jack Cambrian's fault. It was Morris's fault. It was . . .

Cassie stared at the ugly truth.

. . . her fault.

And it had nothing to do with the magazine. It had been a year since Morris sold the magazine, but that was not the only landmark event of a year ago. One year ago, Andy MacTavish had gone to prison for murder, put there on the strength of Cassie's story.

For fifteen years, she struggled to move beyond the death of her late husband Rob. For fifteen years she had mourned. And then she met Andy and she knew that finally, after all that time, her life was going to make sense again. It was okay to mourn Rob and to love Andy. And then she sent him to prison. Cassie stared at her computer screen and sipped her Irish whiskey.

Once upon a time, Cassie lived in the hour between night and day, in that space between sleep and wakefulness. She had been avoiding that place for a year. It scared her now, that place in her bed, in her head, that she used to go to see Rob. It scared her, but it was where she needed to be.

Cassie turned off her computer and got ready for bed. She dug deep into the dark places in her closet and found an old cotton nightgown, one of Rob's favorites. It was not fancy, certainly not sexy, but Cassie knew that Rob loved the way her body moved inside that nightgown. As she drifted off to sleep, Cassie could almost remember the young bride she had once been, married right out of college, and that young bride's plans for the life they were supposed to spend together.

They were twenty. In her dreams they were always twenty. Cassie wanted desperately to have a dream of Rob, but when she opened her eyes in the morning, she could not remember anything. She lay in bed, half awake, her eyes half-open, the view out her bedroom window still more night than morning. Rob had not come to her in a dream, but he would come to her in this place. She lay in bed, her tears soaking the pillow. It wasn't fair.

She buried her head in Rob's chest and cried. She felt his arms around her, and she cried. It's not fair.

No, it's not, he whispered, *and it may not get any better.*

She cried for Rob. She cried for Andy. She cried for Cassie. It's not fair.

No, it's not, he whispered, *but you have to believe that it will be.*

Rob was gone. The morning sun streamed in her window. It was time for Cassie to face the day.

The air was fragrant with the smell of pine and the sound of Miles's trumpet. Cassie was tempted to take the top down, but December is not convertible weather in New Jersey, even on the best of days. Instead she rolled down her window, letting the pine in and Miles out. She zipped her coat against the early morning chill.

Cassie was in no great hurry. She knew where she was heading, and for a change it wasn't the Mall of New Jersey. So she wandered through the Barrens, on roads both strange and familiar, but always heading southeast, the forest gradually thinning, the scent of pine surrendering to saltwater and seaweed.

She had no trouble finding the turn and followed the road until it dead-ended at the water. Except for the "For Sale" sign, Andy's beach house looked just as it had when the police took him away in handcuffs.

Spend, Spend, Spend

Once Tommy got started, he quickly warmed to his new role as Santa Claus, petty thief. The opportunities for thievery were as many and varied as the people who believed in the fat man in the red suit. Each day, Tommy went to work at the mall making children happy, spreading holiday cheer, and gathering holiday lucre. Every night, he made the drive to Woodbine and an appointment with his fence, Louie Feldman. For the first time in a very long time, Tommy had cash in his pocket and a feeling that his life was his to control. *Why can't the Christmas spirit last throughout the year?*

"Hey, Santa . . ." Tommy looked up to find Big Mack filling the walkway.

"Hey, Big. Flying solo today?"

Big Mack grunted and rubbed his hands. Tommy didn't need to know that Little Mack was in Woodbine, discussing business with Louie. "Anythin' you wanna tell me, Tommy, before I beat the ever-lovin' crap outta you?"

"Ho. Ho. Ho. Easy there, big fella. You don't wanna be hittin' Santa Claus. Think of the children."

"You've been cheatin' us, Tommy. I don't like cheats. I take it personal, Tommy. Real personal." Big Mack continued to rub his hands together.

"Whaddya mean I'm cheating? I've been making my payments. Here . . ." And Tommy reached inside his read suit, pulling out his cash. "Here's today's hundred," and Tommy peeled off a couple of bills. "And something a little extra for your effort."

Big Mack glared. "You see, Tommy? That's what I mean. Now where you been getting all this cash?"

"What's the problem, Big? I'm just a man trying to pay off a debt."

"Look, Tommy. I've been patient about the cash. Right? And all I asked was a little favor. Boost some stuff, you know, electronics, jewelry."

Tommy suddenly was starting to sweat inside his Santa suit. "Look at me. I can't be sneaking around dressed like Santa. Who would be easier to identify in a line-up than Santa? I explained all that last week."

Big Mack considered Tommy's explanation. "So tell me, Tommy . . . where's all this extra cash coming from? And how come the security office is getting so many reports of lost and stolen merchandise?"

"It's not me." Tommy looked at Big Mack, looked for understanding. "Gimme another chance."

Big Mack's eyes were cold steel. "I can't, Tommy. It's bad for business. You understand."

Tommy had no answer.

"Let's take a walk, Tommy," said Big Mack.

Working mall security, Oliver Berryhill had taken more than the usual number of complaints this holiday season. Lost and stolen merchandise were definitely on the rise, but when Oliver alerted his supervisors, they told him not to worry about it. Mall management didn't want the bad publicity that would come with news of a Christmas crime spree. He was instructed to downplay the problem, to defuse angry shoppers.

So Oliver went about his business, walking the mall, framing imaginary camera shots and bopping to the piped-in Christmas music. It was going to be a hipster's Christmas this year, he decided, judging from the swinging arrangements. Oliver was singing along to Little Charlie and the Nitecats—"It's Christmas Time Again (so Spend, Spend, Spend)." He wondered whether anyone in mall management realized what was playing on the Christmas tape loop. He stopped to use the men's room.

It was a few minutes too late that Oliver realized there was no toilet paper in the stall. Luckily a man was using the adjacent stall.

"Hey, bud. Pass me some toilet paper, okay?"

It annoyed Oliver when his neighbor ignored his request. Are we not our brother's keeper, Oliver wondered, especially during the holidays?

"How about it, bud? Can't you spare me a coupla sheets?"

When the stranger in the adjacent stall again ignored his plaintive request, Oliver carefully peeked under the composite fiberglass wall which separated the stalls, staring at the fine Italian loafers, the black gabardine suit pants, and the pool of dark red blood spreading across the floor.

Oliver pushed open the door to the adjacent stall. A very large man, fully clothed, sat on the toilet seat, dead from a stab wound in his neck. There was a puddle of blood on the floor, a Henckels carving knife in the puddle. Oliver remembered what they taught him in mall security school.

He checked the man's pulse. And found none. Oliver reached for his walkie-talkie. *Damn.* The batteries were dead too. He would have to walk to the security office at the other end of the mall.

Oliver checked the man's pockets and found a wallet—Thaddeus Maciborski. He also found several pieces of woman's jewelry, but no receipts, the jewelry quite possibly stolen. Something about the man was familiar. Oliver played back the imaginary footage he'd been shooting for weeks. He froze the footage on a scene in the parking lot, the dead guy and his partner hassling an older woman. He considered the recent rash of complaints. An idea began to tug at Oliver. He placed an "Out of Order" sign on the men's room door and hustled down to the security office. The office was empty, security staff out making their rounds. He logged onto the computer. Thaddeus Macibroski, aka Teddy Mack, aka Big Mack, aka Big, had more criminal convictions than aliases. Oliver placed a call to the local police.

"My name is Oliver Berryhill. I'm a security officer at the Mall of New Jersey."

"Yes, Mr. Berryhill, what can I do for you?" The officer who answered the phone seemed less than interested in doing much of anything for Mr. Berryhill.

"There's been an incident at the mall."

"An incident?" The officer was listening now.

"I was making my rounds of the mall today, just like always, and I came upon a man in possession of stolen property."

"And?" The officer prompted Oliver to continue.

"When I confronted the suspect, he pulled a knife on me. I'm sure you realize, as mall security, I don't carry a weapon. The man lunged at me. In the ensuing struggle, as I defended myself from his attack, the man seems to have been cut by his own knife."

"How badly is the man hurt?" the officer asked.

"I'm afraid the man is dead."

"I'll send someone right away," said the officer.

While Oliver waited for the police to arrive, he placed an anonymous call to the local TV station. Oliver was ready for his fifteen minutes of fame.

Sharing His Years of Experience

Two police officers were first to arrive, followed quickly by the medical examiner and the local TV news crew. Mall management was less than pleased to learn the purpose for their unexpected visits and was thrown into chaos at the mention of the dead man. Oliver, however, was ready and waiting, his hair combed and his story straight.

The officers did a quick examination in the men's room, bagging the knife, while the medical examiner confirmed that the large man's death was as it appeared. The director of mall operations was frustrated with the police who denied him access to the men's room, but there was nothing he could do. When Oliver ignored his questions, he nearly went postal, but Oliver patiently explained that he had a responsibility to speak first to the police officers.

The older of the two police officers, Eddie Bebedict, "Eggs," as he was known by his friends, a gruff man with gravel in his voice, approached the mall director. "I need a private spot to talk."

The mall director was nervous, but pleased to finally have the opportunity to find out what was going on. "We can talk in my office."

"Not you. The square badge. Him." And he pointed to Oliver. "But thanks for the use of your office." Eggs gestured to Oliver who showed him the way to the mall director's office.

"So explain to me again what happened."

Oliver and the officer were sitting in the mall director's cubicle, going over the sequence of events. Oliver had watched enough detective movies to understand how this worked. He stayed calm, his voice even, his manner serene, recalling, not reliving the traumatic events of the day.

"I was making my rounds, same as always. I make it a point to check the men's room a couple of times a day, mostly just to roust the smokers. So I walk into the men's room, and I spot the perp standing at the mirror, examining several pieces of ladies' jewelry."

This was the third time Eddie Bebedict had asked Oliver to recount the events. He checked his notes as Oliver spoke, but made no new notes.

"I confronted the perp. He reached into his suit pocket and pulled out a knife. We struggled. I pushed him off of me. He lost his balance, the knife slicing across his neck as he fell back into the stall. Blood spurted from his neck." Oliver shuddered at the memory. "What do they call that? The carotid artery?"

The officer nodded. "So what happened next?"

Oliver continued. "I could tell the man was dead. I put the sign on the door so no one else would walk in, and then I ran down the hall and called you."

"Thank you." The officer made a few notes. "And then you called the reporter."

Oliver did his best to look offended. "Me? Of course not."

Eddie Bebedict shook his head. "No, of course not." He took a moment to collect his thoughts before asking, "You're not planning on going anywhere are you, Oliver?"

"No. Well, maybe to my Mom's for Christmas. She lives the other end of town. Is that okay?"

"Okay then. You're free to go . . . for now."

Oliver smiled. "Whatever I can do to help a fellow officer."

The officer walked back down the hall to the crime scene. He was pleased to see that the medical examiner had already transported the body and his partner had already completed the canvass. Bright yellow crime scene tape festooned the entrance to the men's room.

As the officers made ready to leave, the director of mall operations had a question. Pointing to the crime scene tape he asked, "What am I supposed to do about that?"

The gravel settled deep in the police officer's throat. "Use the ladies' room, I guess."

As they walked through the mall, they could see Oliver Berryhill being interviewed, this time on camera, by the local TV reporter. Eggs turned to his partner, mentoring now, sharing his years of experience. He pointed at the preening security cop.

"You think that putz could kill Big Mack, even by accident?"

Crab Salad

Cassie stared at the house. It was weathered wood and glass. It wasn't a person. It wasn't a promise. It wasn't even a home. It was just a building, and it did not hold dominion over her. Cassie turned her car around and followed the coastline, back toward town, toward Main Street, toward the boardwalk.

In the summertime, Cassie could orbit the town without ever finding a parking place, but the beach town was empty in the winter, and Cassie had her choice of thousands of available spaces. She could park in front of any store, any restaurant, any motel in town. It hardly mattered. They were all—well, nearly all—closed for the season. Cassie pulled into a spot and climbed up onto the boardwalk. The arcades were closed, the pizza joints closed, the bars closed. Even the psychic had shut down for the season, the neon eyeball turned off at Om Depot, Madame Alexina having correctly foreseen the limited demand for off-season psychic advice.

Cassie was surprised to find that the downstairs room at White Sands Blues was open. No live music, of course, and no customers either, but there was mellow jazz playing on the sound system, and a youthful bartender relaxing behind the bar, watching television with the sound muted.

"Come on in, ma'am. We're open."

Cassie took a seat at the bar. "I'd like an Irish whiskey and water."

The bartender went off in search of whiskey, returning with a bottle of Jameson's. "Is this okay?"

Cassie nodded.

The bartender extended his hand. "I'm Glenn."

"Cassie," she answered, and sipped the Jameson's and water. "Thanks."

"What brings you to the beach this time of year?" Glenn wondered.

"What keeps you open this time of year?"

Glenn smiled. "*Touché.*"

"Can I get something to eat?"

"Well," Glenn explained, "the kitchen's not really open, but let me see what I can find."

Glenn disappeared in back and returned ten minutes later with a tin of crabmeat. "I think it's still good. How about I make a crab salad?"

"That would be wonderful!"

Glenn again disappeared, returning shortly with two small plates of crab salad, on Boston lettuce, with a light mustard-wasabi dressing. "I hope this will be okay." He topped up Cassie's whiskey and poured himself a glass of Pinot Grigio.

Jimmy Heath was playing saxophone on the sound system. On the muted TV behind the bar, a news story came onscreen from the Mall of New Jersey. The reporter was interviewing a security guard.

"Holy crap, Glenn. Turn the sound up."

Glenn increased the volume on the sound system.

"Not the music. The TV."

Glen fixed the sound just in time for Cassie to hear Oliver Berryhill explain. "I thought about all the shoppers, especially the moms with their young children waiting to meet Santa Claus. I couldn't let the madman get past me. I couldn't let any of the children be put in danger."

"What the hell was that all about?" She had spent weeks at the mall, day after boring day, and nothing ever happened. *What a piece of bad luck,* she thought. *For the dead guy, too.*

Cassie checked her cell phone. Jack Cambrian had already left a message.

"O'Malley. My gut told me there was a story at the mall. And my star writer is on scene when the whole thing goes down. What a piece of good luck. Call me as soon as you can."

Cassie gulped down the rest of her Jameson's and threw a twenty on the bar. "Sorry, Glenn. I gotta run."

The Code

Driving to Woodbine, Little Mack could picture his upcoming visit to Louie's pawnshop. At first, Louie would deny any knowledge of Tommy V. Little would get up in his face, and still Louie would resist giving Tommy up. The code.

Probably Little would have to threaten violence. He might even have to hit the guy. Little Mack shook his head in the car on the way down to Woodbine, imagining the violence. *It was all so tedious.*

And it was also unnecessary. Even as Little Mack was driving to Woodbine, Big Mack was on his way to the mall. The Macks already knew that Tommy was playing them, running some kind of scam. The details really didn't matter. But still, there he was, driving the Lincoln Town Car to Woodbine. The code.

Little Mack thought about the code. Every business has its own peculiar set of rules. In that regard, the enforcement business was no different. It was a matter of honor. After all, it was the business he chose. It was the business his father chose for him. After his brothers died, Big Mack informed his only living son that he was going into the family business. Most of the time, Little Mack enjoyed a day "at the office." But recently, all he felt about work was tired.

When he parked the Town Car in front of Louie's pawnshop, he said a quick prayer that Louie might allow him to bypass the ritual confrontation, but the patron saint of enforcers must not have been listening.

Louie denied knowing Tommy V. Little Mack got in his face, and he could tell that Louie was scared silly, but he was stubborn and he played by the rules. Louie was not going to give Tommy up. Little Mack would have to play the scene out.

He threatened violence, and Louie started to cry, but still he refused to talk until Little Mack hit him one time, not too hard, but enough that Louie cowered in the corner, his glasses flying across the pawnshop. Louie told Little Mack how Tommy had come in almost every night for a week, to unload stolen goods. *It was all so tedious.*

Little Mack walked out of the pawnshop and started up the Town Car. He pointed the car north, leaving Woodbine in his rearview window. *What the fuck is wrong with me?*

Little Mack was halfway home when he heard the report on his car radio. During an attempted robbery, career criminal, Teddy Maciborski was killed at the Mall of New Jersey. There was a brief audio clip of Oliver Berryhill explaining how he had to protect the women and children.

Little Mack pulled the Town Car onto the shoulder. He wanted to feel anger. He tried really hard to locate the anger in the pit of his stomach, but he could not find anger. What he found there surprised him. Little Mack sat in the Town Car on the side of the road and cried.

Jesus, it's a good thing no one's here to see this.

Little Mack cried like a baby. Like a pawnshop owner about to get hit.

Events Unfolding like a Movie

Word spread through the mall like a fungus. There was a dead body in the men's room, or was it the food court or the bath shop? No one was quite sure what was going on, but everyone knew there was a dead body. Was there a killer on the loose? No one knew, but that didn't stop everyone from expressing an expert opinion. The mall was about to be locked down. The police were setting up checkpoints all along the mall's perimeter. SWAT teams were already sweeping through the mall, store by store. It made no difference that there were neither SWAT teams nor checkpoints because there was gossip. And gossip fueled rumor. And rumor fueled hysteria. And amidst the commotion, no one noticed when Santa failed to return from his break.

Tommy grabbed his bag of purloined presents and ran for his car. Life really can change completely, he thought, in an instant. He drove poorly, distracted by the events of the day, nearly hitting two cars in the parking lot and one more on the road. He thought about his confrontation with Big Mack, the ugly words that were exchanged, the ultimatum. He drove recklessly, weaving in and out of traffic, uncertain as to his final destination even as he pulled to a stop in front of Greta's house. He jumped out of the car, grabbing the bag of stolen goods, banging at Greta's front door.

When Greta opened the door, she found Tommy still dressed as Santa, with a bag of gifts slung over his shoulder, muttering to himself, pacing in front of the door.

"Tommy! Aren't you—grr—supposed . . . ?"

Tommy pushed past her into the house, dropping his bag on the floor in the family room. "Can I leave this here for a couple of days?"

"Shit, Tommy. Don't get me involved in one of your schemes." When they were married, Greta often had the chance to observe Tommy in the midst of a scheme gone bad. She recognized the herky-jerky motion in his arms and legs, the odd angle of his head, the look of desperation in his eyes. This one was bad. "What's wrong?"

"Nothing . . . really, Greta. Look, I'm just gonna stash this bag in the basement for a coupla three days. Okay?" Tommy carried the bag down the stairs without waiting for an answer.

He looked around the unfinished basement, left the bag in the utility closet and ran back up the stairs, taking two steps at a time.

"You know, Greta, I really had fun at dinner."

Greta was still angry about dinner. "I—grr—did too, Tommy. Until you left me the damn check."

"I'm gonna pay you back, Greta."

"Sure you are, Tommy."

"Really." Tommy's hand was on the doorknob. "I gotta go."

"If you don't—grr—mind one question, Tommy, how come you're wearing your Santa suit?"

Tommy stopped half-way out the door and smacked himself in the head. "Holy shit, Greta. You're right. Do you have any of my old clothes packed away in the attic?"

Greta laughed. "I burned whatever you didn't take."

"I gotta go, Greta." Santa sprinted for his car.

Tommy wondered if it was safe to stop at his apartment, but he didn't really have a choice. He had to change out of the Santa suit. He drove past his apartment three times before pulling into a parking place. He saw no evidence that anyone was sitting on his apartment. He moved cautiously as he entered. The tiny apartment was quiet and dark. Tommy threw the Santa suit on the floor, climbing into an old pair of jeans and a grey hooded sweatshirt.

Tommy still hadn't figured out where he was going or how long he would be gone. As he rifled through his bureau, trying to decide what he might need, he flipped on the TV. On TV, Oliver Berryhill was explaining to the reporter how he subdued the enraged criminal.

"Say what?" Tommy stopped what he was doing to watch the special news bulletin.

Oliver Berryhill told quite a story. Tommy pictured the events unfolding like a movie. Oliver walking into the bathroom, checking for cigarette smokers and finding instead the very large and very dangerous Teddy Maciborski. Teddy examining the stolen jewelry, startled by Oliver's appearance, trying to hide the stolen goods before his illegal activity might be uncovered. Oliver, always on the alert, recognizing the telltale signs of a criminal mind, confronting the man, cool and relaxed in the face of danger. "I approached the man carefully and said, 'Hey Mac. How ya doin'?' " Oliver looked at the reporter and smiled, a grim smile, the smile of a man who had looked at danger and danger blinked. "I remember exactly because it seems funny now, ironic, that I called him Mac and then I learned that was the guy's name, Mack."

Oliver explained how Mack tried to double-talk his way out of trouble, and when he realized Oliver was not going to be fooled, he pulled a knife. Sitting in his apartment, watching the interview on TV, Tommy tried to imagine the ensuing struggle, Oliver pushing the armed and dangerous Big Mack off of him, Mack losing his balance, tripping, his arms reaching out as he tried to catch himself, falling backwards into the stall, accidentally slitting his own throat as he fell.

"It was horrible," Oliver admitted to the reporter. "The blood spurting from the man's neck. It's a picture I won't ever forget."

Oliver told the story so well that Tommy, sitting in his apartment, could picture the blood spurting from Big Mack's neck wound nearly as clearly as Oliver.

Tommy stared at the television. "Maybe things will work out after all."

Her Mother's Logic

Rae Harbrough dialed her daughter's phone number. "Have you been watching the news, dear?"

"Hello, mother. What are they reporting on the news today?"

"You mean you don't know?"

"No, mother. I'm very busy today." Cheyenne had spent the day reviewing departmental proposals for the township budget plan.

"Mayor busy?"

"Yes mother, mayor busy."

Rae Harbrough frowned. "Don't you worry that being mayor is taking up too much of your time?"

"Mother!"

"I'm sorry, dear. It's just that I worry about you sometimes. You look tired."

"I'm fine, Mother. Now why is it that you called?"

"There was an incident at the mall today. A security officer had to kill a dangerous criminal."

"What?" Cheyenne turned on her TV.

"Turn on you television dear."

"I just did, Mother." Cheyenne flipped channels, quickly finding a report on the incident at the mall. "Wow."

Rae got to the purpose of her call. "I think you should give that nice young officer a proclamation."

"The rent-a-cop? Why on earth should I do that?" Cheyenne never could quite follow her mother's logic.

"He did a brave thing, Cheyenne, protecting the women at the mall. Imagine if you and I had been there."

Cheyenne felt guilty, but for just the briefest moment she did imagine her mother at the mall. "But why should I give the man a proclamation? You realize the mall isn't in Doah, don't you?"

"I'm not going senile yet, dear. I think a proclamation is just a nice way to say thank you. After all, people from towns all over south Jersey, including many voters in Doah, shop at the mall."

Cheyenne knew that her mother was not thinking about how Cheyenne might enhance her appeal to Doah's voters. She waited for the real reason, and her mother did not disappoint.

"Do you realize that the man who died today, the dangerous criminal, was the same man that tried to steal my cashmere scarf last week?"

Audrey Hepburn

Cassie did not return Jack Cambrian's first phone message, and she ducked two more after that. She didn't want to talk to Jack until she learned more about what really happened at the mall. She watched the news reports, watched as Oliver Berryhill refined the story with each retelling. He was remarkably adept for a security guard. By the time the mall re-opened in the morning, his story would be too rehearsed to be of much interest. It was, Cassie decided, probably too late already.

She needed to talk to someone who was there. It didn't have to be someone with direct knowledge of the killing. After all, there were no eye witnesses to the fatal encounter between Teddy Maciborski and Oliver Berryhill. When she spoke to Jack Cambrian, she needed to sound like she had been there. She needed to get a feel for the chaos in the mall. She needed a source at the mall. She needed, Cassie decided, to bum an early morning cigarette from Santa Claus.

Santa would know what it felt like in the mall. He would have seen the children crying and the mothers yelling. He would know who'd been bad and who'd been good.

She might have writer's block, but Cassie still had a writer's instinct. She had stumbled upon an angle for her story—the killing at the Mall of New Jersey as seen through the eyes of Santa Claus. She still had to do her research and write the damn thing, but she could already picture the finished piece. Cassie O'Malley was back. She would have a story for Jack Cambrian, and not just any story. She would have a damn fine story for the magazine.

Cassie turned off the news reports and switched on a Dave Brubeck CD, the tune "Audrey," an homage to Audrey Hepburn, floating like Ms. Hepburn herself through the condo. Cassie poured herself an inch of Tullamore Dew and logged onto the computer. "Go ahead," she urged, "you can do this."

But she was wrong. She stared at the computer screen, her fingers poised above the keyboard, but the idea would not gel, the words would not flow. Cassie freshened her Tullamore Dew.

That night Cassie dreamt of Christmases past. She dreamt of her freshman year in college, spending Christmas in the dorm with her roommate, Cheyenne. The random room assignments of freshman year had thrown Cassie and Cheyenne together. It was a pairing that would never work, Cassie told herself. They were The Odd Couple, Cassie's Felix to Cheyenne's Oscar. When they decided to throw a tree-trimming party for the dormitory, Cassie fretted over every detail. Cheyenne popped a beer and announced that it was all good.

The dorm was nearly empty, most of the girls having gone home for the holidays. And so, in the dormitory, in her freshman year at Princeton, the tree-trimming party had been poorly attended. But in her dream, nearly twenty years later, the dorm room was filled with guests. Cassie's parents were there, as was her husband. Morris was there, and Jack too. Oliver Berryhill was a guest at the party, explaining once again how he fought off Big Mack's attack. And Big Mack himself made a brief appearance at the tree-trimming party. Cassie awoke in the morning, Christmas carols still ringing in her ears. It was time to pay a visit to Santa Claus.

Cassie parked her car at the front of the lot, some twenty minutes before the Mall of New Jersey was scheduled to open for business. As she expected, Santa Claus was standing out front, puffing on a Newport. She took a deep breath and walked over.

"You are looking powerful sexy this morning, Santa Claus." Actually, Cassie thought that Santa looked anxious, nearly nauseous, but the situation did not call for such candor.

Tommy blushed behind his white whiskers. "I haven't seen you in a couple of days. Need a cig?"

Tommy held out the pack of Newports, and Cassie took one. She waited until Santa pulled out a lighter. "Let me light that for you."

"Thank you." Cassie giggled. She was disgusted with herself for giggling, but she was pleased as well. A quick peek told her Santa was enjoying the attention.

They stood in front of the entrance and smoked their cigarettes, sharing an intimate nicotine moment. As shoppers moved around them and entered the mall, Cassie turned to Santa Claus, asking, "Aren't you going to be late?"

Santa stubbed out his cigarette. "Yeah. I gotta go."

Cassie smiled up at Santa. "I'm working on a Christmas story. How about I buy you a cup of coffee on your morning break? You can tell me what it's like to be Santa Claus."

Tommy sipped his hot coffee, careful not to burn the inside of his mouth, and looked across the table at Cassie taking notes. "Don't get me wrong. Most days it's just a job. Kids screaming. Moms bitching. The elves can be a royal pain in the ass. And Mrs. Claus . . . Let me tell you, when it's her time of the month, Mrs. Claus can be a bitch. But for all that, I think I'm beginning to like being Santa Claus." Tommy took a bite of corn muffin and another sip of coffee, black, two sugars. How about you? Do you like being a writer?"

"I love being a writer." Cassie thought about her answer. "At least I used to. Lately I'm not so sure."

"What's changed?" Tommy wondered.

"I don't know. Anyway, I'm the one who's supposed to be asking the questions. So tell me about yesterday. I hear it got pretty crazy here."

Tommy laughed. "Yeah, that's what I hear too."

Cassie was surprised by Tommy's answer. "On TV, they've been reporting that the mall was in a state of panic yesterday. Are you saying it's being exaggerated?"

"I'm sure some folks panicked, but a lot of people probably didn't know that anything happened yesterday until they got home and saw the reports on television."

While Tommy talked, he kept an eye on the line growing ever longer at Santa's Workshop. "I gotta go. Thanks." He gulped down the rest of his coffee, searing the roof of his mouth. "Damn."

Cabin Twelve

Little Mack sat on the side of the road and cried. *Stop acting like such a pussy.* He told himself to just stop crying, but he didn't know how. He didn't get weepy like this very often, but when he did it tore right at the heart of who he was. *My daddy was a tough guy. My brothers were tough guys. I'm supposed to be a tough guy. So what am I doing sitting here crying like a friggin' baby?*

Oh, shit. In his rearview mirror, Little Mack spotted the police car pulling up behind him, the patrol cop getting out of the squad car, walking up to his driver's side window.

"Is everything okay, sir?"

Little Mack looked at the patrol cop. He couldn't stop crying long enough to answer.

"Are you okay, sir?" the officer repeated.

"I'm . . ." Little Mack wiped his nose, ". . . fine."

The cop was unconvinced. "If you don't mind my saying so, it doesn't look like everything is fine. Can I see your license and registration sir?"

Little Mack reached into his glove compartment and handed the officer his counterfeit documents. The officer took the cards. "Wait here." He went back to his squad car. While the cop called in to check the identification, Little Mack sat in the Town Car and cried.

The officer returned to the driver's side window of the Town Car and handed Little Mack his license and registration.

"Are you planning to drive home to Trenton tonight, Mr. Smith?"

Crying softly, Little Mack nodded yes.

"I am afraid I can't let you do that. Not in your current condition. I'd like you to follow me back to Woodbine, sir."

Little Mack knew that the cop was right. He was in no shape to drive home. He turned the car around and, following the patrol car, made the short drive back to Woodbine, peering out from between his tears. When the cop car came to a stop in front of Bhait's Motel, Little Mack pulled in behind him. He wiped his eyes and blew his nose and managed to reduce his embarrassing display to watery eyes and sniffles before entering the motel lobby. The officer was huddled with the motel manager when Little Mack walked in.

Beejit Bhait examined the large man with weepy eyes and custom-tailored suit. "Ah, my good sir. You will be needing a room?"

Little Mack picked up a whiff of sandalwood. He wasn't sure if it was coming from the incense burner sitting on the shelf behind the check-in counter or whether it was coming from Mr. Bhait himself.

"Yeah, I need a room. Somethin' private."

Beejit Bhait looked at the patrol cop and nodded. "I understand, good sir. You will be wanting cabin twelve. Please to be pulling your car around to the back."

Little Mack took the cabin key and drove his car around to the back of the motel property. As Mr. Bhait had promised, cabin twelve was indeed in a very private location. Little Mack didn't want to be seen crying like a baby.

Cop Humor

Cassie decided it was time for her to pay a visit to the officer handling the death of Teddy Maciborski. It took only a couple of phone calls to determine that the officer handling the case was Detective Eddie Bebedict, but the detective made it clear over the phone that he had no interest in speaking to a member of the press.

"But I'm not a reporter," Cassie had explained, "I write features for the *Jersey Knews*."

Eddie Bebedict snorted, just one time. "That piece of garbage? I wouldn't use the *Jersey Knews* to line my bird cage."

Cassie loved the sound of gravel grinding in Eddie's throat as he talked. "But I'd like to talk to you about Oliver Berryhill."

Eddie Bebedict was unimpressed. "Why are you interested? No space alien abductions this month?"

Cassie found herself liking the detective, even though he wouldn't speak to her, quite possibly because he wouldn't speak to her. The *Jersey Knews* was hardly the most reputable of periodicals. Still, Cassie was not about to be discouraged by the detective's lack of interest. Half an hour later she was standing at the detective's desk, introducing herself.

"I thought I told you I wasn't gonna talk to you," Eddie reminded her.

Cassie pushed. "I figured it was worth the trip to make you turn me down face-to-face."

Eddie, however, wasn't staring at her face. "Oh, what the hell. Take a load off, Ms. . . ."

"O'Malley. But my friends call me Cassie," she said as she took a seat alongside the detective's desk.

"Eddie Bebedict," he replied, "My friends call me Eggs."

"Eggs?"

"Eggs . . . Bebedict," he explained. "Get it, eggs benedict?"

Cassie chuckled. "What's that, cop humor?"

Eddie smiled. "Yeah, cop humor. So what can I do for you Cassie?"

"What can you tell me about Teddy Maciborski?"

Eddie opened the file on his desk. "Teddy Maciborski was a goon. Blackmail. Illegal gaming. Dealing in stolen goods. Assault and battery."

"And his death?"

"Why do you ask?" Eggs Bebedict watched Cassie closely.

"I've spent the last couple of weeks at the mall, trying to write a sappy story about the Christmas shoppers."

Eggs was suddenly more interested. "So you were at the mall yesterday when Big Mack died?"

Cassie shook her head. "No, and that's the problem. I was supposed to be. Now my boss thinks I've got this great story for him, and the truth is I've got jackshit."

Eggs was understanding. "So now you're trying to cobble together a story before your boss figures out you screwed up."

Cassie nodded.

Eddie snorted a second time. "I can respect that. Tell you what, Cassie, maybe we can help one another."

"I'll be happy to do whatever I can, Detective."

"Thank you, Cassie. I was wondering if you got to know this Oliver Berryhill in the last couple of weeks."

"I saw him, of course. I guess I talked to him a couple of times. Nothing memorable."

"So here's what I'm curious about, Cassie. Do you think that Oliver Berryhill was capable of killing Teddy Maciborski?"

Cassie was surprised by the detective's question. "I thought it was an accident."

"You're right, Cassie. Of course it was an accident. What I mean is, when you listen to Oliver Berryhill describe the struggle in the men's room with Teddy Macibroski, Teddy coming at him with a knife, can you picture Oliver, in any event, being the one who emerges from the men's room alive?"

Cassie hadn't asked herself the question in quite the same way, but the thought had crossed her mind. "No, Detective. I guess when you put it that way, I picture Teddy walking out of the bathroom very much alive and Oliver sitting on the toilet, dead."

Eggs nodded. "Me too, Cassie. Me too."

For a moment, they sat in the squad room, imagining the scene in the men's room at the Mall of New Jersey.

Cassie spoke first. "So what are you doing with the case?"

Eggs snorted a third time. "Nothing. The captain is satisfied with the outcome. The case is closed."

Cassie rose to leave. "Thank you, Eggs."

"You're welcome, Cassie. Keep in touch, okay?"

"Of course, Detective."

A Light Visible in the Window

When the police car pulled up in front of the Bhait's Motel, Morris peeked out his cabin window, curious to know what had brought the police to this deserted spot on the outskirts of town. During his forced respite at the motel, there had been no other guests. Beejit Bhait kept largely to himself. The arguments between Beejit and his mother that bled through his wall at odd hours of the day and night hardly seemed a sufficient reason for the police presence. Then Morris saw the Town Car pull in behind the patrol car. A very large man dragged his tired body from the car.

Morris had seen that very large body once before. There was something different about the man on this occasion. It was more than just the absence of his equally large partner. It was something else. Morris had the feeling that this man had somehow shrunk inside his very large body. It was not that he looked smaller to Morris. It was as if the man no longer fully filled his very large body. But despite the deterioration, Morris had no doubt that it was the same man. How had he traced Morris to the motel? What were his intentions? Morris was certain that this was a man who preferred to keep his business activities invisible. For what possible reason had he involved the local police? Morris sank back away from the window, only to creep back, needing to watch, as his pursuer checked into the Bhait's Motel.

Morris watched the patrol car depart. He watched the Lincoln Town Car pull to the rear of the motel property. In a panic, Morris realized that his was the only cabin with a light visible in the window. Had his pursuer seen the light in cabin number one? Morris turned the light off and waited.

Morris passed fifteen excruciating minutes alone in the dark in cabin number one. He picked up the telephone and dialed Cassie's number, listening to the ring. *Pick up, Cassie*, he begged, *please pick up.*

"I'm sorry, but I am unavailable to take your call right now. Please leave your name and number, and I'll get back to you as soon as possible."

"Cassie. It's me. Morris. Pick up the damn phone, Cassie. He's here. What am I gonna do, Cassie? Pick up the damn phone. Please."

Morris placed the receiver down on its cradle. He would have to face this on his own. He sat in the dark and watched the clock. Five minutes passed. Ten. Twenty. Thirty minutes went by and nothing happened. The absence of any immediate threat seemed to Morris to be especially sinister. What was his pursuer waiting for? His partner? Morris needed to know what was happening. More stupid than brave, he slipped quietly out of his cabin, and hugging the wall, walked in the shadows down to the end of the row of cabins. As he went around to the back, he spotted the Town Car outside cabin twelve. Morris moved slowly now, careful not to make noise. For just a moment, Morris thought he saw someone hidden in a stand of trees behind the cabins, but he rubbed his eyes and the shadowy figure was gone. Sweating now, Morris crept up to cabin twelve. He knew that what he was doing was stupid, but he'd come this far. Morris peeked in at the edge of the window. What he saw took him by surprise.

Lying on the bed in cabin twelve, this very large man, still wearing his custom-tailored suit and fine Italian shoes, was bawling like a baby.

Oliver Berryhill Day

When Tommy arrived at the mall for another day of Santa duty, he discovered that Santa's Workshop had been dismantled overnight, leaving a small stage and a modest display of Christmas decorations. "Don't worry about it," the mall manager explained. "It's just for one day."

Tommy tried to imagine what event was pushing Santa off the schedule for a day.

"It's Oliver Berryhill Day here at the Mall of New Jersey. Shoppers can get their picture taken with a genuine hero." Something in the manager's tone suggested a lack of enthusiasm for the event.

"So what am I supposed to do?" Tommy wondered.

"Take the day off, Tommy. Have fun. Shop." The manager laughed. "I've got an idea. You could get your picture taken with Oliver Berryhill."

"Maybe I will."

"Just remember," the manager advised Tommy, "don't clock in today. If you stick around, you're doing it on your own time."

Tommy watched as mall maintenance workers put the finishing touches on the display. Oliver would sit where Santa usually sat. The line would follow the same path, shoppers waiting in line to shake Oliver's hand and get their picture taken. The giant candy canes had been removed from Santa's Workshop to create a spot for media. Mall management had invited the local TV station to cover the event, along with the radio stations and the local print media. They were hoping for a large turn-out, good coverage and an upbeat day.

To mall management, Oliver Berryhill was just a prop at the event. The real focus, as always, was the shopper. They hoped that by throwing this day-long event, complete with refreshments, give-aways and unadvertised sales, the mall could negate the loss of shoppers that might otherwise be expected after the fatal encounter in the men's room.

It was obvious that Oliver Berryhill didn't know he was just a prop, sweeping into the mall twenty minutes late, surrounded by his posse (looking on, Tommy wondered about rent-a-cop groupies) and trailed by his own private film crew, who was recording the event for O.B. Productions.

Tommy had to laugh when he got a clear look at Oliver Berryhill. Overnight, his brown Mall of New Jersey security guard uniform had sprouted gold epaulets and trim. Tommy had seen enough. He made his way to the exit, unwilling to waste any more of his unexpected day off hanging out at the mall.

Oliver Berryhill Day started slowly as small children, eager to sit on Santa's hospitable lap, arrived dragging adults behind them. The toddlers were not impressed by a preening security guard. The supervisor of special events, on behalf of mall management and all of the storeowners and their employees, welcomed the disappointed children and their impatient parents to Oliver Berryhill Day. Oliver smiled broadly, causing several small children to break out in tearful sobs and screams. The supervisor gave Oliver a dirty look and gave the children lollipops.

By late morning, the mood began to shift. The mid-day team of Dick Joakes and Lou Spowels showed up from radio station WWEX to do an onsite remote.

"Okay, boys and girls. We're comin' at ya today from the Mall of New Jersey. It's a party down here. So drop whatever you're doing and come down to the mall for Dick Joakes and Lou Spowels. We're gonna be here until two p.m. What've you got there Lou?"

Lou Spowels leaned into his microphone. "Hey, Dick. Someone just handed me this." Lou waved a piece of paper, for his radio listeners. "We're supposed to let everyone know that it's Oliver Berryhill Day here at the Mall of New Jersey. Come meet a genuine local hero."

"That's right, Lou. Later we'll see if we can get a few words with Mr. Berryhill. Right now though, we're gonna sit back and listen to some tunes. We're taking requests from our listeners here in the mall."

Actually, Dick and Lou took their song requests from mall management, who had very specific ideas about what music should be piped through the mall's sound system. The first song was the latest single from Kelly Clarkson.

Gradually the crowd grew larger and the mood more festive. A line began to form as shoppers took the opportunity to shake hands with local hero Oliver Berryhill. At noon, the supervisor of special events paused the photo line as well as the pop music. She motioned to Oliver Berryhill to join her on stage.

"We have a very special guest joining us today to read a special proclamation. From nearby Doah Township, I would like to introduce Mayor Cheyenne Harbrough."

There was a polite smattering of applause, the crowd hoping that this would be a brief interruption.

Cheyenne looked out at the crowd. "Thank you. I am very pleased to be here today representing the wonderful town of Doah." Cheyenne Harbrough took a framed document from her briefcase and began to read.

"Whereas the Mall of New Jersey provides a world class shopping experience for thousands of citizens from all over the great state of New Jersey and beyond; and

"Whereas citizens from Doah Township travel daily to the Mall of New Jersey for their shopping and entertainment needs; and

"Whereas it is the private security officers who are at the front lines, creating a safe and enjoyable shopping experience for those shoppers from Doah, from New Jersey and beyond; and

"Whereas acting in the face of great personal danger, one security officer, Mr. Oliver Berryhill, demonstrated extraordinary bravery in order to protect shoppers from an armed felon; and

"Whereas that felon has on at least one other occasion accosted unsuspecting shoppers here at the Mall of New Jersey;

"Then therefore, be it resolved that the town council of Doah Township, New Jersey, on behalf of its grateful citizenry, does hereby thank and commend Oliver Berryhill for his act of selfless courage.

"Signed on this fourteenth day of December, 2007, by myself, Cheyenne Harbrough, Mayor of Doah Township."

Cheyenne handed the plaque to Oliver Berryhill. "Thank you, Mr. Berryhill."

Oliver reached past the plaque for the microphone. "Thank you, Mayor Harbrough. This is indeed an honor. As public servants, you and I both have a duty to protect civilians. In that respect, I only did what any security officer is pledged to do."

Oliver was just getting warmed up when Lou Spowels opened up the channel for his own microphone. "Okay, boys and girls, that was Mayor Harbrough and Oliver Berryhill." He popped a cart into the machine, turning the volume up louder. "And this is Kid Rock and the Howling Diablos."

Paternal Pride

Tommy's first stop after leaving the mall on this unexpected day off was the home of his ex-wife Greta. He knocked on the door and was pleased when his son, Tommy Junior, answered.

"Mom's at work."

"That's okay, kiddo. I didn't come to see your mom."

"Hey, Pop, cool. Is this your weekend? Gimme a minute, okay?" Tommy Junior was running to his room before his dad had a chance to enter or answer.

Tommy yelled to his son's disappearing back. "C'mon back, kiddo."

Tommy Junior turned and walked back into the living room, wary of yet another paternal disappointment. "What's up?"

"I'm sorry, Tommy. It's not my weekend. I just came by to get some of my stuff out of the basement."

"Pop, you don't have anything down there. Mom burned it all years ago." Tommy Junior remembered the day his mother built a bonfire in the backyard. It was a violation of a township ordinance, but his mother always said it was the best fine she ever had to pay.

"It's okay. I came by a coupla days ago while you were at school. Your mom stashed a bag in the basement for me. Look, kiddo, I'm in kind of a hurry." Tommy headed for the basement stairs, Tommy Junior following closely.

When Tommy grabbed the bag of stolen goods, his son was curious. "What you got there, Pop?"

"Nothing. Just some stuff I gotta take to a guy in Woodbine."

Tommy Junior sensed an impending adventure. "Can I come along?"

"You'll just be bored, Tommy. There's nothing for you to do in Woodbine."

"C'mon, Pop. We never spend any time together. Whaddya say? Please?" Like most kids his age, Tommy Junior had a smile he saved for special occasions, for when he needed to get one over on a reluctant parent. He trotted out the special smile now.

"Oh, what the hell. You're old enough. And you're mother's always on me to spend more time with you."

"You mean it, Pop? Thanks. I'll just be a minute."

Tommy Junior disappeared into his bedroom, reappearing with his iPod plugged into his ear. "I'm ready."

His dad said something, but Tommy Junior had the volume turned up too high to care.

They rode in silence to Woodbine, Tommy listening to the car radio, his son listening to his personal library of tunes.

As they neared Woodbine, Tommy's teenage son turned off the iPod and looked at his father. "So what's the plan?"

Tommy was surprised by the question. "What do you mean?"

"I mean we're in the middle of nowhere with a bag full of jewelry and electronics I'm pretty sure you didn't pay for. I figure we came down here to sell the stuff. So what's the plan?"

Tommy was secretly pleased, but he was not going to confirm his son's suspicions. "Nah. It's nothing like that. I'm just making a delivery for a guy I know's got a store in town." Tommy pulled the car to a stop in front of Louie's.

"It's a pawnshop, Pop. Really, Pop, I wanna know how this stuff works."

Tommy swelled with paternal pride. "I go inside and sell the stuff while you wait here in the car."

"How am I gonna learn anything sitting in the car?" Tommy Junior doled out another special smile and watched his father's resolve crumble.

"What do you think your mother would do if she found out?"

Tommy Junior laughed. "I think she'd burn the rest of your clothes . . . this time with you still wearing them."

Tommy's laugh was more nervous than his son's. "Here. You carry the bag."

Tommy and Tommy Junior entered Louie's pawnshop. Louie's laugh was more nervous than Tommy's. "Hey Tommy. Good to see you. That your boy?"

Tommy grunted, "Yeah."

"He's a looker, that's for sure." Louie turned to face Tommy Junior.

"You got a girlfriend?"

Tommy Junior grunted like his dad. "Yeah."

The pleasantries out of the way, Louie turned to business. "So what's in the bag?"

Tommy signaled to his son, who dumped the contents of the bag on Louie's counter.

"I can give you six hundred for the lot of it."

Tommy snorted at the number. "The bracelet alone's worth two large."

Louie took a handkerchief from his pocket and wiped his forehead. "Do we really have to do this every time, Tommy? Six hundred dollars is a fair offer."

"I need a grand, Louie."

"I'm sorry, Tommy. Really. As it is, I'm gonna take a loss at six hundred."

Tommy pulled Louie aside and whispered. "Listen, Louie. You're making me look like a real loser in front of my kid. You gotta give me somethin' . . . I'll make it up to you next time." Tommy backed away and waited to see what Louie was willing to do.

"Tell you what, Tommy. I shouldn't do this, but we're friends. Right? I'll go for eight hundred. Do we have a deal?"

Tommy nodded, pleased. "Yeah, we have a deal." He looked at his son to see if Tommy Junior was impressed.

Louie took eight one-hundred dollar bills from the cash box and handed them to Tommy. "Sure was a shame about Big Mack."

Tommy nodded.

"What happened?" asked Louie.

"How should I know? I saw it on TV, same as you did."

"It's just, well, you know how it looks. You were playing the Macks and now, well, now Big Mack's dead."

"It doesn't look like nothin', Louie," said Tommy. "The security cop did it. Ain't you been payin' attention."

"Easy, Tommy. I didn't mean anything. I was just thinking out loud, is all."

"Well, don't be. And don't be thinkin' I was cheating the Macks either. 'Cause I wasn't."

Louie retreated farther behind the counter. "Okay, Tommy. I believe you. Even if Little Mack says otherwise."

Tommy nearly came across the counter at Louie. He was screaming now. "What did you say to Little Mack?"

"Nothing, Tommy. Really, nothing."

"If you told the Macks you were fencing stuff for me . . ." Tommy glared at Louie and sputtered to a stop.

"Relax, Tommy. When you run a pawnshop, you hear all kinds of stories. But I treat my customers like a doctor treats a patient, like a lawyer treats a client. What's the word, you know?"

Tommy Junior piped up from the corner. "Confidential."

"That's right, Junior. Confidential. Your dad's business here is all strictly confidential."

"For your sake, Louie, I hope so," said Tommy Junior.

In the car, driving home from Woodbine, Tommy could feel his son's eyes locked on him. "What?"

"Nothing, Pop."

"Spill it, kiddo. What's on your mind?"

Tommy Junior didn't know how to ask. "Nothing, Pop. Really." And he retreated behind a sullen teenage face.

They drove the rest of the way home in silence. When they pulled up in front of Greta's house, Tommy took the bills from his shirt pocket and peeled one of the hundred dollar bills from the wad. "Here Tommy. This is for you."

"Wow, Pop. Thanks."

"When you share in the risks, kiddo, you share in the reward. Don't ever forget that."

"I won't, Pop."

"See ya round, kiddo."

"Yeah, Pop." Tommy Junior stepped out of Tommy's Plymouth and let himself into the house.

Brown Uniforms

Little Mack slept poorly on the cheap motel mattress, too small for his extra-large frame and with an exposed bedspring poking at his side. He was still tired when he awoke, and he was cranky after the bad night's sleep. Little Mack stumbled into the bathroom, stubbing his toe on the doorjamb.

"Dammit." Little Mack felt the throbbing in his foot and the growing anger in his gut. Suddenly he laughed. If he was getting angry, he knew the crying shit was finally passing. If he could just get good and angry, he was certain this bout of depression would pass. He took a shower and shaved and retrieved a fresh suit from the back of his car. He had no proof, but a very strong sense, that someone had been messing with the Town Car. He hated when someone messed with his wheels. Little Mack smiled. He was going to be okay after all.

Little Mack drove into town for breakfast. He found a small diner and ordered eggs over easy and a cup of coffee. The eggs were over hard and the coffee was weak. Little Mack felt his anger building and smiled. He lingered over a second bad cup of coffee and flirted with the waitress.

Late in the morning, Little Mack returned to cabin twelve at the Bhait's Motel. He flipped on the radio.

"Okay, boys and girls. We're comin' at ya today from the Mall of New Jersey. It's a party down here. So drop whatever you're doing and come down to the mall for Dick Joakes and Lou Spowels. We're gonna be here until two p.m. What've you got there, Lou?"

Lou Spowels leaned into his microphone. "Hey, Dick. Someone just handed me this." Lou waved a piece of paper for his radio listeners. "We're supposed to let everyone know that it's Oliver Berryhill Day here at the Mall of New Jersey. Come meet a local hero."

Local hero Oliver Berryhill, famous for killing Teddy Maciborski. Little Mack put his fist through the bathroom door and then smiled.

Little Mack stopped in the lobby to settle up his bill. It bugged him that Beejit Bhait was nowhere to be found. Little Mack left the key to cabin twelve and two twenty-dollar bills on the counter. Making a mental note never to return to this dump, he climbed into the Lincoln Town Car, his right foot heavy on the accelerator, Woodbine receding rapidly in the rearview mirror.

Everything on the return trip angered Little Mack. It bugged him when there were other cars on the road. It bugged him when his was the only car on the road. The weather bugged him. The road signs bugged him. The radio bugged him. WWEX. Dick Joakes and Lou Spowels. Oliver Berryhill Day especially bugged him.

It was nearly two o'clock when Little Mack pulled his Town Car into the mall's parking lot. He walked inside and surveyed the festivities. Little Mack joined the line of shoppers waiting to meet the local hero. The line moved slowly. By the time he reached the head of the line, Little Mack was seething.

Oliver Berryhill was startled by the heat that emanated off this very large shopper with a grim smile and an uncanny resemblance to Teddy Maciborski. Little Mack shook Oliver's hand and leaned in close, whispering into Oliver's ear.

"My name is Augie Maciborski. I believe you knew my father."

Oliver tried to pull away, but Augie's enormous right hand held the smaller man in its firm grip. "You can't live the rest of your life surrounded by crowds in public places."

Little Mack wondered if his message was clear enough. "I will see you again, Mr. Local Hero." Little Mack stepped back, released Oliver's hand and smiled broadly.

Oliver felt a sudden onrush of gastrointestinal distress. Waving at the event supervisor, he duck-walked off to the men's room, grateful that security officers at the Mall of New Jersey wore brown uniforms.

"This is Lou Spowels thanking all you boys and girls for joining us here at the Mall of New Jersey."

From her customary spot on the edge of the food court, Cassie O'Malley watched the progress of Oliver Berryhill Day, taking notes and snapping digital pictures. It was time for her to respond to Jack Cambrian's phone messages.

Clean Lines and Technology Upgrades

Oliver Berryhill Day was a feel-good story about a local hero. Cassie was certain it would appeal to Jack Cambrian. But on another level, it was a story populated with odd characters, both dead and alive, which made it just bizarre enough to appeal to her own slightly off-kilter sensibilities. Cassie realized that this was the story to get her writing again. Perhaps it was also the story to mend fences with her editor. She called the magazine and left a message, suggesting a meeting in the office on the morrow.

Cassie looked forward to a story meeting with Jack Cambrian. It felt good to stop hiding from the magazine's new owner. She poured herself a Tullamore Dew. As she sipped the whiskey, Cassie remembered there was also the matter of the magazine's former owner. She had been ducking phone calls from both the current and former owners of the *Jersey Knews*. It was time for Cassie to find out why Morris was freaking out in Woodbine. She placed a second phone call.

"Morris."

"Cassie. What took you so long?' Morris hated himself for whining.

"What's going on, Morris?"

"They know I'm down here, Cassie."

"Who knows?"

"You know, Cassie. The guys that are looking for me. The Macks. Somehow they followed me."

Cassie was familiar with Morris's over-active imagination. "Are you sure, Morris?"

"One of them spent the night at the motel."

"Did he see you?"

"I don't think so," said Morris.

"Then you're probably okay," Cassie said, although she was beginning to think otherwise. "What's he been doing all day?"

"I don't know, Cassie. I've been hiding in my room. But his car's not around anymore."

Cassie thought Morris was probably over-reacting, but then again, she wondered if there was more to the story. "Look, Morris, if you think maybe it's not safe at the motel, get in your car and leave already."

Morris coughed. "That's a problem, Cassie."

"Don't tell me your car's still in the shop Morris?"

"It's a long story. Look, I hate to ask, but I really need you to come get me."

Cassie wanted to be annoyed, but after all, this was Morris. Fifteen years of friendship had to mean something.

"Okay, Morris. Here's the thing. I'm stopping at the office in the morning. I'll come get you when I finish up."

"You're going to the office?" Morris forgot about his troubles in Woodbine. "You never go into the office."

Cassie knew that was true. "Don't exaggerate, Morris. I went to the office sometimes when you owned the magazine."

"Four times, Cassie." Morris knew he sounded pitiful, but he could not stop. "Four times in fifteen years."

Cassie didn't want to get drawn into an argument with Morris. They both understood that Morris had always wanted more from their relationship than Cassie was willing to give.

"I'll see you tomorrow, Morris. Around noon. Be ready."

Morris looked around the empty motel room. "I'll be here."

The state capitol held no appeal for Cassie, but it was home to the offices of the *Jersey Knews Magazine* and it was, on a Sunday, deserted, state officials and bureaucrats alike having retreated to their suburban homes. Cassie easily found a parking space in front of the converted row house that served as the magazine's office.

The office was empty on a Sunday, but Jack had come in for the meeting. Cassie looked around the office. Jack had redecorated, or perhaps Morris. It had been so long between visits, the improvements could date back to Morris, but Cassie decided the clean lines and technology upgrades were a reflection of the new owner.

"Good morning, O'Malley. This is a pleasant surprise."

"Thanks for coming in on a Sunday," Cassie said.

Jack Cambrian was tempted to point out the obvious, that he often worked on Sunday, that Cassie should know that after a year. "No problem, O'Malley. So what've you got?"

Cassie described Oliver Berryhill Day.

"It's a good story, O'Malley, the local hero angle and all. How soon can you have it ready?"

"I need a few days. I haven't actually interviewed the security guard yet. Let me reach out to Mr. Berryhill, and then we'll see where we are with the story. Okay?"

"Okay." Jack Cambrian smiled. "You'll keep me in the loop?"

"Yeah, boss," said Cassie. "In the loop."

"And you'll start coming to staff meetings?"

Cassie thought about it before answering. "One step at a time, boss. One step at a time."

Jack Cambrian laughed. "But you'll think about it?"

Cassie smiled. "Yeah. I'll think about it."

Fifteen Minutes of Fame

Oliver was twelve minutes into his fifteen minutes of fame. He was the center of attention and thoroughly enjoying every minute of the experience. Oliver had always wondered about the celebrities he read about in the tabloids, the ones who complained about all the attention. There was, he decided, no downside to fame. Twelve minutes into his fifteen minutes of fame, Oliver's only concern was how to extend his time in the spotlight. And then Little Mack whispered in his ear.

Oliver had told the story so many times that he began to believe he really had fought off the dangerous felon. And then, twelve minutes into his fifteen minutes of fame, Little Mack reminded him that he was not so tough after all. When Oliver Berryhill Day ended at the mall, Oliver Berryhill was afraid to leave. He had arrived with an entourage, but when the media cameras had left, so had the entourage. When the event supervisor thanked him and said goodbye, when his shift supervisor reminded him it was back to a regular work day tomorrow and then departed, Oliver Berryhill found himself dangerously alone.

As he walked to the exit, Oliver was panning three hundred sixty degrees, on full alert for the possible appearance of Little Mack. Walking toward the exit, looking back over his shoulder, Oliver tripped over a large potted plant, ripping his brown Mall of New Jersey pants and cutting his Mall of New Jersey leg just below the knee. Mall of New Jersey blood trickled down his left leg as he walked.

When Oliver reached the exit, he stopped, afraid to venture outside. He stared at the exit, considering his options, failing to generate any options to consider. Slowly he opened the door, feeling the cold December air on his face and on his exposed leg. He had been fashionably late arriving that morning, his car parked at a remote end of the lot. He now faced a long walk across a deserted parking lot alone in the dark of evening, accompanied only by Little Mack's earlier threat, which still echoed in his ears. "I will see you again, Mr. Local Hero."

Oliver started to run for the car, only to stop some twenty feet later, out of breath and embarrassed. He looked around, but, of course, no one had seen. The parking lot was deserted. Slowly he walked to his car, reminding himself as he walked to take deep, even breaths.

He made it to the far end of the lot undisturbed, and as he took his keys out to unlock his Ford Taurus, Oliver had a most disturbing thought. Little Mack didn't need to be there to do him harm. *What if he rigged the car to explode?* He stood in the parking lot, wondering if it was safe to unlock the door. After fifteen minutes, he unlocked the door and climbed in, panting. He wondered if it was safe to turn the ignition. Ten minutes later, he started up the car, gasping for air. He pulled out of the parking lot and onto the access road. As he approached the highway entrance, preparing to merge into heavy highway traffic, Oliver wondered if Little Mack had cut his brake line. He held his breathe, tapped the brakes, and squeezed between a panel truck and a tour bus. The panel truck swerved, nearly forcing Oliver off the road, clipping Oliver's fender. *Was the driver simply distracted inside his panel truck, or had Little Mack arranged for this automotive encounter?*

Oliver cautiously climbed out of the Taurus, the driver of the panel truck already out of the truck, examining the damage and screaming. "Where the hell did you learn to drive?"

"I'm sorry," Oliver mumbled. "A problem with my brakes."

"Look at this," the other driver said, pointing to the damage to his truck.

Oliver didn't think the damage to either vehicle was significant. "Maybe we're better off if we just call it a wash and take care of our own repairs. If you report it to the insurance company, you know what's gonna happen to our rates."

"The accident was your fault. If you don't want to report it, that's fine with me. Gimme five hundred cash, and we can be done right now."

"I don't carry that kind of cash," Oliver said.

"Then I need to see your license and registration."

Oliver traded identification information with the truck driver, and when they were finished, he pulled back out into traffic. He slowed his car to old-lady speed and puttered along in the right lane, angry drivers cutting around him, but he made it home without further mishap.

As Oliver pulled into his apartment complex a thought came to him unbidden. *What if the accident had been staged by Little Mack?* The driver had written down his address. *What if Little Mack knew where he lived?*

One Forty-Six a.m.

The first thing Oliver did was to turn on all the lights in his apartment. Even so, he discovered dark corners in the apartment, where the light thrown off by his cheap lamps failed to penetrate the shadows. Or perhaps the darkness was all in his imagination. Oliver couldn't be certain. He switched on the television and watched footage from Oliver Berryhill Day. He watched as Mayor Harbrough read her proclamation. Barely ten hours had elapsed since the clip being shown on the TV, but to Oliver it seemed quaint, archival footage from a more innocent era. A line had been drawn in the sand that was Oliver's life. "I will see you again, Mr. Local Hero."

Oliver lay in bed but could not sleep. An old movie came on after the news. Oliver loved the old movies, but this one was colorized. Edward G. Robinson did not belong in color. He flipped channels, but nothing held his attention. Finally he felt himself nodding off.

Oliver was sleeping deeply when the telephone jolted him awake. He sat up in bed, disoriented and disturbed. He looked at his clock radio. One forty-six a.m. Feeling clammy and feverish, Oliver reached for the phone.

"Hello."

The phone line was silent.

"Hello?" asked Oliver.

Silence. Oliver thought he might have heard someone breathing into the receiver.

"Is anyone there?"

It promised to be a long night.

Sleep was no longer an option. Oliver lay in bed and listened to the sound of night inside and outside his apartment, the odd creaking, the clock ticking, the occasional car in the parking lot, neighbors at odd hours coming and going, but mostly the deep silence of insomnia mixed with fear. It was a toxic mixture.

Oliver lay in bed and tried to focus on the positives. He was a big shot at the Mall of New Jersey, having jumped from the bottom of the mall's pecking order to the very top. He was known by everyone at work, respected by many, liked by some. No longer hanging around on the edge of life, Oliver had become the center of attention. He hoped to parlay that attention into a job with the local media; with a little luck, one day he'd be making films for real. Anything was possible. After all, he was a local hero.

"I will see you again, Mr. Local Hero."

Oliver broke into a cold sweat, remembering Little Mack's promise. With the first light of morning, he dragged his tired body from bed and got ready for work. Oliver looked forward to spending the day surrounded by crowds in the very public spaces at the Mall of New Jersey. He put on a clean Mall of New Jersey security uniform, ready for work. He looked at his watch. It was only six-thirty.

It was a long night, as well, in Woodbine. Morris barely slept as the off-again, on-again argument between Beejit Bhait and his mother raged throughout the night. As usual, Morris could not make out the words as they bled through the adjoining wall, but the tones were especially nasty. Morris buried his head under his pillow in an unsuccessful attempt to block out the Bhait family dispute.

He looked at his watch sitting on the nightstand. One forty-six a.m. Morris slept fitfully, grateful at least that the argument offered distraction from his own mounting troubles.

At six fifteen, Morris climbed from bed and took a quick shower, the old motel plumbing giving complaint as the hot water heater came to life. Cassie told him to be ready by noon. At six thirty, Morris was ready to check-out.

He was tired of hiding from Little Mack. Morris stepped outside into the early morning, early winter chill. He walked toward the rear of the motel property. There was no sign of Little Mack's Town Car. Cabin twelve was empty. Little Mack, apparently, had not returned.

Morris walked down the street in search of breakfast. Beejit's cousin Gupta welcomed him warmly. "Ah, good sir, yes, the restaurant is open. Please to be sitting." Gupta offered Morris the choice of a table or a seat at the counter. Morris sat at the counter and examined the breakfast menu before ordering a cup of coffee and a plate of curried eggs and potatoes.

"Would you be liking bread with your eggs and potatoes? We have onion kulcha this morning."

"No bread this morning," Morris said. "Thank you."

Gupta returned with a carafe and poured Morris a cup of viscous coffee. It poured slowly, in a thick, black stream, more solid than liquid. Morris added cream, but the coffee held tight to its deep black color. He continued to pour cream into the mug, waiting for the coffee to lighten, but he gave up when the mug began to overflow, the coffee still dark black and evil. Morris sipped cautiously and waited for his eggs.

Gupta was in a talkative mood. "You are enjoying your vacation, good sir?"

Morris nodded and sipped his coffee.

"And my cousin Beejit, it is a fine motel, yes?

Again Morris nodded, not wanting to appear ungrateful.

Gupta excused himself and disappeared into the kitchen, returning with Morris's breakfast. "There is much to be sightseeing in Woodbine. Please to enjoy your breakfast, good sir." Gupta retreated so that Morris might enjoy his eggs undisturbed.

Morris made short work of the curried eggs and potatoes, which were surprisingly good. He sipped the intense cup of coffee and perused the morning paper. Morris had lost touch with the news during his time in Woodbine. He looked at the photograph on the front page. "Local hero honored at the Mall of New Jersey," the caption read.

"I don't understand," said Cassie. Sitting with Morris in his cabin at the Bhait's Motel. There was a lot she didn't understand, but for the moment she was referring specifically to Morris's finances.

"It's really not very complicated," Morris began again. "I needed the money."

"But the magazine was doing well."

Morris stared past Cassie at a stain on the cabin's wood paneled wall. "Maybe it wasn't high art, but we did find our niche in the marketplace. I should have brought someone in to help me with the business though."

"I always thought you did a good job managing the business end of things."

Morris laughed. "That's why you're a writer and not an accountant, Cassie. The magazine did well, but all I was building in the ledger book was debt." Morris remembered just how bad things got. "I had to keep borrowing to cover the cost of operations."

Cassie was beginning to understand why Morris sold the magazine. "But if the debt was piling up all that time, why'd you wait so long to sell?"

Morris couldn't meet Cassie's gaze.

"Oh. Morris. No." Cassie shook her head sadly. "For me?"

Morris put on a half-hearted smile. "For you."

"You didn't think . . . ?" Cassie didn't finish her thought, and thankfully Morris didn't answer.

Cassie asked a different question instead. "So these guys who are looking for you? You owe them money?"

Morris nodded.

"And one of them tracked you to the motel?"

Again he nodded.

"And you didn't leave because you couldn't afford to pay for the repair to your car?"

Morris sat there, too embarrassed to answer.

"Oh, Morris."

Cassie and Morris sat in cabin one at the Bhait's Motel saying nothing because there was nothing left to say. There was a polite knock on the door.

"Please, good sir, but guests are not allowed to be having visitors in the room."

Morris let out a mournful laugh. "That's all right. Ms. O'Malley is here to give me a ride home."

Beejit Bhait looked troubled. "You will be leaving us then, good sir?"

"Yes."

"It is a good motel?"

"It is a fine motel, Mr. Bhait."

"But you still have to be meeting my mother."

Morris exited the cabin. "I am sorry."

Beejit scurried after him. "Perhaps you will be coming here again?"

Morris grinned. "Perhaps I will. Thank you, Mr. Bhait. For everything."

Of Cumin and Coriander

Cassie popped a disc in the Mustang's CD player, picking something powerful, McCoy Tyner, because she loved the music, but, even more, because she didn't want to talk and she didn't want to think. She liked Morris when he was the iconoclastic magazine owner. He was tough-minded, independent, verging on the obnoxious, nothing special in the looks department, her long-time editor and friend. She was not prepared for this new Morris, the needy, moonfaced, pathetic debtor. She wanted to yell at him, to shake some sense into him, to smack him upside the head. She wanted to . . . Cassie turned the volume up even louder, focusing her attention on Tyner's poly-rhythms, on his powerful left hand, and as circumstances required, on the local traffic. She just wanted to get Morris home and then get home safely herself.

But Morris had been holed up in a motel in Woodbine for a week. His body craved conversation. Cassie turned down the volume on the CD and listened as Morris talked about the mess that was his life. When she got to Morris's house, Cassie agreed to go inside for just a minute. And when she got inside, she agreed to have one drink. Morris uncorked an inexpensive bottle of merlot. She drank the first glass quickly, too quickly, or perhaps just as quickly as she needed, and held her wine glass out for a refill.

Cassie found Morris's music and put on Marvin Gaye. They talked quietly and sipped red wine, lapsing into silence, listening to Marvin Gaye, "Let's get it on." Morris leaned in toward Cassie.

She had spent the last fifteen years avoiding just such a moment with her friend and editor, and they both expected that she would pull back, mumbling well-practiced excuses. But this was a different Morris now, or perhaps she was a different Cassie, and she did not pull away this time. Morris kissed her on the lips.

His kiss tasted vaguely of turmeric, of cumin and coriander. Otherwise, the kiss was remarkably unremarkable. Cassie wanted the kiss to matter.

She tried again. Wrapping her arms around his neck, her lips parted ever so slightly, she gave Morris a languorous kiss. She lingered in his mouth, inviting passion into her life, or at least into her mouth, but the kiss refused to spark. She backed off for a moment, taking a breath and looking into Morris's eyes. "That was . . ."

Morris finished her thought. ". . . Ordinary."

Cassie laughed. "Very ordinary."

Morris grinned. "Well, at least we found out."

Cassie wasn't certain if the feeling in her chest was relief or disappointment. "You know what I miss?" She didn't wait for Morris to answer. "I miss talking story ideas with you."

Morris refilled their wine glasses. "So what are you working on?"

Cassie began telling him all about Oliver Berryhill Day.

"I think I saw something in the newspaper at breakfast," Morris said, "but I've been out of the loop these past few days. What's your take on the story?"

Cassie jumped up. "I've got pictures in the car. I'll be right back." She ran out to her car and returned with her digital camera. "I haven't had a chance to look at these yet. Let's see if I got anything good." She popped the memory card into Morris's computer.

The slide show booted up automatically, pictures popping up in sequence, pictures of Oliver Berryhill, of Mayor Harbrough, of Dick Joakes and Lou Spowels, pictures of random shoppers shaking Oliver's hand, pictures of . . .

"Holy shit, Cassie! That's him!"

Cassie looked at the photo of the very large man whispering in Oliver's ear. "Who's him?"

Morris was astounded. "That's Little Mack . . . the guy I've been hiding from."

"Are you sure it's him?"

"Look at him, Cassie. Do you think I'd mistake him for someone else? Except maybe his father."

"His father?"

"Yeah, the Macks. Double-wide loans harks."

"I don't know what this is all about," Cassie said, "but his father, Teddy Maciborski, Big Mack as you know him, I'm pretty sure that's the same guy died in the confrontation with Oliver Berryhill."

Morris was stunned. "Big Mack is dead?"

"Yeah." Cassie described Oliver's version of the fatal encounter in the men's room.

"I'll be damned."

"How well did you know Big Mack?" asked Cassie.

"What do you mean?"

"I mean, was he really a tough guy, or was it just an image?"

"No, Cassie. He was dangerous . . . the real deal. Where are you going with this? What's your angle on the story?"

Cassie thought for a moment before responding. "Does the security guard's story sound plausible to you? I mean, if Big Mack really got into it with Oliver Berryhill, do you think that Big Mack would be the one turns up dead?"

Morris tried to imagine the scene in the men's room. "Look, Cassie, I don't know squat about the rent-a-cop, but I do know Big Mack. Seems to me, you'd have to be pretty tough or pretty desperate to survive that kind of confrontation with Big Mack."

"You mean desperate, like late on loan payments desperate?"

Morris nodded. "Yeah . . . hey, wait a minute. You don't think I had anything to do with this?"

"Of course not, Morris. I'm just trying to understand is all. Besides, you were stuck in Woodbine." She watched Morris closely. "Weren't you?"

Cassie's Blueberry Pancakes

"So, let me see if I've got this right." Cheyenne looked up from the breakfast menu. "You were with Morris last night. You wanted to do it. He wanted to do it. But you didn't do it. What am I missing here?"

From Cassie's perspective, the answer was simple. "No spark. When we kissed."

"You always were a romantic." Cheyenne chuckled. "Does sex always have to mean something? Can't it just be mindless fun? Aerobic exercise? Can't it just be sex?"

"Do you really want me to answer that, Chey?"

"No, I guess not." Cheyenne put her menu down and looked across the table at Cassie. "Deep down, I always figured you'd wind up with Morris one day. I don't know why exactly, but there's always been something very intimate about your friendship."

Cassie thought about her relationship with Morris. "I don't know, Chey. Maybe."

"So how did Morris take the rejection? It must have crushed him."

"No, Chey. That's not how it was. It was a mutual decision."

"Really? And you believed him?"

Cassie didn't bother to respond. "So how about you, Chey? Any new guys in your life?"

Cheyenne laughed bitterly. "You know the expression, 'Power is the ultimate aphrodisiac?' I guess that's only true if the man's the one with the power."

"I've never known you to go this long without a man."

Cheyenne shook her head. "If I'd known what being mayor was going to do to my sex life, I don't think I would have run for office."

"Are you girls—grr—ready to order breakfast?"

Cassie and Cheyenne, and all the regulars at the Eggery, had grown accustomed to Greta's growl, but this morning it seemed somehow more urgent, demanding their attention.

"Yes, of course, Greta," Cassie said. "I'll have a short stack of blueberry pancakes."

"I'll have two eggs over easy and a side of home fries," added Cheyenne.

"I'll—grr—be right back with your coffee."

When Greta went back into the kitchen, Cassie turned to Cheyenne. "Does Greta seem more—what's the word I'm looking for, Chey?"

"Twitchy?"

"Yeah, does she seem more twitchy today than usual?"

Before Cheyenne could respond, Greta returned with their coffee. She seemed to be struggling not to spill coffee as she set the mugs on the table.

When Greta left, Cheyenne answered Cassie's question. "I guess. Yeah. Maybe."

Cassie sampled her first cup of the day. "Mmmm. Coffee's good this morning." Cheyenne took a sip and nodded. "A fresh pot."

"How are things with your parents?" asked Cassie.

"After forty years, my mother wants love. What is so all-fired important about love all of a sudden?"

"C'mon, Chey. Be fair."

"Okay, so she wants love. I guess I can understand that. But what's wrong with my dad? Why can't she love him?" Cheyenne took a sip of coffee before continuing. "You saw them at Thanksgiving. I invited them both, thinking that maybe they'd take the opportunity to try to work things out." Cheyenne lapsed into silence.

"Do you really want to have this conversation again, Chey? Isn't it time for you to let it go?' asked Cassie.

"I just don't think I'm ready for my mother to be dating." Cheyenne paused. "And really, after forty years, she had to pick Charles Meriwether the third? That's the man she falls in love with?"

"He was a little . . . hard to take," said Cassie.

Cheyenne quickly agreed. "I'm not especially religious, but I don't think I'm anti-religion. Certainly not anti-God. He tried to make it sound like I was the devil incarnate."

"You're not taking any of that seriously, Chey . . . are you?"

"What really bothers me," Cheyenne explained, "is that I think that Mr. Meriwether is using my mother. I think the man has political ambitions. I just don't want my mother to get hurt."

"What do you mean?"

"I think he wants to make God a bigger part of the political debate here in Doah. You remember the outcry during the election?"

"You're not still worrying about the manger at the municipal building? Really, Chey. That decision was made before you were even elected Mayor. Don't you think maybe you're being paranoid."

"Maybe, Cassie. I hope you're right. But I have the feeling I've inherited the problem. And if Mr. Meriwether's Thanksgiving lecture is any indication, he thinks I'm vulnerable on the subject."

Cassie was having trouble following Cheyenne's argument. "This can't be about the manger. What do you think the man really wants?"

"Near as I can figure," suggested Cheyenne, "he wants to make Doah a God-fearing town again."

Cassie let out a whistle. "Can he do that?"

"I doubt it. But he can sure cause a lot of trouble if he tries."

"You give him too much credit, Chey," said Cassie. "He's just one man . . . isn't he?"

"They live off by themselves, deep in the cranberry bogs. Been there for generations, following their own religious beliefs, developing their own rituals, keeping to themselves, inbreeding, I suppose, living in the shadows. From what I've been reading, they used to think it was safer if they stayed hidden." Cheyenne stared past Cassie, focusing on a spot of dirt on the near wall. "But now they've decided to become active politically, to bring God front-and-center in the political debate. That's where Mr. Meriwether comes in. He's the polished public face of this odd religious cult. They call themselves The Chosen Community of God."

"The—grr—Chosen Community!" Greta, hustling back with their breakfast, stopped dead in her tracks, her central nervous system staging a wildcat strike, her arms flapping out of control, her face all atwitch. For an endless moment, everything grew quiet. No one moved. Conversation stopped. The lighting in the Eggery seemed to grow dimmer as, just for a moment, suspended in time, everything simply stopped. Everything, that is, except for Cassie's blueberry pancakes, which, obeying the immutable laws of inertial motion, continued along their forward trajectory, landing, with eerie accuracy in Cassie's half-open alligator purse.

The fresh blueberries, making all the right contacts inside the expensive purse, jump-started life in the dining room at the Eggery. Cassie didn't know whether to laugh or scream. Without even the pretense of an apology, Greta sat down at the table with Cheyenne and Cassie.

"You want to—grr—know about the Chosen Community? I will tell you all about them."

"How do you know about the Chosen Community of God?" Cheyenne's world narrowed its focus to the Eggery's twitching waitress.

"I—grr—grew up there."

The Eternal Battle
Between Good and Evil

"Actually—grr—it was a lot worse when I was young. You noticed my twitch, yes? When I was younger, I couldn't control it at all. It would start in my feet and travel—grr—in a wave through my legs, building up pressure in my chest and arms until my brain would feel like it was being pressed flat inside my head, my whole body would be twitching, nerve endings rubbed raw, and suddenly—grr—I would be screaming, growling, cursing. It was horrible. I couldn't control it, like I can—grr—now.

"My parents were part of the Chosen Community of God. The Community didn't look kindly on my twitching and screaming, my growling and cursing. Somehow I made it through kindergarten and first grade at the church school.

"I was in second grade, I guess I was—grr—seven years old, the day the archbishop visited the school. Archbishop, hah. Looking back, he was just some poor Piney minister with a flock of maybe a hundred families, but he sure did like his title. Anyway—grr—the archbishop came for a school visit. I remember the day like it was—grr—yesterday. The archbishop walked into my class accompanied by several religious aides and by the headmaster and I—grr—started to twitch. I could tell it was going to be bad, but I couldn't do anything to stop it. The archbishop was introduced to our teacher, Miss Howell. Then he turned to us to—grr—say a few words. Just—grr—as he started to speak, the trembling got worse and I shouted, 'You're a cunt-licking, scum-sucking doodyhead!' Can you believe I called the archbishop a doodyhead? And then, as if—grr—that wasn't enough, I growled. Think about it. I growled at the archbishop.

"I think Miss Howell fainted as soon as she heard me say 'cunt.' The headmaster was apoplectic, sputtering and stammering, his face bright red and—grr—the veins in his neck bulging with disbelief. His mouth began to twitch, and for a moment I thought the headmaster was going to start screaming just like me.

"Meanwhile, the archbishop's aides sprang into action. One of them pushed the archbishop toward the door as if to protect him from my attack, while the second aide wrestled me to the ground.

"They told my parents I was possessed, that the devil was inside me. They ordered an exorcism, and my parents readily agreed. I was locked in my room for a week, until the exorcism could be arranged. It was the most horrible week of my life, locked in my bedroom, waiting to find out if the priests would be able to cast the devil from my seven-year-old body. The eternal battle between good and evil. On one side, the high priests and their attendants, the holy vestments, the chants, the prayers, the holy water, and on the other side, one small child with an uncontrollable twitch and an odd penchant to curse. The exorcism lasted for days, holy incantations and devilish imprecations, and ended unsuccessfully, when I yelled out something about the high priest's sainted mother.

"The Chosen Community of God gave my parents a choice—their daughter or their Lord. My father would not forsake his God. At the age of seven, I was prohibited from having contact with any members of the Chosen Community, with the exception of my mother, and I was banished to the barn behind my parents' house.

"I spent the next six years alone in the barn. By thirteen, I already had great titties. My hormones were running amok. I had no—grr—idea what was happening and no one to talk to. I became fascinated by energy and motion, and—grr—the physics of cause and effect. I spent all my time in the barn, building these fabulous contraptions. They would fill the barn, climbing—grr—along one wall, banking and dipping and setting off the most extraordinary chain reactions. I would sit for hours at a time, alone in the barn, surrounded by my machines, my panties around my ankles, waiting for my own chain reaction.

"By the time I turned fourteen, my situation came to the attention of child welfare. I still don't know for certain, but—grr—I've always suspected my mother called in the anonymous allegation. It destroyed her when I was moved to a foster home. I like to believe that my mother was giving me one last chance.

"It was at the foster home that I first learned about Tourette's. I wasn't—grr—possessed. I wasn't—grr—crazy. I had a neurological disorder. And it could be—grr—controlled with medication.

"It was also at the foster home that I first met Tommy." Greta had been so wrapped up telling her story, she nearly forgot about Cassie and Cheyenne.

"But—grr—you wanted to know about the Chosen Community. That part of the story is—grr—finished."

Cheyenne would never look at the Eggery's twitching waitress the same way again. "Holy crap."

Eighteen Cents

Morris stared at the empty space in his garage where his car used to be. It was not an especially nice car; it was old, uncomfortable and in need of a paint job, but it was his car and he missed it. He was cash poor, deeply in debt, but he was not without assets. Morris knew it was ridiculous that he allowed a flat tire to cost him the title to his car. He had not been carless in more than two decades, and he did not like the feeling.

Morris called Deep's Quick Lube. His car was still on the service lot. When Morris inquired about buying back the car, Deep was not unsympathetic.

"Ah yes, my good sir. You will be missing your car. I understand."

Deep was polite, but firm. He set a price and showed no desire to come down from that number. For the price Deep was asking, Morris knew he would do better at a used car lot, but he wanted his aging Buick. He would not sleep well until that ugly green sedan was again taking up space in his garage. Morris agreed to Deep's price. Deep, in turn, agreed to hold the car until Morris could make arrangements to come to Woodbine with the cash. Morris hung up the phone without asking if Deep could bring the phone out to the lot so that Morris might say a few words to his Buick. Now all he had to do was come up with the cash.

In the last few years before Morris sold the magazine, the *Knews* had achieved a small but loyal cult following, including a few highly successful Jersey rockers. Morris's taste in music ran more to bebop and hard jazz than rock, but he counted the rockers among his friends. When he sold the magazine, he discovered that these celebrities were friends of the magazine, not his personal friends, an important distinction he had not previously recognized. Still, he was loathe to sell the autographed guitar. But he couldn't drive to the grocery store on an autographed Gibson twelve-string. He contacted a couple of reputable dealers, but, without a certificate of authenticity, let alone documented evidence he came by the Gibson legally, he was met by polite rejections or obscenely low-ball offers to buy. Morris worked his way through the phone book before he found himself talking to a pawnbroker in Woodbine.

The trip to Woodbine only reinforced Morris's decision to sell the guitar. A trip that would take him less than one hour by car, required by bus two transfers, took nearly two and a half hours, and he still had to walk the last mile or so. There was a grim smile on his face as he walked past Bhait's Motel heading for Louie's pawnshop on this cold December day.

Louie's pawnshop was a small storefront on a side road in Woodbine, the display window jammed with cheap wristwatches, battered trumpets, and nearly new handguns ("only used one time," the poster in the window promised). When Morris entered the shop, Louie was busy with a teenage boy. Morris couldn't tell if the boy was buying or selling. Louie looked up from the transaction. "I'll be with you in a minute."

When the boy left, Louie said, apparently speaking to Morris, "That's a good kid."

"Huh?" Morris had been looking at Louie's collection of instruments.

"The kid who just left. His father promised to bring me some stuff. Not a lot of stuff, but a deal's a deal. You know what I mean?"

"Yeah, sure." Morris wasn't really listening. He wanted to get the deal done and pick up his Buick.

"So anyway, the kid explains to me his father couldn't get down here today. The kid thumbs a ride, delivers the stuff for his dad. A good kid."

"I see what you mean."

Louie turned to the business at hand. He sized up Morris, standing in his pawnshop carrying a guitar case. "Are you the guy called me about the guitar?"

Morris grunted, "Yeah."

"Let's take a look."

Carefully, Morris took the collectible guitar from its padded case and handed it to Louie.

"Ooooh, that's a nice one." Louie strummed the guitar. "Good sound. How do I know the signature is real?"

"I'm an honest man."

Louie looked at Morris and smiled. "All of my clients are honest. I'm honest. I run an honest business here. But that doesn't answer the question. How do I know the signature is real?"

"I guess you can't really know." Morris heard the sound of a cash drawer closing.

Louie nibbled on a sesame seed bagel sitting on the counter. He made Morris an offer. It was enough to buy back his car, but considerably less than the autographed guitar was worth. "What about the price you quoted me over the phone?"

Louie nearly choked on a sesame seed. "Sorry. It's the best I can do."

"I don't know." Morris was beginning to have second thoughts. "The guitar was a personal gift. If I can get the autograph authenticated, would that make a difference?"

Louie knew his customers. He planned to sell the autographed guitar as authentic, with or without proof. Documentation would be convenient, but at the end of the day, he knew what the guitar would command. Still, convenience had some financial value to Louie, and he suggested that authentication was probably worth a couple of hundred.

Morris was in a bind. He didn't know if he could get the documentation, but he wanted to try. He needed the additional cash that authentication would attract. But he also needed immediate cash if he was going to drive home in his Buick.

As Morris weighed his options, Louie puttered behind the counter, wanting to appear disinterested in the transaction. Finally, he looked up at Morris. "Tell you what I'm gonna do," said Louie, "since we're both honest men here." Louie barely smiled. "I'm gonna give you nine hundred cash today for the guitar, without authentication. That's more than the guitar is worth." Louie tried not to grin. "If you're lying to me about the signature."

"I'm not," Morris said.

"I believe you. That's why I'm willing to give you the cash." That and the fact that Louie was confident he could find a buyer, regardless. "If you get me documentation in the next couple of days, I'll give you another three hundred."

It was still less than the guitar was worth, but it was the best deal he was going to get. Morris handed over the guitar. Louie counted out nine one-hundred dollar bills. Morris folded the cash in his pocket and walked out the door of the pawnshop.

Fifteen minutes later, Morris approached Deep's Quick Lube on foot, his pace quickening at the site of his aging Buick waiting patiently for him in the otherwise empty parking lot. Deep greeted him warmly.

"Ah, good sir. I am pleased to be welcoming you to Deep's Quick Lube.

And how may I be of assistance this day?"

"I'm here for my car," said Morris, a note of annoyance creeping into his voice.

"Yes, yes. Would you be meaning the Buick?"

Morris looked around at the otherwise empty lot. "Yes. I would be meaning the Buick."

"Ah, yes. The Buick. It can be yours for only eight hundred and fifty dollars."

Morris was too tired to haggle. He took out the nine bills, pleased to be getting his car back plus fifty dollars change. He wasted no time completing the transaction. He climbed into the driver's seat. It felt odd. Deep had pulled the seat forward. Morris adjusted the seat and smiled. He rolled down the window to say good-bye to Deep forever. As he prepared to pull away, Deep reached out his hand.

"Please to drive carefully, good sir. The car does not have a spare."

Morris jumped out of the car. He was tired of being ripped off. It was time to stand up for himself, for his honor, for his Buick. "What do you mean it doesn't have a spare? This whole mess started with a flat tire."

"Yes. I am remembering that. You bought a tire." Deep pointed to the left rear tire. "And it is being there, good sir. On your car. But perhaps you will be wanting a spare?"

Morris looked at Deep and sighed. "You have one, I suppose?"

Deep headed for the back of the shop. "I will be checking for you, good sir." Deep returned five minutes later rolling a tire and smiling. "You are being in luck, good sir. Deep's Quick Lube is having a tire sale today. Only forty-seven dollars."

Morris handed Deep the fifty. Deep reached in his pocket, counting out eighteen cents. "Sales tax," he added, by way of explanation.

Morris accepted the eighteen cents change, not even enough for the parkway toll. He would have to drive home on the back roads. At least Deep hadn't changed his pre-sets. Morris turned on the radio, Joshua Redman on sax, Nicholas Payton on trumpet.

Dirty Laundry

After finishing her shift at the Eggery, her feet and head aching from a full day of waitressing, wanting nothing more than a rosewater bubble bath, Greta came home to a house full of chores, hers and Tommy Junior's.

"Grr—Tommy!" she yelled, but no one answered. "Tommy!" The house was empty, her son out with friends without completing his chores.

Tommy Junior was a good kid, but Greta knew he was at a dangerous age: fifteen, going on forty, staying out late, the surge of adolescent testosterone, at risk of making the big mistakes, the ones that you carry around for the rest of your miserable life. She just wanted to see Tommy Junior get through the next few years without doing anything irreversibly stupid.

She also wanted him to clean his room, to put his dirty dishes in the sink, his dirty clothes in the laundry basket, his dirty magazines back in their hiding place under his box spring, but that, she knew, was too much for a mother to ask of her fifteen year-old son.

Greta started in the kitchen, cleaning up after her son. She found an empty can of Spaghettios and tossed it in the trash. She found a bag of buffalo wings partially defrosted in the microwave and returned it to the freezer. She rinsed the plates and cups and put the cookies back in the cupboard.

Greta turned her attention to Tommy's dirty laundry. She gathered up the clothes scattered around his room and carried them to the closet that housed her compact washing machine. Out of habit, she checked the pockets in his shirts and jeans before throwing her son's clothes in the machine. Somehow, there was always something that Tommy Junior would leave in his pocket, sometimes his school I.D. card, sometimes a scribbled phone number, a note from his teacher, and this time, Greta found a dollar bill. She set the bill aside, making a mental note to lecture Tommy Junior one more time about checking his pockets. Tired and annoyed, it took Greta another moment to fully process what she'd seen. She retrieved the bill and looked at it again, not believing her own eyes. Greta wandered into the living room and stuffed the bill in her pocket, leaving the dirty laundry half in the machine, half in a pile on the floor. What was Tommy Junior doing with a hundred dollar bill?

Greta asked the question again, an hour later, when Tommy Junior wandered in the front door.

"Where'd you find it?" Tommy Junior glared at his mother.

"It was in the pocket of your jeans."

"Mom, you know I don't want you going through my things."

"Excuse—grr—me, young man, but you don't want to go there. Not unless you're prepared to start doing your own laundry."

"But the jeans weren't even dirty, Mom."

Greta was not going to have this argument. "Don't, Tommy. Just don't."

Mother and son stared at each other. When Greta was satisfied that Tommy got the message, she asked again, "Where did you get the hundred dollar bill?"

"It's kind of a funny story, Mom."

"That's—grr—good, Tommy, 'cause I could use a good laugh after such a long day."

"Well, you see . . ." but Tommy lapsed into silence as he searched for a plausible explanation.

Greta waited. "I'm waiting, Tommy."

Tommy tried out several stories silently, in his head, but one look at his mother told him that only the truth would set him free.

"I took a ride to Woodbine with Dad."

When Tommy Junior was finished telling the story, Greta sent him to his room. He looked at his mother. "Mom?"

"Yes, Tommy?"

"Can I have my money back?"

Greta saved them both the trouble of forming an answer and simply pointed to his bedroom. "Go."

Greta called her ex-husband and left a nasty message on his answering machine. She was spoiling for a fight and felt cheated by the recording. She sensed that Tommy's father was sitting in his apartment, listening to her yelling at the answering machine. She hung up the phone and grabbed her coat. "I'm going out. Behave yourself while I'm gone."

By the time Greta arrived at Tommy's apartment, she was wound up tight. She was yelling even before her ex-husband opened the door.

Tommy looked at his ex-wife screaming at his front door and tried to calm her down. "Relax, Greta. What's the matter?"

"Don't you tell me to relax, Tommy. What the hell is the matter with you anyway?" Greta picked up Tommy's cell phone and threw it, hitting him in the chest.

"Hey, watch it, Greta. That hurt."

Greta laughed. "My tics, Tommy. I'm sorry, but that was a tic."

"Bullshit, Greta. I know your tics, and that was no goddamn tic. You threw the phone at me."

Greta picked up the TV remote and, aiming at his head, let the remote fly.

"Shit, Greta. What's with you?"

Greta pulled the hundred from her purse. "This, Tommy."

"Damn. Where'd you find that?" Like father, like son.

"Tommy Junior told me all about your trip to—grr—Woodbine. Now you listen to me. Do not even think about enlisting your son in your scams."

Tommy tried to object, but Greta just waved him off.

"I'm not kidding, Tommy. Look, you and I, we're not—grr—exactly model citizens, but our son is gonna make it. He's gonna finish high school and get himself a real job, maybe even go to college. You think I've been hard on you these last—grr—few years? You don't wanna know me if I think you're getting Tommy Junior involved in criminal activity."

Greta snatched the phone book off the table and flung it at Tommy. "Damn. My tics are bad tonight." She stormed out of the apartment, slamming the door behind her.

Tommy picked up the phone book and found the telephone number. "We need to talk."

Fingerprints

As a frustrated filmmaker and security guard, Oliver had often looked at shoppers, framing a shot in his imaginary camera, and wondered about their motivation in coming to the mall. He quickly learned to distinguish the serious shoppers from the social set, the ones with no time to waste and those with nothing but time. In the imaginary documentary he was shooting, Oliver would highlight the bargain hunters, the mall walkers, the seasonal and the regular wage slaves and would ascribe to each his own unique motivations.

Until that morning, he never considered that any of them went to the mall to be surrounded by eye witnesses, but that was the motivation which drew Oliver to the mall several hours before the start of his shift. If Little Mack came after him, Oliver wanted there to be plenty of witnesses.

Oliver was nervous in the car en route to the mall. He was so busy watching a car in his mirror, so convinced that he was being tailed, that he nearly rear-ended a police car sitting at a red light. Oliver couldn't begin to relax until he pulled his car into the mall parking lot, finding a space just a short walk to the entrance. Having arrived safely at the mall, Oliver breathed a deep sigh of relief. There was very nearly a bounce in his step, a song on his lips, as he walked from his car to the mall entrance.

"Hey, Berryhill. This is a pleasant surprise." Standing by the door, smoking a cigarette, waiting not for Oliver Berryhill, but for Santa Claus, Little Mack greeted Oliver warmly. "We need to talk."

"G-good morning." Oliver swallowed hard. "N-no time to talk. I'll be late for work."

Little Mack snorted. "You're a hero, Berryhill, right? Nobody's gonna give you crap if you're a coupla three minutes late."

"I-I-I don't know."

"Are you afraid of me, Berryhill?" Little Mack stared straight into Oliver's rapidly blinking eyes.

"No. I don't think so. Should I be?"

"Relax, Berryhill. I'm a pussycat." Little Mack snorted a second time. "Just like my dad."

"It was an accident."

Did I say it wasn't, Berryhill?"

It's ju-just I thought you should know," Oliver explained, his stammer returning. "He fell."

"You sure are taking a lot of credit for an accident."

"I can't help it of the media runs with the story," Oliver said.

"It just seems you're enjoying it a little too much." Little Mack's gaze pierced Oliver. "You know what I mean, Berryhill?"

"Look. I'm sorry about your father, but I've gotta get inside before I'm late." Oliver started walking toward the door.

"Go ahead, Berryhill." Little Mack smiled. "We can talk some more later."

Detective Bebedict sat at his desk and thought about fingerprints, those idiosyncratic whorls that are left behind, manual markers in a digital world, digital markers in a manual world. He thought about fingerprints on the knife that killed Teddy Maciborski. More to the point, he thought about the absence of fingerprints on the knife that killed Big Mack. *There should have been fingerprints,* Eddie kept repeating.

He said it the first time that morning, standing in his captain's office. "There should have been fingerprints."

But his captain, a good cop grown weary, wasn't interested. He had a dead bad guy and a live local hero, and he didn't need a messy murder investigation. That's what he said to Eggs Bebedict that morning. He said, "I've got a dead bad guy and a live local hero, and I don't need a messy murder investigation."

Eggs visualized the incident in the men's room, the story according to Oliver Berryhill. *There should have been fingerprints.* Sometimes, as a detective, Eggs would fixate on one troubling piece of information, one incongruity in the story, would allow that clue to percolate in his head, waiting for the universe to re-align itself, for the real story to reveal itself. Detective Bebedict's head was filled with the absence of fingerprints.

Eggs wanted to talk to Oliver Berryhill, but his captain reminded him that officially the case was closed. Detective Bebedict needed to understand the absence of fingerprints. He would get no other police work done until he could shake this nagging doubt. Detective Bebedict needed someone to do his talking for him. He thumbed through his rolodex until he located the misfiled card with Cassie O'Malley's phone number. He stood up from his desk, left the building, and placed the call from his cell phone.

"Ms. O'Malley? This is Detective Bebedict . . . Eggs."

"Detective Bebedict. So nice of you to call. What can I do for you, Detective?"

"Well, for starters," he said, "you can call me Eggs."

"Okay, what can I do for you . . . Eggs?"

"Actually Ms. O'Malley . . . Cassie. May I call you Cassie? Actually Cassie, it's what I can do for you."

"And what might that be, Eggs?"

"Are you still working on that story about Oliver Berryhill and Teddy Maciborski?"

Cassie was curious where the detective was leading her. "Yes."

"Well then, I have something that might be of interest to you."

"Yes?"

"You understand this is strictly confidential, Cassie?"

"Of course." The writer in Cassie appreciated the detective's knack for ratcheting up the suspense.

"And that you didn't hear this from me?"

"Absolutely."

Detective Bebedict took a deep breath. "I've never done this before."

"Done what, Detective?"

"Eggs."

"Done what, Eggs?"

"I've never leaked police information."

"Is that what you're doing, Detective?"

"Eggs."

"Is that what you're doing, Eggs?"

Eggs Bebedict nodded into the telephone. "There were no fingerprints on the knife."

"What?" Cassie didn't understand the detective's point.

"No fingerprints. On the knife. There should have been fingerprints."

"But that makes sense. If Teddy Maciborski stumbled and fell, accidentally slitting his own throat, Oliver's fingerprints wouldn't be on the knife." Cassie was pleased with her bit of amateur detective work.

"No, Cassie. You don't understand. There weren't any fingerprints on the knife. Not Oliver's and not Teddy's either." It was fast becoming the detective's mantra. "There should have been fingerprints."

"I see what you mean." Cassie thought for a minute. "Why are you telling me this?"

Eggs Bebedict considered his choices. He could tell her that the case was officially closed. He could tell her that his captain, nearing retirement, wished to avoid a messy murder case. He could tell her that he needed her to do his leg work for him. "I guess I'm just a sucker for a beautiful blond writer."

Cassie knew right away there was another explanation. But that didn't stop her from liking the explanation he volunteered.

"Why, Detective," she said, batting her eyelashes into the phone and feeling suddenly very southern, "you do say the sweetest things."

Safe at the other end of the satellite transmission, Eggs Bebedict blushed into the telephone. "Keep in touch, Ms. O'Malley, okay?"

Detective Bebedict's phone call left Cassie with a brainteaser . . . not the puzzle of the absent fingerprints, but the puzzle of the detective's motive. Why did the detective . . . Cassie corrected herself. Why did *Eggs* call her with this evidence? She was a feature writer for a low-circulation quarterly magazine. How did it benefit the detective to have this information released months later, in a barely reputable magazine?

Cassie was tired of the Mall of New Jersey. She wanted to write her odd little account of Oliver Berryhill Day and move on to other stories. She didn't care especially about the absence of fingerprints. She pulled her Mustang into the mall parking lot, circling, waiting for a spot to open up, and listening to the last bit of Muddy Waters before turning off the CD player.

Cassie made her way into the mall along with the mass of Christmas shoppers. She wanted to find Oliver Berryhill, ask him a few questions about Oliver Berryhill Day, slip in a question or two about the fingerprints and go home. She had made enough visits to the mall that she knew his routine. She staked out her table at the edge of the food court and waited. Santa's Workshop was back to its normal holiday routine. There was a long line of children on this busy day at the mall waiting for Santa to return from his break. Cassie checked her watch. Oliver would also be on a midmorning break. She slipped through the closed double doors, off the main hallway, leaving the shoppers behind, past the electrical panels and the utility closets, hoping to find Oliver alone in the employee break-room.

The break-room was empty. Well, nearly empty. Cassie was startled by the dead body propped at a table in the rear corner of the room. "Holy crap!" She pulled out her cell phone and called Eggs Bebedict.

"Hello, Detective. It's Cassie. I'm at the mall."

"This is a pleasant surprise. I didn't expect to hear back from you so soon. And please, I've told you this before. Call me Eggs."

Cassie had no time for pleasantries. "There's another dead body."

"What?" Detective Bebedict suddenly was paying attention.

"I found a dead body in the employee break-room."

"Is anyone with you?"

"No. Just the dead body and me, perfect together."

"I'll be right there, Cassie." Detective Bebedict was pulling on his coat as he spoke. "Don't let any of those damn rent-a-cops disturb the crime scene."

"I'll do the best I can, Detective."

"Thank you, Cassie. By the way, do you have any idea who the dead man is?"

"You're gonna think I'm crazy, Detective . . ." Cassie wondered herself if finding the corpse had somehow distorted her perceptions. "I think the dead man is Woody Allen!"

With their Latex Gloves and their Ziploc Baggies

Detective Bebedict had spent more than a decade on the job without investigating even one suspicious death, and now he had two in two weeks. He raced to his car and to the crime scene that awaited him at the Mall of New Jersey. First Teddy Maciborski and now Woody Allen. En route to the mall, the detective made several telephone calls. On the third call, he reached Mr. Allen's management who insisted that Mr. Allen was currently doing lunch with an investor in Manhattan and very much alive. It was, evidently, Mr. Allen's doppelganger who was dead in the break-room at the Mall of New Jersey. Unless, as Eggs found himself wondering, it was Mr. Allen's doppelganger doing lunch in Manhattan.

When Eggs arrived at the mall, he found Cassie barricading the door to the break-room, holding off Oliver and two additional members of mall security who were demanding, but not gaining, admittance.

"Am I glad to see you, Detective!" Cassie stepped aside to permit Eggs Bebedict access to the crime scene. One of the rent-a-cops made a half-hearted attempt to follow the detective into the break-room, but Eggs turned, holding his hand out, like a cop directing traffic or a dog trainer teaching obedience. "Stay!" The rent-a-cop stopped. Then Detective Bebedict waved Cassie into the break-room. "Tell me exactly what happened."

Cassie explained that nothing had happened. She had entered the break-room looking for Oliver, and instead found this dead man who could be Woody Allen. Eggs took a closer look at the dead man. He did look remarkably like the famous movie-maker, but Detective Bebedict decided with a mixture of relief and disappointment that Mr. Allen's management was undoubtedly correct regarding their client's whereabouts.

Detective Bebedict went through the man's pockets and found no identification. No wallet, no money, no identifying documents. Eggs knew who the dead man wasn't. He needed to get to work if he was going to learn who the dead man was.

"Did you see anyone leaving as you came down the hall?"

Cassie shook her head no. "The hall was empty."

"Are you sure?"

Cassie nodded her head yes. "I'm sure."

Detective Bebedict returned his attention to the dead man sitting quietly in the rear corner of the break-room with the bullet wound in his abdomen.

"Well, at least we know the cause of death," Eggs said, talking to the dead man. The dead man, however, didn't answer.

Eggs looked around the break-room, hoping to find a gun. It was a small room, with several cheap, industrial strength folding tables and chairs, a vinyl couch with a wood-crate coffee table, covered in old newspapers and department store advertising supplements. There was an alcove with a coffee pot, a microwave, and a mini-refrigerator. Eggs found cigarette butts in the employee break-room of the "smoke-free mall." He found a half-eaten bran muffin and a nearly empty cup of coffee. He found three dollars and twenty-seven cents in loose change. But he didn't find the murder weapon.

Cassie watched as Detective Bebedict searched the room for evidence. "Don't you have crime scene guys to do that?"

Eggs Bebedict let loose a gravelly laugh. "You've been watching way too much television." But he did call the department and ask them to send a couple of men.

Cassie watched as they gathered the evidence. Eggs was right. It was nothing like TV. Where was the babe-alicious forensics expert in her short red dress and her long blond hair, talking lab tech jargon and thrusting out her chest? Where the nerdy guy with the funny accent, mapping the geometry of the crime, proving with a mathematical precision, like a landlocked Captain Queeg, his theory of the crime? Where was the kind, but flawed, supervisor, dispensing words of wisdom, calming a nervous crowd of onlookers?

Detective Bebedict left the evidence collection to the two good ol' boys, Piney policemen, with their latex gloves and their Ziploc baggies. Eggs wanted a few words with Oliver Berryhill.

To the Best of my Memory

Detective Bebedict thought Oliver Berryhill seemed nervous about answering his questions. The Detective found it necessary to do his best Detective impersonation, suggesting ominously to Mr. Berryhill that, if it were necessary, they could do the interview "down at the station house." Still, Oliver was acting all fidgety.

"I thought the case was closed, Detective. I thought your Captain was satisfied," said Oliver.

Detective Bebedict stared at Oliver, dropping his already deep voice another full octave. "Don't you think a second dead body changes things just a little, Mr. Berryhill?"

A nervous laugh leaked from the corner of Oliver's mouth. "I guess maybe it does."

"Good. I'm glad you understand. Now, I know you've done this before, but one more time, Mr. Berryhill. What exactly happened when you walked into the men's room two weeks ago?"

Oliver Berryhill got a faraway look in his eye, as if he were watching the incident on videotape. "I was making my regular rounds, checking the men's room, looking for smokers, not expecting any real trouble, when I walked in on Mr. Maciborski standing at one of the sinks." He looked at the detective. "Of course, at the time, I didn't know his name was Maciborski. He was just a guy, standing at he sink, looking at a piece of jewelry."

Detective Bebedict nodded ever so slightly. "Go on."

"I'm not sure what tipped me off," Oliver Berryhill taking a modest approach to the story this time, "but something told me the bracelet had been illegally obtained."

"So there was nothing specific you can point to? You just had a hunch?" asked the detective.

Oliver Berryhill agreed quickly. "A hunch, yes. Exactly. I had a hunch the bracelet was stolen, so I confronted Mr. Maciborski."

"Okay then. Do you remember exactly what you did next?"

Oliver thought for a minute. "Well, yes. I asked Mr. Maciborski if he would mind showing me his receipt for the bracelet."

"And then?"

"Mr. Maciborski reached into his coat pocket. I guess I should have seen it coming, but when he pulled his hand out from inside his coat, instead of the receipt, he was brandishing a knife."

Oliver Berryhill shuddered as he recounted the events that followed. "I tried to remember my crisis training, tried to block Mr. Maciborski's attack. We got tangled up and Mr. Maciborski lost his balance and stumbled, falling backwards. As he tried to catch his balance, he reached out, but before he could right himself, he banged into the edge of the stall, falling backwards and accidentally slitting his throat."

Oliver paused, remembering the blood. "I thought I was going to be sick."

Eggs watched a wave of nausea cross Oliver's features. "Then what happened?"

"Blood was spurting everywhere. It was horrible. I realized he must have hit that artery. You know the one I mean."

"The carotid artery," volunteered Detective Bebedict.

"Yeah. That's right. Anyway, I knew right away that he was gone. I ran down the hall to call the police. And then I ran back to the men's room and waited for you to show up."

Oliver Berryhill fell silent. Detective Bebedict allowed the silence to deepen before asking his question. "So was it before you called the police, or afterwards, that you wiped down the knife?"

"Huh?" Oliver didn't understand the question.

"It's a simple question. Did you wipe the knife before you left the men's room, or when you first returned?"

"I don't know what you're talking about, Detective."

Eggs Bebedict looked for evidence on Oliver's face. "I mean the lab found no fingerprints on the knife." He paused. "There should have been fingerprints."

"I didn't do anything with the blade, Detective. Really."

"So how do you explain that Big Mack's prints weren't on the knife?"

"I can't explain it, Detective."

"If things didn't happen in quite the way you've told me," suggested Detective Bebedict, "this would be a good time to tell me, Oliver."

"No, Detective. To the best of my memory, that's exactly how it happened." Oliver took a deep breath. "I guess it's possible that my memory could be playing a trick on me. After all," he added, taking another deep breath, "it was a pretty traumatic experience."

Eggs Bebedict waited, but Oliver volunteered no further explanation. "Are you telling me that your memory is playing a trick on you . . . on us both?"

"No, Detective. No. No. No. No. No. I'm just saying if it was, I wouldn't know that, now would I?"

"No, Oliver. I guess you wouldn't. Do you think it's possible that maybe, in some small way, your memory of this tragic accident is flawed? Is it possible that your police report doesn't reflect the full story?"

"I don't think so, Detective." Oliver paused, considering how to ask his question. "If I remember something differently now, what kind of trouble would I be in?"

"I'm no psychologist, but I know that sometimes the brain protects itself from traumatic memories by blocking them out. If you're starting to remember things differently now, I think it would be very wise of you to tell me those new memories."

"I'll try to keep that in mind, Detective . . . in case that starts to happen."

Detective Bebedict watched Oliver closely. "But those new memories . . . that hasn't started yet?"

Oliver Berryhill stared at the ceiling. "Not yet."

On the Road to Manderley

When word spread throughout the mall of a second dead body, even the most avid of shoppers stopped mid-list, and streamed for the mall exit. Within an hour, the final die-hard shoppers were pulling out of the parking lots. They would go home and tell all their friends about the horrible experience, and then, in a day or so, they would return in even greater numbers to finish their holiday shopping. Not even two dead bodies could permanently kill the Mall of New Jersey.

The police had finished up at the mall and, except for one remaining officer there to protect the integrity of the crime scene, there was no evidence of an ongoing investigation. Salespeople stood around wondering what to do; cashiers and clerks made small talk. To Oliver, it seemed as though everyone was looking at him; their whispers confirmed his suspicion that they were talking about him as well. It was as if they held Oliver responsible for the second dead body. As if the dead man was somehow his fault. He'd brought murder to the mall and now it refused to depart.

Cassie wasn't sure why she was still hanging around the mall. She needed a smoke and went in search of Santa, hoping to bum a cigarette. Santa's Workshop was deserted, shoppers long gone, their children gone with them, the photographer gone, even the elves had wasted little time packing up, waiting impatiently for mall management to give them permission to leave early. It saddened Cassie, so close to Christmas, to see a lonely Santa Claus, sitting by himself, alone in his workshop.

"Hey, Santa."

Santa looked up at Cassie and smiled. "Hi."

"Strange, huh?"

Santa nodded. "Yeah."

"Smoke?"

Santa dug inside his red coat for a pack of Newports.

Cassie started to get up, heading for their cigarette spot just outside the mall, but Santa didn't bother to get up. "The hell with them." He lit a cigarette and handed it to Cassie. She took the cigarette and sat back down.

"The hell with all of them." Santa peeled off the itchy Santa beard. He was going to enjoy his Newport.

Cassie stared at the beardless Santa Claus. There was something oddly familiar about Santa's five o'clock shadow.

For Oliver Berryhill, the rest of his shift passed by in a paranoid blur. He wasn't sure which was worse, that Detective Bebedict didn't believe his story, or that Little Mack did. Oliver had no doubt that Little Mack intended to avenge his father's death. He had no clear sense of the detective's intentions.

When Oliver left the Mall of New Jersey at the end of his shift, it was early in the evening. The sky was gradually darkening, a winter chill in the air, a light rain starting to fall. He looked but did not see Little Mack anywhere. He was not comforted by Little Mack's absence. Oliver Berryhill thought about the second dead body. He did not believe in coincidence. Two dead bodies don't just happen.

Oliver wondered about the relationship between Teddy Maciborski and this latest dead body. There was a connection between the two deaths, of that Oliver was certain. There was at least one killer on the loose. Oliver realized there was more for him to worry about than Little Mack. More than Detective Bebedict. He just didn't know who or why.

Oliver walked to his car and got in. He started up the ignition, turning on the headlights and the windshield wipers. It promised to be a gloomy ride home. As he pulled out of the lot, he kept his eyes focused on the road ahead. He tried not to think about the dangers. It was an uneventful drive home, but Oliver had seen enough movies to know that the solitary drive—peering out through the rain streaked-windshield, the wipers keeping time like a metronome, the headlights illuminating a quiet country road—would be scored with an ominous soundtrack, cuing the movie audience to the impending danger. It was an uneventful drive home, but if Oliver listened hard enough, he could hear the ominous soundtrack as clearly as if he were already home watching the DVD release of one of the old Hitchcock classics. He was Joan Fontaine, in the car with Laurence Olivier, on the road to Manderley. Or Joan Fontaine, in the car with Cary Grant, driving along the cliff. In either case, he was Joan Fontaine. The ominous soundtrack was scored for him.

Oliver breathed a sigh of relief when he pulled into the parking lot at his apartment complex.

Official Police Business

Morris spent two days trying to make contact with a certain Jersey rocker. After perhaps a dozen phone calls, Morris had to admit that the multiple layers of management served the rock star well. Email was no better. Morris sent missives to everyone associated with the rocker, his manager, agent, body guard, tour director, road crew, and nanny, without success. Finally, he received a return email, threatening legal action if Morris didn't cease and desist. Morris read the email and smiled. Let 'em sue. The text of the message threatened a lawsuit, but the subtext—Morris was an expert at reading between the lines—the subtext clearly implied the guitar was legitimate. Morris printed out a copy of the threatening email for Louie. Late the next morning, he hopped in his aging Buick—the engine rattle was new since its extended stay at Deep's Quick Lube—and set out for Woodbine.

Morris parked in front of the pawnshop and immediately noticed the autographed guitar displayed prominently in the window. He looked at the price tag—$1500—and let out a string of invective. Louie better be prepared, he decided, to put more cash on the table.

Morris turned the doorknob and pushed, but the front door to the pawnshop failed to open. He looked in the window. All the lights were off. The store was empty. Louie's was closed in the middle of the day. Counting on the additional cash payment, uncertain what else to do, where else to go, Morris pounded on the locked door at Louie's.

It didn't take long before Detective Bebedict had a positive identification on the second dead body at the mall. Louie Feldman was a small businessman from Woodbine, a mostly honest pawnbroker who was not above fencing stolen property when the circumstances were favorable. The detective decided to make a visit to the dead man's storefront in Woodbine. He called Cassie and asked her to ride along.

Something about the detective's gruff but gentlemanly demeanor struck

Cassie once again as vaguely southern. Batting her eyelashes, she responded in kind. "Why, Detective, are you asking me out on a date?"

Eggs let loose a gravelly guffaw. "You're a pistol, Cassie, you know that?"

"Well . . . are you?"

"When I ask you out on a date, you'll know it."

When, not if. Cassie liked that. "Okay, then. When are we leaving for Woodbine?"

"I'll pick you up in half an hour."

"Okay, then."

"Yeah," said the detective. "Okay."

Cassie felt foolish, running around her condo, changing clothes for her official police business, unofficial date with Eggs Bebedict. She hated thinking about clothes, especially in the winter. Finally she settled on a tight pair of low-riders, cashmere sweater, and kickass pair of pointy-toed boots. Detective Bebedict pulled up in front of her condo right on schedule. He didn't bother to get out of his car, honking the horn and waiting in the parking lot for Cassie to come down. She was ready but decided to make the detective wait. Next time, she told herself, he'll get out of the car. Cassie was surprised to discover she was already imagining a next time.

Cassie felt awkward in the detective's car on the ride to Woodbine. Eggs Bebedict was apparently a fan of conservative talk radio. Cassie tried to change the station, but Eggs growled and she pulled her hand back from the radio controls.

"Sorry," she said.

"Maybe later," Eggs offered.

Cassie listened to the local talk show. They were talking about the recent killings at the mall. Cassie realized Eggs was working. She sat back in the passenger seat and relaxed, allowing Eggs to monitor public opinion about the killings as he drove.

"Anything new being reported?"

"Not really. But everyone's got something to say about it." Eggs took a philosophical approach. "Opinions are kinda like bellybuttons, you know? Everyone's got one." He grinned. "But they're all pretty damn useless."

When they pulled up in front of Louie's, the first thing they noticed was Morris pounding on the door.

Eggs was suddenly on full alert. "What the hell is going on here?"

"Holy shit, Eggs. That's Morris."

"Who?" Eggs was already climbing out of the car, turning his attention to Morris. He flashed his badge. "Police."

Morris turned red and gradually stopped pounding on the door, caught in the act of . . . well, he realized, in the act of nothing. He wasn't doing anything wrong.

"What's the matter, Officer?"

There was an awkward moment as Cassie scrambled out of the car, explaining to the detective who Morris was, explaining to Morris who Eggs was.

"But what are you doing here, Morris?" asked Cassie.

"Yeah," growled Eggs. "What she said."

Morris pointed at the display window. It took Cassie a moment. "Your guitar! Why? How?"

"What?" growled Eggs. "Where?"

Morris pointed to his aging green Buick parked across the street. "I hocked the guitar so I could get my car back."

"So you came back today to get your guitar out of hock?"

"No, I came back today 'cause Louie owes me another three bills." Morris explained the situation to Detective Bebedict.

"I'm sorry to have to tell you this," Eggs growled, "but you're not gonna get anything more from Louie."

"I don't understand. Is he under arrest or something?"

Cassie stepped back into the conversation. "He's dead, Morris."

"That doesn't make sense. I just saw him a coupla three days ago. When did he die? How did he die?"

Detective Bebedict stared at Morris. "Someone shot him. A coupla three days ago."

The Great Directors

"I didn't do it!" blurted Oliver when he discovered Little Mack sitting at his kitchen table. "I didn't do it," he repeated, as he tried to modulate his tone.

Little Mack stared at Oliver Berryhill, saying nothing.

"You gotta believe me."

Little Mack smiled. "Sit down, Oliver."

Oliver sat down.

Little Mack sighed. It seemed to Oliver that he was distracted. "I came here tonight to avenge my father's death. Do you understand?"

Oliver didn't know what to say, so he said nothing.

"I ask myself what my father woulda done, you know, if it was me dead. My pop, no problem, you wouldn'ta seen Oliver Berryhill Day."

"Please." Oliver searched Little Mack's face, hoping for a chance to explain. He saw no empathy, but he did see fatigue in Little Mack's blood-shot eyes.

"I got obligations here. It's a matter of honor." Little Mack pulled himself up straight in the chair.

"Just hear me out, okay?"

Little Mack nodded imperceptibly. "Go ahead," he mumbled.

Oliver Berryhill had told the phony version so many times, it took effort to get the real story straight.

"I was making my rounds in the mall." Oliver started slowly, easing his way into the truth. "But I didn't go in the men's room looking for anything. Truth is, I had to take a dump." Oliver looked at Little Mack who sat there impassive, at his kitchen table.

"I didn't even realize your father was in the men's room until I discovered there was no toilet paper in my stall."

Oliver remembered feeling trapped in the stall without paper; he remembered the frustration when the man in the adjoining stall ignored his plaintive request. He looked up at the ceiling in his kitchen.

"Your father was already dead when I found him sitting on the toilet, fully dressed, blood pooled around him on the bathroom floor." He looked at Little Mack. "I'm sorry." Oliver found it nearly impossible to read Little Mack's reaction.

Little Mack stood up from the table, unkinking his back, rolling his shoulders, the shoulder holster peeking out from under his jacket as he stretched. "You told the police my father was a thief. You said he died fighting with you in the bathroom. You said the same and more to the press." Little Mack towered over Oliver.

Sitting at his kitchen table, looking up at Little Mack, Oliver Berryhill began to cry.

"Be a man, Berryhill."

Oliver sat at the table, blubbering.

"You're pathetic, Berryhill."

Oliver wiped his nose with the back of his sleeve, trying to compose himself.

Little Mack's voice grew icy cold. "We're going for a ride."

"Where?" Oliver sniffled.

"You'll see."

When Oliver didn't stand up, Little Mack patted his jacket, on top of the shoulder holster. "Now, Berryhill."

"I didn't do it," said Oliver, but he stood up. Little Mack unholstered his piece and used it to point to the door.

Oliver followed the gun's direction. "Where are we going?" But the gun didn't answer.

Outside the house, even in the dark, the moon mostly hidden behind clouds, Oliver wondered how he had missed the black Lincoln Town Car.

"Get in." Little Mack waved at Oliver with the gun.

Oliver opened the passenger side door and climbed in. "Where are we going?"

Little Mack turned the key in the ignition and pulled the car into the street, saying nothing.

Oliver Berryhill talked nervously, continuously, about nothing, about everything, his life, his job, the mall, his childhood, movies.

At the mention of movies, Little Mack grunted. "You a movie buff, Berryhill?"

Oliver thought maybe he had found a common interest, launching into a monologue about the great directors—Capra, Hitchcock, Spielberg,

Coppola—and the great movies—*Manchurian Candidate, Cuckoo's Nest, Casablanca, Lord of the Rings, The Godfather . . .*"

"You like the Godfather movies?" asked Little Mack.

"Yeah," said Oliver, concerned he had wandered into dangerous territory.

Little Mack smiled. "Me too."

Meanwhile, Little Mack drove the car, heading deeper and deeper into the Pine Barrens. For the first ten or fifteen minutes, Oliver was able to recognize landmarks and maintain his bearings, but gradually he lost all sense of place. When Little Mack pulled the car to a stop, at the end of an old abandoned road, deep in the forest, Oliver was completely disoriented.

"Let's take a little walk, okay, Berryhill?" Little Mack wasn't asking. He pulled a small flashlight from his pocket and used it to point to a barely noticeable trailhead heading off to the right. The two men started walking, picking their way slowly along the overgrown trail, following the beam from Little Mack's flashlight.

Oliver tried to restart their conversation, but for the first time in his adult life, Oliver could not think of anything to say about film. He stumbled on a tree root, twisting his ankle. "Dammit!"

"What's the matter, Berryhill?"

"My ankle. Damn."

"Just keep walking."

After some thirty minutes of walking along the old trail, Little Mack stopped abruptly, pointing his flashlight at an abandoned smelt iron bog. Oliver could smell the brackish water and, when the flashlight panned across the area, he saw bits of abandoned brick structures, one of the many "lost" towns deep within the Pine Barrens.

Little Mack turned to face Oliver. "My plan was to bring you out here and leave you."

Oliver began to panic. "But I'd never find my way back."

Little Mack roared with laughter, and Oliver understood Little Mack's intentions.

"Relax, Berryhill. I've changed my mind."

Oliver was relieved, but confused. He was afraid to ask.

"I'm not gonna kill you. Not today, anyway. But I am gonna expect something in return."

"Anything. Anything at all. Just ask."

"I'm glad you feel that way." Even in the dark of night, Oliver could see

Little Mack smile. "Let me explain," said Little Mack. "If I believe you . . ."

"You can," Oliver assured him.

"If I believe you, then someone else is responsible for my father's murder."

"That's right. It was someone else." Oliver was nodding like a bobble-head doll, a collectible Local Hero Security Guard figurine.

"So here's what you're gonna do for me, Berryhill. Well, not so much for me, but for my father."

Suddenly, Oliver felt sick to his stomach.

"You're gonna find the killer for me, and you're gonna avenge my father's murder."

Oliver grabbed his stomach. Deep in the Pine Barrens, in the dead of night, Oliver Berryhill threw up.

Little Mack chuckled. "I feel better already."

Oliver sank to his knees in the heavy underbrush at the edge of the bog and, for a second time, he threw up.

Planning a Good Dinner Party

"I didn't do it." Morris looked defiantly at Detective Bebedict, standing on the sidewalk in front of Louie's pawnshop. He turned to Cassie for help. "Tell him. Just 'cause I saw Louie a coupla three days ago doesn't mean anything."

Detective Bebedict growled. "What it means is maybe you saw something could help us solve the case."

Morris shrank back, exhaling deeply. "Oh . . . of course."

Eggs waited, growing impatient. "Well?"

"Well what?"

Eggs controlled the urge to unleash a string of insults. "Did you," he said, "see something?"

Morris thought for a moment before answering. "No. Not that I can remember. I came in with the guitar. We argued a little about the autograph, about price, but otherwise, nothing. I gave him the guitar and a promise to come back with authentication. He gave me cash and a promise of more cash when I returned. I took the money and went straight to Deep's to buy back my car."

Eggs looked across the street at Morris's aging green Buick and laughed. "That piece of shit?" He caught a look in Cassie's eyes that told him not to make fun of Morris's car. "Sorry."

Morris turned red. "It's a long story."

Eggs wasn't really interested in the car. What he was interested in was Louie. "How did you meet Louie?"

Morris didn't understand the question. "I met him when I walked into the pawnshop."

"No, Morris. I mean, why did you pick Louie? There must be plenty of places would buy your guitar."

"I found him listed in the yellow pages." Morris explained that more reputable dealers wanted to see a certificate of authenticity.

* * *

A million questions bounced around inside Oliver's head and in his gut. Ethical questions. Ten Commandment questions. Life and death questions. Thou shalt not kill. And more practical questions. Like, where and how to buy a gun. What kind of gun to buy? Who has the best prices? Oliver had thought of nothing else since his walk in the woods with Little Mack. He couldn't think clearly. His head was too cluttered with questions.

Oliver pulled out a yellow legal pad and began writing down questions. Any question. Every question. No question was too big or too small. Oliver quickly filled the top page on the legal pad and flipped to a second. Will I need to show identification? How much will it cost to buy a phony driver's license? Is it always wrong to kill? Will I go to hell? Will I go to jail? Will I know how to load the bullets? What kind of gun should I buy? Does *Consumer Reports* have a gun issue? How close will I need to stand to be sure not to miss the target? Who is the target? Can I trust Little Mack? Do I have a choice? Oliver got the questions down on paper, freeing up much-needed file space in his cerebral cortex.

Oliver reread his list of questions. He felt better, just knowing he'd gotten them down on paper. And he realized that he had some answers. After Little Mack announced that Oliver was going to avenge Big Mack's murder, he volunteered the name of a gun dealer in Woodbine who would ask no questions. Oliver told himself he could get through this if he just took things one step at a time. It was critical, Oliver realized, to think just enough, but not too much; to think ahead, but not too far. In that respect, Oliver realized, planning a murder was not unlike planning a good dinner party.

Oliver decided to think only as far as the drive to Woodbine. He put the yellow legal pad in the junk drawer in his kitchen.

A Weird Coincidence

Oliver Berryhill drove to Woodbine, slowly, wondering if New Jersey had a minimum speed limit. He would hate to be ticketed for driving too slowly. He eased his foot off the accelerator, coasting south to Woodbine.

While the car coasted, Oliver rehearsed, trying out one unsatisfactory opening after another, starting with the simple, "I'd like to buy a gun." He rejected the simple declarative, hoping to come up with something that would make him sound more . . . well, dangerous.

"Can you show me something in a forty-five caliber?" (Oliver realized he didn't even know what a caliber was).

Oliver searched his memory for a movie scene that he could play when he got to Louie's. There had to be hundreds of old gangster movies, but Oliver couldn't remember a single one. He thought of Charlie Chaplin in *The Pawnshop*, but he wasn't going to get his opening line of dialogue from a silent movie.

Meanwhile, even at coasting speed, Woodbine approached.

Oliver had no trouble locating Louie's in the small town. As he looked for a spot to park his car, Oliver noticed two men and a woman engaged in an animated conversation on the sidewalk right in front of the pawnshop. He couldn't be certain, but it appeared that the store was closed. Oliver slowed the car and took a closer look, suddenly recognizing one of the men as the officer who had investigated the death of Big Mack. Then he realized the woman was that writer who'd been hanging around the mall. Oliver stomped on the accelerator, passing the pawnshop and continuing on down the rural route, hoping they hadn't noticed the driver of the speeding Subaru.

Oliver's head, once again, was crammed with questions. He drove for another mile or so before he pulled his car to a stop at the side of the road and mopped the cold sweat from his forehead. He wondered what they were doing outside Louie's pawnshop. He wondered if they had seen him behind the wheel of the Subaru. He wondered about the identity of the second man.

Detective Bebedict watched as the Subaru sped down the otherwise quiet street. "Did you see that?"

Cassie nodded. "Yeah."

"I mean did you see the driver?"

"I'm not sure. He looked familiar though. Did you get a good look?"

Eggs grinned. "It was Oliver."

"Holy shit. You're right."

Morris's head bounced back and forth between Eggs and Cassie, trying to follow the conversation. Finally, he interrupted. "Who's Oliver?"

Eggs looked at Cassie. "Go ahead."

"When Big Mack died," Cassie explained. "Oliver is the rent-a-cop at the mall."

Morris looked down the street, as though he could still see the Subaru. "The security guard? But what's he doing here?"

Eggs growled. "I think we ought to get off the street. Anybody else hungry?"

Morris said, "I know a pretty good Indian luncheonette not far from here."

Cassie was in the mood for a plate of chicken tikka masala, but Eggs vetoed the idea. "Curry? I don't think so. C'mon. I think there's a burger joint just up the road a ways."

Morris walked to his Buick and Eggs to his car. Cassie was momentarily stuck between rides. Turn to her left and go with Morris or to her right and Eggs? She turned to her right.

Eggs pointed up the street for Morris's benefit. "We're going that way. Follow me."

As they drove up the street, Cassie noticed the Subaru parked at the curb, Oliver sitting behind the wheel. She turned to Eggs, "Over there." She pointed to the Subaru.

"Yeah. Thanks."

"What do you think he's up to?" But Eggs wasn't ready to answer Cassie's question. He waited until they arrived at the burger joint and placed their order.

"When two people are killed at the Mall of New Jersey in the space of a couple of weeks, it can't be coincidence," Eggs explained between bites of cheeseburger. "I was looking for a connection between the knifing of Teddy Maciborski and the shooting of Louie Feldman."

"And?" Morris asked, prompting Eggs to continue.

"And we just saw the connection sitting in the Subaru."

"Oliver Berryhill?" asked Morris.

"Yeah." Eggs thought for a moment. "Oliver is the link between the two dead bodies."

Cassie picked at a French fry, dreaming of tikka masala. "I agree. But why?"

"Let's review," growled Eggs. "What do we know for sure?"

Cassie started them off. "We know that Big Mack died of a knife wound to the throat in the men's room."

"Okay, good. What else?"

"He was stealing jewelry from the mall," she added.

"Maybe," suggested Eggs, "maybe not." Eggs saw Cassie's puzzled look and explained. "We know Big Mack was a career criminal and we know he was found with stolen jewelry, but shoplifting . . . well, that's small potatoes for Big Mack."

Cassie began to see where Eggs was going. "So you're thinking . . . ?"

"I'm thinking Big Mack wasn't at the mall to steal jewelry."

Cassie jumped in, finishing the detective's train of thought. "He was there to receive stolen jewelry."

Eggs was pleased with Cassie's intuitive grasp of the case. "And that means . . ." He waited for Cassie to answer.

"And that means," she said, "that Big Mack had a partner at the mall."

Morris blurted out the answer. "Little Mack."

Eggs barely looked at him, dismissing Morris's too-obvious answer. "Well, yeah, Big Mack always worked with his son, but I mean someone on the inside . . . someone at the mall."

Morris tried again, more tentative this time. "Oliver?"

Eggs nodded. "Yeah, Oliver."

"So Oliver was using the cover of his position as a security guard," said Cassie, "to steal jewelry at the mall. Then he'd pass the stuff to the Macks."

Eggs agreed with Cassie. "That's right. Then the Macks would use Louie to fence the stolen goods."

Cassie jumped back in. "Making Oliver the prime suspect in two murders."

"That's what I'm thinking," growled Eggs. "But I woulda expected Little Mack to be with his father at the mall. I guess they figured it was an easy job, no real danger."

Morris suddenly remembered. "Little Mack was in Woodbine the day his father was killed."

"Huh?" Detective Bebedict turned and stared at Morris. The first time Morris made mention of Little Mack, the comment had barely registered with the detective. "How do you know so much about Little Mack?"

"I saw him register at the Bhait's Motel."

Cassie nearly jumped out of her chair. "That's right, Morris."

Eggs looked from Morris to Cassie and back to Morris. "What am I missing here?"

"Little Mack was looking for me."

"How come."

"I borrowed some money and fell behind in the payments."

Detective Bebedict measured his words with care. "If you have anything to do with this, anything at all, this is your only chance to get out from under, Morris. Right here. Right now."

Morris tried to maintain eye contact with the detective. "It's just a weird coincidence."

Eggs spoke slowly, so slowly you could drive a truck between his words. "I . . . don't . . . believe . . . in . . . coincidence."

Morris squirmed in his seat.

A Couple of Fire Trucks, a Few Cars, and Some Tractors

"So what do we do now?" Cassie directed her question at Eggs, ending the awkward exchange between Eggs and Morris.

"We? What do we do now?" Eggs got serious. "We take you home."

Cassie was surprised by the detective's answer and waited for him to continue.

"This case is now a double murder investigation, and that's no place for amateurs," he explained.

"Do you have a plan?"

"Yeah," growled Eggs. "I gotta search the pawnshop."

"What are you looking for?" wondered Morris.

"Stuff from the mall. Stuff showing the chain from Oliver to Big Mack to Louie. Jewelry, most likely."

Morris was nodding his head in agreement. "That shouldn't be too hard."

Eggs snorted. "It shouldn't be, but it's gonna be a royal pain. I don't have jurisdiction in Woodbine," he said. "So I gotta talk to my captain, who's gotta talk to the captain in Woodbine, who's gotta . . . look, you don't need a friggin' lecture on inter-governmental police work. Trust me on this. It's gonna be a pain in the ass."

Cassie saw that Eggs was correct. "We should get going."

"Yeah. I'll take you home and head back to the station house. If my captain agrees, I'll be back here tomorrow to look inside."

Cassie looked at Morris. "You gonna be okay?"

"Yeah, Cassie. Thanks. I can drive myself home. It'll feel good to be behind the wheel of the Buick."

They settled up the bill and left, Cassie with Eggs, Morris with his Buick.

In the car, riding home to Doah, an uneasy silence enveloped Cassie and Eggs. They rode in silence for half an hour. As they approached Doah, Eggs cleared his throat.

"How well do you know Morris?"

"He's just a good friend." But Cassie had misunderstood the detective's point.

"Do you think he could be involved in this somehow?"

Cassie felt her face turn red. Of course, Detective Bebedict was thinking about the investigation. "No. No way. Not Morris."

"Are you sure?"

Cassie thought about the changes since Morris sold the magazine. "He's gotten himself in some kind of money trouble, that much is obvious, but I've known him almost twenty years. He's really a sweet guy. A good editor too. No. No way." Cassie thought for a moment, adding, "At least I don't think so."

Eggs pulled into the parking lot in front of Cassie's condominium. "Remember what I told you," he growled.

"About the investigation? The fingerprints?"

"When I ask you out on a date, you'll know it."

There it was again. When, not if. Cassie didn't let him see her smile as she walked from the car to her condo.

Morris took his time getting into his car, fumbling with the keys, waiting for Cassie and Eggs to drive away before starting up the Buick. He didn't want them to notice he wasn't leaving Woodbine just yet. He had several hours to kill before nightfall.

Morris considered his options. He had no place to be until nighttime and nearly no money in his wallet. It would not be smart to attract undue attention. Morris knew he couldn't sit in his parked car for hours. Eventually, it would attract attention. Even if it didn't, he'd get so antsy sitting in the car, he'd probably do something stupid. Like not wait for the cover of darkness. Morris considered where he could go, just a couple of gallons of gas in the tank, just a couple of bucks in his wallet, a place to blend in, to kill time.

Morris sat in his car, knowing he should be moving along, but without a place to go. With a knock on his passenger window, the decision was made for him.

"Excuse me, sir."

Morris was startled by the appearance of a local Woodbine police officer. He told himself to stay calm, that he hadn't done anything wrong . . . yet.

"Yes, Officer?"

"I need you to move your car."

"Of course. Is everything okay?"

The officer looked closely at Morris. "You're not from around here. Are you?"

"No."

"Well, today's the annual Christmas parade and party. Before you know it, the parade's going to be coming down the street and, well, it's not the biggest parade, not the fanciest, but we kinda like it."

Morris smiled. "It sounds very nice."

"So if you would move the car around the corner, I sure would appreciate it. You can watch the parade from here and if you like, stop by the firehouse for the after party."

"Thank you, Officer. I think I'll do that."

Morris had lived in New Jersey for more than twenty years, but he grew up a New Yorker, and a parade, to Morris, meant the Macy's Thanksgiving Day parade. Anything else was a pale imitation at best. Woodbine's parade was not much, by those standards: a couple of fire trucks, a few cars and some tractors, the mayor on foot, the Cub Scouts, the Brownies, Future Farmers of America.

It was, Morris decided, the nicest parade he'd ever seen, a town getting together to celebrate the holiday, a town borne of Jewish roots joyously celebrating Christmas. After a while, it was impossible to distinguish who was marching and who was watching, as family and friends simply mingled on the street, with all of them eventually making their way to the firehouse for a low-key community party.

Morris was having such a good time, sipping punch at the firehouse and chatting with strangers, that he failed to notice as the sky outside the firehouse darkened. When he stepped outside for a cigarette, he was startled by the night sky. It was time.

Morris pulled his car into the alley that ran behind Louie's Pawnshop. The pawnshop was dark. The street was dark at this end, away from the Christmas lights and the community gathering. He hoped the pawnshop wasn't alarmed. He hoped he could jimmy the lock.

Years ago, the magazine had done a series of articles about a small-time burglar turned cult hero. Morris hoped he could remember what the

B and E artist had taught him about locks.

Most storefronts are rented, Morris knew. And most landlords go for the cheapest locksets in the hardware store. So unless the guy renting the space invests in better security, it doesn't take much to pop the lock. Just a little patience. A soft touch. And practice.

Morris was out of practice. He worked the lock quickly but carefully, one eye on the door and the other on the street. He could sense that the lock wanted to open; he could feel it begging to be released, but still the entrance to the pawnshop remained shut. Working the hardware in the cold December night, Morris began to lose feeling in his fingertips. He had gloves in his coat pocket, but he'd never be able to feel the cylinders through gloves. He looked around. The street was quiet, but he could not expect it to stay quiet indefinitely. He blew on his fingers until the feeling returned. He took a deep breath, forcing himself to slow down, to listen with his fingertips, working the lock patiently, caressing the lock.

Morris felt the change moments before the cylinders released. He opened the door and stepped inside, closing the door quietly behind him. He would have to remember to wipe the door for prints as he was leaving. Inside the store, the lock no longer an issue, Morris pulled on his gloves. He had no flashlight, but dared not turn on a light. He would have to work in the dark.

Morris fumbled his way through the pawnshop. He knew what he was looking for, but even if he found it, Morris wondered, would he recognize it? He would take nothing. Morris was there for information only. He was not a thief. But when he found two hundred dollars in the cashbox, well, he told himself, it was a dead pawnbroker, so it wasn't really stealing, and he really needed the money. He didn't have time for an internal debate. Morris stuffed the cash in his pocket and continued to search in the dark until he found what he was looking for.

He left everything as he found it and peeked out the window. There were a few party stragglers on the street. Morris waited until everything was quiet and slipped out the door, hurrying to his car before any more partiers appeared on the street. He hoped no one heard his Buick coughing as he pulled the car out of the alley, turning in the direction away from the firehouse and the Christmas lights.

Talking to a Source

It was well past midnight when Morris dialed Cassie's phone number. "Tell the detective he was right."

"Hunnnnh? Who is this?" Cassie was sleeping deeply, dreaming about eggs over easy when the telephone woke her.

"It's me, Cassie."

"Morris?"

"Pay attention, Cassie. I found jewelry in the pawnshop."

"What?" Cassie was still trying to wake up.

"From the new jewelry store in the mall. The one that just opened."

"What are you talking about, Morris?"

"The detective is right, Cassie. Oliver must have been stealing jewelry and passing it to Big Mack. Then Big Mack would sell it to Louie. Just like the detective explained it."

The fog lifted from Cassie's head. "Hold on, Morris. How do you know this?" She remembered Detective Bebedict's concern. "Are you involved in this, Morris?"

"No."

"Then how do you know about the jewelry."

"I can't tell you, Cassie."

"But you want me to tell the detective."

"That's right."

"Just like that? Call him up and tell him what? That Morris says there's stolen jewelry in the pawnshop?"

"Yeah."

"And you don't think he's gonna ask me how you know about the jewelry?"

Morris didn't answer.

"Morris, you still there?"

"Yeah."

"Well?"

"If I tell you, you have to promise not to tell the detective."

Cassie was no longer talking to her friend, Morris. Suddenly she was the investigative reporter talking to a source. "Of course. Anything you tell me is strictly confidential."

"Okay, then." Morris took a deep breath. "I broke into the pawnshop tonight."

"Are you crazy, Morris?" Cassie got out of bed and began pacing with the phone. "Have you lost your mind?"

But Morris had an explanation. "The detective thinks I'm involved in this somehow, but I'm not. I needed a way to show him I'm on his side in this."

"And breaking into the pawnshop, that shows him he can trust you?"

"When he started talking about what a pain it was going to be for him to get inside, I figured maybe I could help him out, find what he was looking for. And I did."

"You didn't take anything, did you, Morris?"

Morris thought about the two hundred dollars in his pocket. "No."

"Well, that's gotta count for something."

"What do you mean, Cassie?"

"Shit, Morris. Think about it. Detective Bebedict tells you that he plans to search the pawnshop tomorrow for evidence of a double homicide. So what do you do? You break into the pawnshop before the police have the chance to conduct the search. You think that looks like someone who's trying to help the police? Don't you realize to the detective it's gonna look like you broke in to destroy incriminating evidence?"

Morris was genuinely surprised to see his actions from this new perspective. "I never thought about it like that. I just wanted to be helpful." Morris grew silent.

"Morris?"

"Yeah?"

"You weren't, were you?"

"Weren't what?"

"Destroying evidence?"

They had been friends and colleagues for nearly twenty years. Morris wished she didn't need to ask. "No, Cassie. So will you tell Detective Bebedict to look for the jewelry? It's in a small case behind the counter. It's still in the original box from the jewelry store."

"I need to think about it, Morris."

"I'm not involved in this, Cassie."

"If you weren't before, you sure as hell are involved now." Cassie hung up the phone without saying good-bye.

Cassie barely had time to roll over and go back to sleep before the phone rang again.

"I forgot to tell you . . ."

"Get off my phone, Morris."

"Listen. Your friend Cheyenne, is she still under attack for canceling the town's Christmas display?"

Cassie was too tired to explain. "I'm begging you, Morris. Let me sleep."

"Well, tell her that Woodbine has a really nice Christmas parade and town Christmas party."

"I'm hanging up the phone, Morris."

"I just thought . . ."

A Beer and Two Pickled Eggs

Oliver watched from a distance as the car that held the detective and the writer pulled out of town. He didn't know what they were doing at Louie's, but at least they were doing it no longer. Oliver relaxed, tried to relax, feeling the knot in his neck, his muscles locked up from stress.

Rubbing his neck, Oliver walked up the street, turning into an "old man" bar, nothing fancy, no signature drinks (excepting Augustus Busch's signature on the beer bottles), a small, poorly lit bar, and sitting on the barstools, several small, poorly lit men, retired factory workers and machinists. Oliver ordered a beer and two pickled eggs and listened in on the conversation.

Not wishing to appear to be intruding on their privacy, Oliver only caught bits and pieces of the conversations. Mostly, he heard talk of a Christmas parade. Oliver was on his second beer before he realized said parade would be just outside the bar within the hour. He nursed the second Budweiser and decided to stick around for the parade.

By now, Oliver's ears had adjusted to the acoustics in the old barroom, or perhaps, after two beers, he was simply more obviously eavesdropping, but he began to hear much juicier tidbits, rumors of a local man gone dead. The police had not released a name. The media outlets were not yet reporting the identity, but the gossip was spreading in Woodbine that the man murdered in the Mall of New Jersey was local storeowner Louis Feldman.

Oliver had been listening intently to the murder gossip, nearly falling off his barstool at the mention of Louis Feldman. So that explained what the detective and the writer were doing outside the pawnshop. Oliver wondered again about the identity of the third member of that little group.

He settled up with the bartender and wandered out onto the sidewalk where the community was already gathering for the Christmas parade. The parade held little interest for Oliver, nothing but a couple of cars, some fire trucks and tractors, children on parade, their parents cheering from the sidewalk, but moving quietly along the parade route, Oliver continued to hear random gossip regarding the dead pawnbroker, a simple man who stayed in the background, a deeply religious man who happened to sell guns and stuff and who floated loans for anyone in the neighborhood whose cash was low and whose credit score even lower.

Oliver wondered what Little Mack knew. Did he know, when he sent Oliver to Woodbine, that Louie was dead? Is that what Little Mack meant when he said Louie would ask no questions? Did Little Mack expect him to break into the pawnshop and steal a gun?

As the parade reached its terminus, Oliver followed the sparse crowd to the firehouse for an after-parade party. It was as he neared the firehouse that Oliver noticed the other man, the one he'd seen earlier with the detective and the writer. He was an average looking man, a little older than he dressed, a little heavier, his hair a little thinner. Oliver had not forgotten about this unidentified man; he was part of the scene outside Louie's pawnshop that afternoon and therefore dangerous. Oliver moved carefully, blending in with a knot of locals drinking punch and swapping Christmas stories. From a shadowy corner of the firehouse, Oliver kept an eye on the unidentified man.

When the man stepped outside for a cigarette, Oliver moved from his corner position, trying to keep the man in his line of sight. He was surprised to see the man look around, checking for something, and then take off quickly down the street. Oliver followed at a safe distance, hugging the sides of the buildings.

The man got in his car but wasn't driving fast or far. Oliver guessed correctly that he would catch up with the Buick outside the pawnshop. Oliver hurried around the corner and down the street, moving as quickly as he could, without attracting attention.

Sure enough, when he approached the pawnshop, he spied the Buick parked in the alley around back. The mystery man was attempting to open the locked pawnshop door. Oliver hung back, hidden in the dark of night between buildings on the opposite side of the street. From this vantage point, he watched the man jimmy the lock. He dared not get closer, waiting in the dark some ten, maybe fifteen minutes, until he saw the man leave the pawnshop, closing the door quietly behind him.

Oliver remained hidden in the space between the buildings on the opposite side of the street, trying to decide his next move. He stood there, marking time, until he was sure it was safe to cross the street. Finally, Oliver scurried over to the pawnshop. There was nothing out of the ordinary, just a pawnshop closed for the night. He saw the guns beckoning from the display window, inviting him to bust in the door, to throw a rock through the window. Oliver didn't see how he could manage it. He had come down to Woodbine uncertain whether he had the nerve to buy a gun. Stealing a gun was not an option. There was nothing left for Oliver to do in Woodbine. He hustled down the empty street, found his parked car and turned the music on loud to drown out the questions imploding inside his head.

Eating Breakfast
and Dishing about Boys

Cassie's phone rang one more time, waking her yet again, only this time she opened her eyes and the sun was up. She rolled over and looked at the clock on her night stand. It was nearly ten in the morning.

Cassie picked up her telephone. "Hello?"

"Did you forget about breakfast?" It was Cheyenne. "I'm at the Eggery."

"Omigod, Chey. I'm sorry." She was already climbing out of bed, running around her bedroom. "I'll be right there."

"Are you sure, Cassie?"

"Yeah, it's okay. Just give me two minutes in the shower, and I'll be out the door."

It wasn't exactly two minutes, but Cassie did move quickly, and twenty minutes later she arrived at the Eggery, her hair still damp from the shower.

"Thanks for waiting, Chey. I overslept."

"Everything okay with you?" wondered Cheyenne.

"Yeah, fine. Did you order?"

Greta stopped at the table with two cups of rich, dark coffee. "I'll—grr—be right back."

"So I haven't heard from you in a couple of days. What have you been up to?"

Cassie was about to tell Cheyenne about her day in Woodbine when she remembered Morris's phone call. "I'm sorry, Chey. I almost forgot. I need to make a phone call. I won't be but a minute."

Cassie pulled out her cell phone and dialed the non-emergency number for the police. "Detective Bebedict, please."

"I'm sorry, ma'am, but the detective is not available at the moment. Can I connect you to another officer?"

"No. I need to speak to Detective Bebedict. Is he on his way to Woodbine? This is important."

"Could I have your name, ma'am? Are you sure I can't transfer you to another detective?"

"This is Cassie O'Malley. It's very important that I speak to Detective Bebedict. Please tell him to call me right away."

"I'll see what I can do, Ms. O'Malley."

Cheyenne waited for Cassie to hang up her cell phone before asking, "What was that all about?"

"I have information for the detective about the murders at the mall." Cassie realized a lot had happened since she last spoke to Cheyenne. "It looks like there's a connection between the deaths of Teddy Maciborski and Louis Feldman."

Cheyenne put down her cup of coffee and stared at her best friend. "And you have information about that connection?"

"I believe I do."

Just then Cassie's cell phone rang.

"Hello."

"This is Detective Harding. Am I speaking to Ms. O'Malley?"

"Yes, Detective. You are speaking to Cassie O'Malley." She continued, "but I am not speaking to anyone but Detective Bebedict."

"Detective Bebedict is not available right now. He asked me to call you." Detective Harding hoped that Cassie would believe him.

"Sorry, Detective. If Detective Bebedict really asked you to call me, when you talk to him next time . . . when you talk to him for the first time . . . tell him to call me." She hung up her cell.

Cheyenne sat across the table, mouth agape. "Was that really necessary?"

Cassie sipped her coffee. "We'll know soon enough."

Greta stopped back at their table, refilling their coffee cups and taking their breakfast order—two eggs over easy with a side of bacon extra-crispy and an egg white omelet ("The doctor told me my cholesterol is too high," Cheyenne explained, embarrassed by her heart healthy order) and dry toast.

Even before they were finished placing their order, Cassie's cell phone was ringing once again.

"Okay, Cassie, what do you want?" growled Eggs Bebedict.

"Good morning, Eggs. Thanks for returning my call."

"This damn well better be important, Cassie." Eggs paused, not meaning to sound harsh. "Truth is, I always like talking to you, Cassie, but right now I'm sitting in my car outside Louie's, getting ready to search the place."

"That's better." Cassie paused, not meaning to sound petulant. "I always like talking to you too, but right now I've got some information about the search."

"What've you got, Cassie?"

"Look for jewelry."

"I know that already, Cassie. Is there more?"

"Behind the counter. Look for jewelry behind the counter. It's still in the original boxes."

"How do you know about the jewelry?"

"Eggs . . . Detective Bebedict . . . I think we could be friends, you know what I mean?" Cassie didn't wait for an answer. "But you're a cop and I'm a reporter. We both need to remember that. I have to protect the confidentiality of my sources."

"Of course you do, Cassie. I understand . . . So was it Morris that told you?"

Cassie forced herself to laugh. "I'll pretend I didn't hear that . . . Eggs."

Detective Bebedict snorted. "Thanks for the tip, Cassie."

Cheyenne barely knew where to begin. "You call the detective Eggs?"

Cassie smiled. "Yeah. He told me all his friends call him Eggs."

"You like him, don't you?"

"Yeah. I think I do."

And for the next few minutes they forgot about the double murders at the mall. They forgot about Cheyenne's mayoral difficulties. They forgot about all manner of adult concerns, and were college roommates again, eating breakfast and dishing about boys.

"So what's he like?"

"Older, I'd guess fifty, kinda rough around the edges, not much to look at . . ." Cassie saw Cheyenne's quizzical expression. "Well, not hideous, really kinda cute, but he'd hate it if he heard me call him cute. He's a gentleman, not an Emily Post kinda gentleman, but I think he'd treat a woman with respect."

"You do like him." Cheyenne was pleased. "You're due for a good man, Cassie. Overdue. Does he like you?"

That was the question. "I think maybe he does . . . At least, I think he will, when he figures it out."

Close to the Edge

"**G**rr—you're late."

    "Take a chill pill, Mom."

"Tell me you didn't—grr—just say what I think you said."

Cassie and Cheyenne buried their heads in their breakfast plates, pretending not to hear the argument that had broken out scant feet from their table. Cassie whispered, "Is that her son?"

Cheyenne shrugged her shoulders, concentrating on her egg white omelet. "I'll never get used to this low cholesterol diet."

Cassie chuckled. "I guess I shouldn't offer you a piece of my bacon."

Meanwhile the argument was escalating, becoming more difficult to ignore.

"Look, Mom. I don't even want to be here. But I came. Isn't that enough?"

"No. That's—grr—not enough. My boss expected you thirty minutes ago."

"But I don't want to be a busboy, mom."

"What kind of impression do you think you make when you're half an hour late? What do you think it does to my relationship with my boss? Did you think of that? We count on my job here to pay the bills. Lord knows, we can't count on your father. How about—grr—that?"

Tommy stared at his feet, scuffing one shoe with the other. "I'm sorry, Mom."

"I know you are, son."

"But I don't want to be a busboy."

"Well you're not. Not—grr—yet, anyway. Go on home. We'll talk some more later."

Cassie watched Greta's son run out the restaurant door. Safely outside, she heard him whoop through the closed door.

Cassie didn't mean to, but she caught Greta's eye. "Kids," she mumbled, as if to commiserate with the red-faced waitress.

"Do you—grr—have children?"

"Not yet."

Greta turned to Cheyenne. "How about you?"

Cheyenne shook her head no.

"Then you—grr—wouldn't understand." Greta continued talking, more to herself than to the two ladies eating a late breakfast. "He's a good kid. Really he is. But he's living too close to the edge."

Cassie couldn't help asking. "Too close to the edge?"

"A boy of fifteen, nearly—grr—sixteen already, can get hisself in a helluva lot of trouble."

Cassie tried to remember what boys were like in high school. "I guess."

"I've tried to raise him good, but there's a lot of his father in him."

"His father?"

"My ex-husband Tommy."

"Doesn't anybody stay together anymore?" asked Cheyenne, thinking about her own parents.

"My ex was a real loser. Is a real loser." Greta thought about the many ways that Tommy screwed up his life and theirs. "It's funny. He's working now as Santa Claus. At the mall. Almost three weeks and it's—grr—the longest he's ever held onto a job.

"It—grr—figures. Tommy finds something he's good at and it's a paying gig maybe a month each year. Another week until Christmas and he's out of work again." Greta laughed. "I wonder if the mall would—grr—keep him on doing something else?"

Cassie picked her head up. "The mall?"

"Yeah. Tommy's working as—grr—Santa Claus at the Mall of New Jersey." Greta looked around. "My tables—grr—are backing up." She turned and walked off, checking on the rest of her tables.

Cheyenne grinned, waiting for Greta to move beyond earshot. "That was odd."

But Cassie was thinking about Santa Claus.

"Doesn't anyone stay married anymore?" Cheyenne and Cassie stood in the Eggery's parking lot, talking.

"Your parents . . . ?"

"Yeah," said Cheyenne, self-pity lurking just below the surface of her words.

"You know," Cassie said, even though she didn't really mean it, "your mom and dad could still get back together."

Cheyenne groaned. "I don't think so, Cassie. My mother served him with the divorce papers."

"I'm so sorry, Chey. Is she still seeing . . . ?"

"Charles Meriwether the third. No, at least that's over."

Cassie felt for Cheyenne. "Well, that's a good thing."

Cheyenne tried to smile. "If he tries to cause trouble at the town council, at least my mother won't get caught in the middle now."

Cassie still thought that Cheyenne was exaggerating the man's ability to cause trouble. "I thought that was settled for now. You have all year to work on it with the attorney. Nothing's going to happen this year, right?"

"There's still one council meeting before Christmas," said Cheyenne before returning to the situation with her parents. "If Rob hadn't died, do you think your marriage would have lasted all these years?"

Cassie thought about her wedding day, the summer after graduation, in the garden on campus. "It would have been sixteen years, last summer."

Cheyenne did a quick mental calculation. "Last summer was forty years."

"Maybe it's for the best," Cassie said.

"Maybe." But Cheyenne didn't think so. "Doesn't anyone stay married anymore?"

Good Cop—Bad Cop

Detective Bebedict waited for his counterpart from the Woodbine police force to pull up in front of Louie's before making his approach to the closed pawnshop. His captain was a stickler for protocol and made it clear that he didn't want Eggs to ignore the local jurisdiction. So Eggs was polite when the young officer met him at the door.

He was polite, but just barely. Detective Bebedict began a thorough investigation of the shop, growling from time to time, but otherwise keeping his own counsel. Eggs didn't think the rookie cop was paying attention, but just in case, he took his time before checking behind the display counter. Eggs was surprised to realize that the young officer was carefully dusting for prints.

The store was organized in a jumbled sort of way, a repository for objects once considered desirable: musical instruments and household appliances, wristwatches, pinkie rings and hunting rifles, anything that a down on his luck owner might pawn for rent money or grain alcohol.

The jewelry was just as Cassie had described it. Eggs bagged the evidence without fanfare, all in a day's work. In the back office, he found a ledger book, but as he suspected, only a handful of transactions listed either buyers or sellers. And in a cash business, there were neither credit slips nor bank checks to be found. Still, the jewelry was a start.

Detective Bebedict thanked the Woodbine officer for his assistance and exited the pawnshop. After twenty years on the job, he knew there would be no report of stolen jewelry. Still, it was his job to check. A quick call to the station house confirmed the detective's intuition. If the jewelry was pawned by the rightful owner, it would be useful to know who that owner was. And if the jewelry was stolen, Eggs wanted to know why the theft went unreported. Either way, Eggs knew that his next stop was the Mall of New Jersey.

There was only one saleswoman in the store and she was busy with a customer. Detective Bebedict decided he could afford to be patient. It was, the detective decided, just about the only thing he could afford in the froufrou jewelry store. And that, he realized, was true even after the "amazing holiday prices" touted proudly on the cardboard display boards. To Detective Bebedict, jewelry stores were all the same, places designed to intimidate the unsophisticated shopper, to separate a man from his hard-earned money. Eggs didn't know a carat from a cubic zirconium, gold plate from gold foil from tin foil. He stared at the display case, wondering if Cassie O'Malley could tell the difference between the expensive and the affordable gold.

"May I help you, sir?"

Detective Bebedict looked at the cute salesgirl, half his age, gold at her neck and her wrist and her ankle, with her stylish but short business skirt showing off her legs, tanned even in December, and he showed the girl his badge. She looked around nervously, but nothing appeared to be amiss. "Detective . . ." And she peered more closely at the officer's identification. ". . . Bebedict, is it? How can I help you, Officer?"

He regretted that he had not asked his partner to meet him at the mall. It was so much easier to play good cop-bad cop with a partner. Detective Bebedict smiled at the young woman. "I understand that you've had a problem recently with some stolen merchandise."

To the detective's trained eye, the salesgirl's confusion appeared genuine. "I don't think so. I mean, I'm not the manager or anything, so maybe they just didn't tell me, but I think I would have heard something."

"Is the manager available, Miss . . . ?"

"Judy," said the salesgirl. "Judy Heffernan. No, the manager slipped out to do her own Christmas shopping. I don't know when she'll be back." Judy quickly added, "But I'll be sure to let her know the police were here." Judy turned as if to check on a customer, but the store was empty.

"That's all right, Judy. Perhaps you can help me." Detective Bebedict took the bracelet, still in the embossed gift box, from his pocket. He showed Judy the gold bracelet.

"Ah, that's a very nice piece Detective, Venetian link. Is it for your girlfriend?"

Detective Bebedict ignored the salesgirl's question and asked one of his own. "I was hoping you might tell me who purchased this particular piece."

Judy squirmed behind the counter. "I don't know if I'm allowed to do that, Officer."

"You're allowed." Good cop, Detective Bebedict smiled at the young girl.

Judy reached out her hand, and Detective Bebedict handed her the box. "Let me see." The salesgirl checked the bracelet carefully, examining the box as well, before checking the store's sales records.

"You're in luck, Detective. We've only sold one of these in the last month."

"Thank you, Judy. Now I just need the name and address of the buyer."

Judy frowned. "Isn't that what they call confidential? I don't want to get in any trouble."

It was time to play bad cop. Detective Bebedict glared. "I've never heard of jeweler-client privilege. But if you're not comfortable about this"—and Detective Bebedict continued glaring at the young girl—"I can explain it to you down at the station house."

Judy was no match for the detective. "But I can't leave the store in the middle of my shift."

"Actually, yes you can."

Detective Bebedict smiled—good cop again. "But that really isn't necessary. Now how about that name?"

Judy had an idea. She swiveled the computer screen so the detective could read the purchaser's identifying information: name, address, credit card number. If the customer complained, she could honestly say she didn't tell the officer anything.

Detective Bebedict scribbled in a small notebook. "Thank you, Judy. You've been most helpful." He smiled broadly. "Merry Christmas to you, Judy."

"And to you, Detective Bebedict."

What Eggs liked most about being a detective was the feeling that he got as he followed a trail of evidence. Teddy Maciborski, Louis Feldman, Oliver Berryhill and now Mrs. Pamela Bayardi. He avoided the temptation to speculate as he drove from the mall to the brand new development of expensive colonials some forty minutes from the mall, and the stately brick colonial with the white portico that was the address for one Pamela Bayardi. Detective Bebedict figured he could fit his house three times into the enormous colonial and still have room for an indoor bocce court. He wondered why anyone needed such a large house. He wondered how much it cost to heat.

Mrs. Bayardi answered the door herself. She was, the detective guessed, still in her thirties, a lawyer's wife, or financial advisor's, with two young boys giggling somewhere in the background. "Yes?"

Detective Bebedict showed Mrs. Bayardi his badge. "Of course," she said, "the Patrolman's Benevolent Fund. Let me go get my checkbook." And she turned to leave before the detective could explain. A moment later she returned, already writing. "How much?"

"No, ma'am. I'm here investigating a crime." The gravel vibrated deep in the detective's throat. He wondered if Mrs. Bayardi would apologize for her first impression.

"A crime? Not in this neighborhood?" She didn't.

Eggs blew on his hands to keep warm. "Can we talk inside, ma'am."

Eggs could tell that Mrs. Bayardi would prefer to have this conversation at her front door, but she did not wish to appear rude. "Yes. Please come in."

Eggs wasted no time. "Did you lose a bracelet, ma'am?"

"Is that what this is about?"

"So you did?"

"Yes." She noticed the box in the detective's hand. "Is that it? Thank you for returning it, Detective." And she reached out for the bracelet.

Detective Bebedict pulled back. "I'm sorry ma'am. This bracelet is evidence in a double homicide."

"A double homicide!" Pamela Bayardi sat down suddenly.

"I don't understand." Mrs. Bayardi looked at the detective. "What does my bracelet have to do with a double murder?"

"I was hoping you could tell me that," said Eggs.

"I'm sure I don't know."

"Tell you what, ma'am. Why don't we start at the beginning," suggested the detective.

"I was shopping at the mall. Let me think . . . it was a week ago Tuesday, I think. Or maybe Wednesday. I'm not sure."

"That's okay, ma'am."

"I was doing my Christmas shopping. I didn't plan on buying the bracelet. I was looking for a pocket watch for my husband." Mrs. Bayardi thought back to her day of shopping at the mall. "But it was such a pretty bracelet and such a good price. I just had to buy myself a little present."

"I can understand that, I suppose."

"I remember I already had a shopping bag with things for my boys, and

I put the bracelet in the top of the bag. Then I had a light lunch in the food court . . . a chicken Caesar salad, I believe."

"That's okay, ma'am. I don't think your lunch selection really matters."

"Oh, but it does officer. You see, I'm on a diet." Detective Bebedict guessed her weight at barely a hundred pounds. "Anyway, I realized they gave me the regular Caesar dressing, when I distinctly asked for the lite Caesar."

"My table was barely twelve feet from the counter. I thought the bag would be safe. But later, I realized the bracelet was missing."

"Is it possible that the bracelet fell out of the bag?"

Pamela Bayardi looked at the detective and wondered silently if he'd been listening at all. "No. I am convinced the bracelet was stolen out of my bag in the food court."

"But you didn't file a police report." Years of these interviews suggested to Detective Bebedict that this woman had nothing useful to tell him.

"I reported it to mall security . . . of course," she added for emphasis.

Christmas Fireworks

When Oliver left Woodbine, questions were exploding in his head like Christmas fireworks, and each question, each explosion had a name—the dead man Teddy Maciborski, the one who started all this trouble, and then the second dead guy Louis Feldman, the detective Eddie Bebedict, the lady writer, Oliver realized they didn't all have names after all, the writer, and the other guy, the one he spied breaking into Louie's—but no question exploded in his head more forcefully than the very large, very angry Little Mack. Little Mack was most definitely the grand finale in the Christmas firework extravaganza exploding in Oliver's cerebral cortex.

Passing an old-fashioned row of cottages on the outskirts of Woodbine—Bhait's Motel the sign read, or would read, Oliver noted, if not for the burned-out bulbs—Oliver took his foot off the gas pedal, allowing the car to decelerate, while he debated the merits of hiding out, hoping for an end to his troubles.

But there was, Oliver decided, something eerie about the Bhait's Motel, and the thought of spending Christmas alone, hiding in a cottage in the woods was just too depressing. Oliver pressed down on the gas pedal, heading for home and whatever dangers might await him there.

From the outside, Oliver's home looked empty and quiet, but he remembered how last time, Little Mack had been sitting quietly at his kitchen table. He took his time unlocking the front door, moving cautiously through his small apartment. There were no uninvited guests, no unwanted surprises, not even a telephone message. Still, Oliver was jittery. He poured himself a small glass of cream sherry and popped a DVD in the machine, Tim Burton's *The Nightmare before Christmas*. He finished the cream sherry and fell asleep, the television on, the movie still playing, and slept surprisingly well, waking the next morning, having shaken off the nighttime jitters, pulling on his brown mall of New Jersey uniform and getting ready for work.

* * *

Detective Bebedict climbed into his car, heading for the Mall of New Jersey. He could feel the investigation moving quickly now, drawing to a close. He didn't have all the details yet, but the basic elements of the case were clear, thanks to the help of Mrs. Pamela Bayardi. The Detective had to guard against jumping to conclusions, getting ahead of himself. What he had to do now was to follow the evidence, Eggs reminded himself, and that was exactly what he was doing. The evidence led back to the shopping mall.

Detective Bebedict couldn't find a single damn parking space in the lot, pulling up to an entrance, leaving his car in a fire lane, one of the many benefits of his job. As Christmas drew closer, the crowds at the mall grew larger, more hurried, more harried. In a mob of shoppers going full tilt, Detective Bebedict took his time, admiring the Christmas decorations, stopping for a moment to say hello to Santa, strolling along the main hall, window shopping, waving to the salesgirl in the jewelry store, making his way to the hallway that lead to the mall offices.

A teenage girl was talking on the phone in the otherwise empty mall office. She looked up for a moment, cupped her hand over the phone's mouthpiece, and offered up a hurried, "I'll be right with you."

He showed the girl his badge.

"I've gotta go," she said into the phone. She placed the phone back on its base and smiled at the detective. "I'm sorry."

Detective Bebedict smiled. "That's okay. I need to speak to the mall manager."

"I'll see what I can do," the girl answered. "This'll just take a minute." And she got back on the phone, talking quickly and quietly. "He's just down the hall. He's on his way back."

"Thank you."

The girl smiled. "So what's it like being a cop?"

Detective Bebedict figured the girl was just making small talk. "I like it just fine."

"My father was a policeman."

"Really?"

"Died when I was just a little kid."

"On the job?"

The girl nodded.

"I'm sorry."

* * *

"Can I help you, Detective?"

Eggs turned to face the young man with short blonde hair and tortoise shell glasses, wearing khaki chinos and blue golf shirt, the Mall of New Jersey embroidered on the pocket.

"Are you the mall manager?" Eggs asked.

"Assistant manager." He pointed toward a side door. "Why don't we talk in my office?"

The Back of the Assistant Manager's Light Blue Shirt

To Detective Bebedict the assistant mall manager looked like Oliver Berryhill after a three-hour management seminar. Even with two dead bodies in two week's time, Eggs felt like he needed to do something to get the young man's attention. He dropped his voice a full octave, allowing the gravel to roll around deep in his throat. "What's the mall's policy about allegations of theft?"

The assistant manager smiled. "We don't like it, certainly."

Detective Bebedict stared at the young man. "You don't like theft or you don't like allegations?"

The young man tried to decide if the detective was asking a trick question. "We don't like either, I suppose."

"So if a shopper were to report that she'd been robbed here in the mall, say just for example, someone took an expensive piece of jewelry, how would the mall handle it?"

The assistant mall manager answered as though he were reading from the manual. "In the event that a customer makes a claim of robbery, it shall be the procedure for mall security to write down the customer's complaint and to initiate an investigation."

"And then?" asked the detective.

"We investigate, I suppose."

"Do you file a police report?"

The assistant manager scratched his head. "I don't think so. No."

It was the detective's turn to scratch his head. "You don't?"

"The owners like to handle things quietly, without fanfare. The customer, of course, can go to the police and file a complaint if he wishes to."

"But," Detective Bebedict's voice dripped with contempt, "doesn't the customer believe that's what they've just done with your security guard?"

The assistant manager had no answer. Thankfully, he made no effort to contrive one.

Detective Bebedict knew it was time to push. "You mentioned before that security writes out the customer's complaint. Is that correct?"

The young man nodded, still saying nothing.

"Okay, then. Here's what we're gonna do. I'm gonna give you the name and date of a report and you're gonna go get me a copy of the written report."

Eggs watched the assistant manager closely as he tried to come up with a way to say no to the detective. He pulled a packet of breath mints from his pocket, popping one in his mouth, stalling for time. Finally he went with a simple answer. "I don't have the authority to give you that, Detective."

"If you want to call the owner, you go right ahead young man." Eggs smiled broadly. "But it seems to me, the owner is gonna want to cooperate with the police. Two dead bodies ain't exactly what I'd call good for business. What do you think happens to business if I come back here tomorrow with a search warrant and a news crew?"

The assistant manager nearly choked on the breath mint. Coughing, he wiped his mouth and said, "I guess if you put it that way, Detective." He walked toward the door. "Please follow me, Detective."

He led Detective Bebedict to a small file room, just down the hall. He scanned the file cabinets, identifying the one he was looking for and opened the top drawer, rifling through the file folders.

"Reports are filed by date." He continued looking through the files. "At least they're supposed to be." He frowned. "I'm sorry, Detective. This may take a while."

"I've got time." Detective Bebedict leaned against the far wall and watched the back of the assistant manager's light blue shirt develop a large sweat stain as he searched, unsuccessfully, for the written report.

"This is most embarrassing," he said, closing the file cabinet and turning to face the detective. The front of his shirt looked even worse than the back, Eggs noted with some small satisfaction.

"So let me see if I have this right," Eggs said quietly, slow playing his cards. "Mrs. Bayardi believes, rightly or wrongly, that someone has stolen an expensive bracelet while she is having a chicken Caesar salad in the food court. She comes down here to the office and reports the robbery. A mall security officer makes a written report. The alleged crime is never made known to the police to conduct a proper investigation. And now, what little paperwork the mall is supposed to maintain cannot be found." Detective Bebedict cracked his knuckles and looked at the sweat-soaked manager. "Do I have that right?"

"You make it sound worse than it is, Detective."

"How so?"

"Well, just, the way you say it, it sounds almost, what's the word, conspiratorial."

Detective Bebedict scowled. "It does seem, let's call it, convenient. Anyone at the mall who was knowledgeable about the haphazard approach to such complaints, well, if he were dishonest, a man might take advantage, don't you think?"

The assistant manager was aghast. "Surely you're not suggesting that the thief is an employee of the Mall of New Jersey?"

Just One More Thing

Of course, that was exactly what Eggs Bebedict was suggesting. "Is Oliver Berryhill working today?"

"Not Oliver," squeaked the assistant manager. Their local hero was just about the only bright spot for the mall in the whole holiday debacle.

"Is he here?" Detective Bebedict was tired of dealing with the assistant manager.

"Let me check." He poked his head out the door and called to the girl working in the outer office. "Robin, do you know if Oliver is working today?"

Robin looked past the assistant manager to the detective, asking "Would you like me to have him come down here?"

"Thank you, yes," Eggs said, nodding respectfully to the daughter of a fallen comrade.

"Yes, please," added the assistant manager.

Waiting for Oliver Berryhill, Detective Bebedict could feel the assistant manager's discomfort. Robin, however, had no such problem. She looked at Eggs and smiled. "So is Oliver a suspect?"

"Robin!" The assistant manager was appalled by her question to the detective. "That's really not appropriate." He would have to put a note in her personnel jacket.

Detective Bebedict smiled. He liked Robin. If he had a daughter, he'd want her to be like this girl. "That's okay," he said to the assistant manager. Then he turned to Robin. "You didn't really expect me to answer that, did you?"

Robin shrugged. "Just making conversation."

Before Robin could make any more conversation, Oliver Berryhill entered the office. "What's up?"

Robin didn't bother letting the assistant manager answer. "Detective Bebedict would like to have a few words with you."

The assistant manager looked from Robin to Oliver to Eggs, settling for a moment, on the detective. "Would you like to use my office?"

"That won't be necessary," Eggs said.

The Detective turned to Oliver Berryhill. "We can talk down at the station house."

Robin whistled. She knew what that meant.

So did Oliver. "Can't we talk here? I'm in the middle of my shift."

Detective Bebedict growled. "The mall will just have to manage without you." He turned to the assistant manager. "Isn't that right?"

"Yes. Yes. Of course." The assistant manager's blue shirt was rapidly developing a new sweat stain. "Whatever you say, Detective."

"Okay then." He looked at Oliver. "Come with me."

As they left the office, Detective Bebedict turned back for just a moment. "Thank you Robin."

"I already told you what I know, Detective."

Eggs ignored Oliver's attempt at conversation as they walked through the mall and out to the parking lot. He said nothing at all to Oliver until they got to the car. "Get in the back."

"Am I in any trouble?"

Eggs walked around to the driver's side and got in the car. "We'll talk when we get to the station house."

Detective Bebedict hummed in the car on the way to the station house. It took Oliver most of the car ride before he realized that the detective was humming the theme songs from classic TV cop shows.

The interview room was much as Oliver had come to expect from television and movies—a table, a couple of chairs, walls in desperate need of a paint job, a mirror (Oliver recognized it as a one-way mirror, designed to permit observers to watch the interview).

"Am I in trouble, Detective?"

"That depends."

"Depends?" Oliver wondered. "On what?"

Detective Bebedict trained his eyes on Oliver, knowing that his answer was going to generate a reaction.

"On whether or not you're guilty of murder."

Oliver Berryhill did not have a face for poker, or apparently, for interrogation. He swallowed hard, trying to remain impassive.

"Not guilty."

Detective Bebedict pursed his lips in a grim smile. "That part comes later, Berryhill. For now, just tell me what happened."

"I've already told what happened to Teddy Maciborski."

"Yes, you did." The Detective nodded, leaning in toward Oliver. "But this would be a good time to tell me what really happened."

Oliver didn't know what else to do, so he told the detective the truth. "When I walked into the men's room, Teddy Maciborski was already dead."

Detective Bebedict leaned back, folding his arms across his chest. "Go on."

"That's all there is to tell. Except maybe I thought if I made up a good story, I could be a hero."

The detective considered Oliver's new version. "Or maybe Big Mack was alive. Maybe you struggled. Maybe you slit his throat."

"No, detective!" Oliver knew he had let this get way out of control. "It was wrong for me to make up a story. It was wrong to take advantage of the dead guy. All's I wanted was my fifteen minutes of fame."

Detective Bebedict resisted the urge to laugh. "What's that expression? Be careful what you wish for."

Oliver Berryhill had been thinking just that. "You've obviously been giving this some thought, Detective, so answer me this. Why would I want to kill Teddy Maciborski?"

"Ah, yes. Motive. I must admit that was troubling me, even before, when I knew you were being less than honest. What would lead you to murder Teddy Maciborski?" Detective Bebedict stood up and walked around the small interview room. "Tell me, Oliver, do you know a Pamela Bayardi?"

"Pamela Bayardi?" Oliver tried to place the name. "No, I don't think I do, Detective. Should I?"

"She shops at the mall."

"Surely you don't think I would know every shopper."

"No," Eggs said. "Not every shopper. Pamela Bayardi recently made a report to mall security of a stolen bracelet." Eggs approached the interview table. "Did you take that report, Oliver?"

"I don't think so, Detective. Anyway, what does Mrs. Bayardi's bracelet have to do with the death of Teddy Maciborski?"

Detective Bebedict ignored Oliver's question. "But you've taken other reports from time to time, right Oliver? Reports of stolen property?"

"Of course. I'm a security guard. It's my job."

"That's right, Oliver. It is your job. So tell me," continued Eggs, "what happens after you take a report of stolen property?"

"Well, we file the report in the manager's office. Sometimes, we investigate."

"Do you file a police report?"

"Do you mean me or the manager?"

"You. Or the manager."

"No. The mall owner likes us to handle these things quietly."

"So most of these complaints of stolen property go unsolved?"

"Yes."

"And a security guard would know that, wouldn't he?"

"Of course."

"Thank you, Oliver."

"You're welcome, Detective. Is that all?"

"Just one more thing." Detective Bebedict reached for Oliver's arm. "You're under arrest for the murder of Teddy Maciborski."

White Chocolate Raspberry Ganache

"It was a helluva long day, I suppose, but productive," Eggs said, stabbing the penne arabiatta with his fork, and looking across the table at Cassie. He took a bite of the penne and smiled, enjoying his non-date with Cassie (that's what he called it when he phoned her up and asked her to dinner, a "non-date"). He topped up her wine glass from the bottle of pinot noir and signaled the waitress to bring another beer for himself. Eggs sat back in his chair, utterly relaxed.

"So you've solved the case then?" Cassie wasn't sure if she had accepted the last minute "non-date" dinner invitation because she wanted to hear about the case or because she thought dinner with Eggs would be fun. Perhaps, she allowed, it was a little of both.

"Well. I did make an arrest."

"But you only charged him with one of the murders?"

"One was enough." Eggs took another bite of his penne. "This is good."

"Enough?"

"Yeah. Enough to get him talking." Eggs grinned. "How's the fettuccini?"

Cassie glared at Eggs. "The fettuccini is wonderful. Now, tell me what happened!"

Eggs remembered that moment when Oliver realized he was being arrested. There's nothing like the threat of incarceration to get the weak ones to start talking.

"At first he talked a lot about Teddy's son, Augie. It seems Little Mack was determined . . . is determined to avenge his father's death."

"So Little Mack doesn't think his father's death was an accident?"

Eggs ate a bite of penne, wiping a touch of red sauce from his mouth with his napkin before continuing. "I don't think it matters to Little Mack. His father is dead. Someone's gotta pay."

"So when Oliver made himself the hero of the story . . ." Cassie said.

"Little Mack went after Oliver," Eggs said, finishing for her. "That's when Oliver began to understand there was a downside to being the local hero. That's when he told Little Mack the same story he eventually told me about walking into the men's room and finding Big Mack's dead body in the stall."

"Did Little Mack believe him?"

Eggs wasn't certain what Little Mack believed. "I don't know. But this much I do know. If Little Mack believes Oliver's story, it means Oliver's not the thief."

"In which case," Cassie suggested, "whoever Big Mack was meeting at the mall becomes the prime suspect in his murder."

"If we can figure that out, Little Mack sure as hell can too," said the detective. "But here's where it really starts to get interesting. Oliver claims that Little Mack expects him to settle the score."

Cassie stopped picking at her fettuccini. "To settle the score? How?"

"Oliver told me if he doesn't dispose of Big Mack's killer, Little Mack is gonna leave him for dead somewhere deep in the Barrens."

"Oh."

"Yeah. Oh."

"So did Oliver tell you who he's supposed to kill?"

This part of the story troubled Eggs. "Oliver says he doesn't know yet. And if Little Mack knows, he hasn't revealed the name."

Cassie was skeptical. "Do you believe Oliver's story?"

"I believe Oliver believes it. Why else would he go to Woodbine to buy a gun from Louis Feldman?"

"What!" Cassie forgot all about her fettuccini. "When did Oliver do that?"

Eggs gulped down his beer. "He was in Woodbine, same time we were."

Cassie was having trouble making sense of the timeline. "But Louie was already dead."

Eggs admitted he had been troubled by the timeline, too, until he looked more closely at the sequence of events. "Louis was already dead, but Oliver didn't know that. He knew someone had died in the break room, but he didn't know who. Remember, it was just an unidentified body at that point, dead of a gunshot."

Cassie nodded, remembering. "But by the time we drove to Woodbine, we knew it was Louie."

"Yeah, we did. But we hadn't released the name. So there was no reason for Oliver to think that Louie was dead. He was surprised to find the pawnshop closed." Eggs paused, for the effect. "Even more surprised, apparently, to find us standing there, out front, talking."

A busboy cleared their plates. Cassie sipped her pinot noir and waited for the busboy to depart. "This just gets curiouser and curiouser."

Eggs knew the conversation was about to be more difficult. He looked at Cassie. "You haven't heard the strange part yet."

"Would you like to see the dessert tray?" Cassie was startled by the waitress and was inclined to send her away, but Eggs answered in the affirmative.

The waitress returned quickly with her samples, like a restaurant spokesmodel, using her free hand, gesturing to highlight each selection. "The white chocolate raspberry ganache is my favorite," she said. "The macadamia nut cheesecake is also very good. We have a carrot cake, apple pie and I think we still have a serving of bananas foster. I'll have to check on that if you're interested. But, like I said, the ganache is my favorite."

"I'll have an espresso," said Eggs. Turning to Cassie, he added, "Would you like something?"

"Just coffee."

"Regular coffee?" asked the waitress.

"Yes, please." As soon as the waitress left the table, Cassie returned to the story. "What's the strange part?"

"When you and I left Woodbine," Eggs said, waiting for Cassie's reaction, "your friend Morris stayed behind."

"What do you mean, 'stayed behind'? Don't you remember? He drove home in that ugly green Buick of his. Why he loves that car, I'll never know."

"No, Cassie. I mean, I guess he did drive home eventually, but it was later, much later. Would you like to know what Morris did in Woodbine after you and I left?"

Of course Cassie knew exactly what Morris had done. Morris had phoned her up and told her. "What did he do?"

"According to Oliver, your good friend Morris broke into the pawnshop." Eggs waited for Cassie to say something. When she sat there and said nothing at all, Eggs continued. "But you knew that already, didn't you?"

Still, Cassie said nothing. Eggs continued. "It was Morris told you about the jewelry."

Finally, Cassie responded. "I told him it made him look guilty of something."

"Breaking and entering for starters," Eggs said. "But that's not what you meant."

"No," Cassie agreed. "I told him you would think he broke in to destroy evidence."

"Would it make you feel better if I told you that I don't think your friend was destroying evidence in the pawnshop?"

Something in Eggs tone of voice told Cassie not to feel good about anything. "Should it?"

"No, I guess not," admitted Eggs. "I don't think Morris broke into the pawnshop to destroy evidence. I think maybe he broke in so he could plant evidence."

"The jewelry?" Cassie asked.

Detective Bebedict nodded. "The jewelry."

They stared at one another over two steaming cups of coffee. "If Morris is involved in this, Little Mack is gonna know," Eggs added. "At some point, he's gonna get tired of dealing with amateurs."

Constitutional Issues

Cassie was unable to sleep. She knew Morris was incapable of murder, but Detective Bebedict told her that in his experience, most murders were committed by people who were incapable of killing, right up until the moment that they weren't. She knew that Morris had an alibi for the Big Mack murder, that he was stranded in Woodbine without a car, but the situation with Louie was more complicated. By his own admission, Morris had serious money problems. By his own admission, Louie had ripped him off for the value of his autographed guitar. When she drove to Woodbine with Eggs, they found Morris pounding on the door of the closed pawn-shop. And later that night, after they left, Morris broke into the shop. She didn't believe Morris was the killer. But she couldn't shake the feeling that he was somehow involved. When Eggs laid it out for her, it was hard to ignore the possibility.

Cassie realized that Eggs didn't have the evidence to arrest Morris for the murder of Louis Feldman. If he did, he would not have approached Cassie for help. The detective's theory of the crime pointed to a single killer responsible for both crimes. It would be an insider at the Mall of New Jersey stealing from unsuspecting shoppers and passing the goods to Big Mack, who would then use Louie to unload the stolen property. The theory pointed to Oliver, not Morris and Oliver was already in custody. Eggs told her more than once that he did not believe in coincidence. Even if it turned out that there were two killers, the detective was convinced these were not two unrelated killings. Until he could nail down the connection, he could neither implicate nor exonerate Morris.

Despite the ache that had settled in her chest, Cassie agreed to help. It was late at night when she placed the call.

"It looks bad, Morris. But I told Eggs it doesn't matter how it looks. I told him you couldn't possibly be involved in a double murder."

"What did he say next?"

"I can't do this over the phone, Morris. Meet me at the Eggery for breakfast."

"But . . ."

"Please, Morris. Let's not do this over the phone."

Cassie was unable to sleep. She poured a Jameson's and water and flipped on the television. cable channel eight was replaying the town council meeting, shown live earlier that evening while Cassie was on her non-date with Eggs Bebedict. She recalled Cheyenne's prediction of trouble at the meeting and sat down to watch the re-broadcast. It occurred to Cassie that the meeting was over. She didn't have to watch the tape; she could call Cheyenne and ask. But Cassie was tired of talking; she was tired of thinking. She sipped her Irish whiskey and watched her friend Cheyenne on TV.

"Many of you will remember," Cheyenne was leaning into the camera, her ample chest dominating the TV screen, speaking directly to Cassie and to the other habitual Council watchers who were following the action on local access cable and to the handful of township residents sitting in the Council room. "Many of you will remember the divisiveness which characterized the previous administration here in Doah."

Cheyenne took her eye off the camera just long enough to look at the former Mayor, "Big Jim" Donovan, sitting in the audience. "Please do not misunderstand. I have the greatest of admiration and a certain undeniable fondness for our former Mayor." In the audience, "Big Jim" stirred. Embarrassed by the attention, Mayor Donovan made his way clumsily to the exit.

Cassie chuckled as the camera followed the former Mayor taking his leave.

"But it is no secret that this town found itself embroiled in a series of nasty disputes involving land use decisions and later about religious displays on municipal property. I believe we have made great progress on the land use issues. I wish we could say the same on the matter of religious tolerance."

Sitting in the audience, Charles Meriwether nearly jumped out of his seat, eager for a fight. Looking around the room, he quickly sat down, waiting to see what Mayor Harbrough would do.

Sitting at home, Cassie refilled her Irish whiskey. She wondered if Cheyenne was really about to take on the issue of religion in public life. She didn't have to wait to find out.

"Fifty years ago, Doah was almost entirely a white, Christian community. I realize that there are some who look back wistfully at that time."

Cheyenne stared directly at Mr. Meriwether. "But I do not believe in look-ing backwards. I believe we must look forwards. Doah has become a town of rich ethnic, cultural and religious diversity. I take great pride in that diversity and have always seen it as a real strength in our community. As long as I am the mayor, we will not apologize for our diversity."

The audience sitting in the Council room was surprisingly quiet. Watching at home on TV, Cassie found it difficult to gauge their reaction. Cheyenne, standing at the podium, was finding it equally difficult.

"I understand," Cheyenne plowed ahead, "that there are some in this community who feel that removing the manger from the municipal build-ing is anti-Christian. I do not need to remind you that decision was made under the previous administration, on the advice of our township attor-ney. I think that a large majority in town would agree that we do not wish any one religion to take precedence over any other religion in the public life of Doah. And so we are faced with a dilemma. How do we create a climate in Doah in which every citizen is free to worship or not, to believe or not, and to share that experience with like-minded neighbors, without marginalizing others in this diverse community of ours?"

Several members of the audience rose to speak, but Cheyenne had no intention of relinquishing the floor.

"It would be easy for me to hide behind constitutional issues, to sug-gest that our religious life should happen in our homes and in our churches and synagogues, but the truth is, I happen to believe there is an appropri-ate role for our public institutions as well. I think that municipal govern-ment can acknowledge Christmas without tearing down the wall between church and state."

"Speaking for a moment not as mayor, but as a private citizen who happens to be Jewish, I have to say that I have never been offended by Christmas displays. To tell you the truth, I kind of like them. And we could all use a little more 'peace on earth, goodwill to men.' It seems to me that the town can acknowledge the events that are important to its citi-zens—Christian, Jewish, Muslim, Hindu. Isn't that after all what it means to celebrate our diversity?"

"I am therefore announcing tonight the formation of an ad hoc Mayor's advisory committee to address these issues directly. If you have an opinion, the committee will want to hear it. In the meantime, this is the last Council meeting before Christmas, so with your permission, I would ask that we table any further township business. I would ask you to join me in the first annual Mayoral Christmas party."

"Ho! Ho! Ho!"

All eyes turned to the rear of the Council room. The doors swung open and Santa strode in, looking very much like the sheriff walking into a barroom in Dodge City, there to restore order and Christmas cheer.

"Ho! Ho! Ho! Merry Christmas everybody."

In the municipal building, Council members and audience alike were stunned by Santa's unscheduled appearance. Watching at home on TV, perhaps it was the surprise, or maybe just one too many Irish whiskeys, but Cassie nearly fell out of her chair.

Cheyenne had arranged for eggnog and pastries and these were carried into the room moments after Santa's arrival. She had also arranged for Santa to deliver gifts. Her favorite was for one of her harshest critics, a Thesaurus with an inscription from the mayor herself—"In case you run out of ways to say I'm doing a crummy job."

After the party, Cheyenne sat in her office in the municipal building. "Thanks for agreeing to play Santa Claus tonight."

"It was fun." Taking off his hat and gloves, peeling off his white whiskers, "Big Jim" Donovan grinned. "There are some in this town who were convinced you were going to do a lousy job as Mayor. You know I was never one of them. You're proving yourself to be an admirable Mayor."

"Thank you, Jim."

"Just so you understand that's not going to stop me from challenging you in the next election.

"I wouldn't have it any other way." She reached out and put her hand on Santa's thigh.

Better Make this One Decaf

Cassie fell asleep with the television on, Santa holding court in the Council room; ho, ho, ho echoing in her dreams. Morris, on the other hand, barely slept at all after Cassie's phone call. He was standing at the Eggery's front door when it opened for business at 6:30 in the morning. When Cassie strolled into the restaurant at 9:00, he was on his third pot of black coffee.

"You look horrible, Morris." Despite all the coffee, his eyes were bloodshot and half shut. What remained of his hair hung off the side of his head in random patches. A farmer had plowed deep furrows in Morris's brow.

"What did you tell him, Cassie?"

"I told him it wasn't you, that when Big Mack was murdered, you were stranded without a car at that motel in Woodbine."

"And then?"

Cassie shook her head. "Detective Bebedict didn't say very much, but he thought it was curious you were in Woodbine, of all places. Tell me again, Morris. You didn't have anything to do with Louie Feldman's murder, did you?"

Morris nearly burned his mouth on his coffee. "After all these years, do you really need to ask?"

"I'm sorry, Morris." Cassie couldn't meet his gaze. "Did you?"

"No, Cassie. I had nothing to do with Louie's murder. And I didn't plant any evidence, either."

"Okay, Morris. I'm sorry. Your connection to Louie is just an unfortunate coincidence. I won't ask you, ever again."

"Thank you, Cassie." Morris was relieved.

"But what about your connection to the Macks? You owed them money, right?"

Morris nodded. "I told you that already."

Cassie tried to remember the conversation. "But you never told me how you hooked up with the Macks. I mean, you were always pretty careful who you did business with."

"I told you, Cassie. The magazine wasn't generating the kind of revenue you thought it was. I was falling deeper and deeper in debt."

"But you sold the magazine. I mean that must have covered the debt, at least. It did cover the debt, didn't it Morris?"

Morris tried to find a simple explanation to a complicated question. "Well, yes . . . and no. I had some rather large gambling debts. I couldn't go to the bank, not while the sale of the magazine was in process."

Cassie had known Morris for nearly two decades and in all that time she hadn't realized he had a gambling problem. "So you went to the Macks."

"Yeah. I went to the Macks."

Cassie didn't know what else to say. "Have you ordered breakfast?" She signaled for the waitress.

"Are you—grr—here again?"

Cassie laughed. "I guess I have been here a lot the last couple of weeks. This is my friend, Morris." She turned to Morris to make the introduction. "Morris, Greta."

"Nice to meet you Greta."

"Same—grr—here."

Cassie asked for her regular. Morris ordered pancakes and a fourth pot of coffee. "Better make this one decaf," he added, as an afterthought.

Greta disappeared into the kitchen.

"So what am I supposed to do now?"

"Detective Bebedict would like you to go to the station house today to answer a few more questions."

"Do I have a choice?"

"Not really."

Morris was feeling sorry for himself. He tried to pinpoint the moment his life had begun to fall apart. All he could think of was when his car got a flat tire deep in the Pine Barrens, but he knew his troubles started years earlier. "Can I eat my breakfast first?"

Cassie tried not to laugh. "Of course you can."

A busboy stopped at the table with a fresh pot of coffee. He didn't seem happy to be working.

"I know that boy," Morris said, as the busboy made his way around the restaurant.

Cassie was surprised. "I don't know how. That's Greta's son. He just started working here."

Morris stared at the busboy's back. "Well, I know him from someplace."

No Witnesses, No Prints

There was a deep chill in the station house. It felt like someone had deposited an enormous block of dry ice right in the center of the squad room. Detective Bebedict looked up and realized that the block of dry ice was none other than his captain, who was definitely not happy to find the local hero still in lock-up. "Bebedict," he roared, "I thought I told you to cut him loose."

Eggs Bebedict didn't like the captain, but he respected the chain of command. "I think we've got enough to charge him, Captain."

"You got jack, Detective. No witnesses, no prints, nothing."

"With all due respect, Captain," Eggs spit the words out, "I've got the stolen jewelry."

The captain looked at his detective. "Ah, that's right. You've got the jewelry." The captain paused. "And what exactly does the jewelry prove?"

Detective Bebedict wanted to smack some sense into his captain. "It all fits, Captain. Don't you see? Oliver was stealing from unsuspecting shoppers at the mall. If, like Mrs. Bayardi, they realized they'd been robbed, he'd make sure nothing ever happened with their complaint. Meanwhile, he was passing the stuff to the Macks."

"I know. I know," the captain said, waving Eggs off. "And the Macks were disposing of the stuff at Louie's pawnshop."

"That's right Captain. Only something blew up between Oliver and Big Mack."

"That's an interesting theory, Bebedict, but you've got no proof. Find me the proof, Bebedict and I'll back you. Meanwhile, cut Berryhill loose."

Eggs had more to say, but his captain cut him off. "That's an order, Detective."

Eggs released Oliver Berryhill and thanked him for his cooperation. If he was going to make the case, Detective Bebedict knew he would have to squeeze Morris. He hoped Cassie would understand.

The detective dialed Cassie's cell phone.

"Cassie, it's me . . . Eggs. Have you talked to him yet?"

"I'm with him now. By the way detective, thanks for dinner last night. It was fun."

"Yeah. Same here. So is he coming in?"

"I'm having trouble hearing you. It's kind of noisy in here." Cassie looked around. In a corner of the restaurant, Greta and her son were arguing again. Cassie figured it was another argument about the busboy job. It seemed pretty clear that Greta was losing.

"I asked if Morris would be coming to the station house this morning."

The argument seemed to be escalating. Cassie walked out to the parking lot, looking for a quieter place to talk.

"We're having breakfast. He'll stop by the station house when we're done."

"Tell him I get cranky when I have to wait."

"Easy, Eggs."

"Just tell him . . . please."

Cassie smiled into the phone. "That's better. Expect him in an hour or so."

"Make it half an hour."

At that moment, Greta's son came storming out of the restaurant, followed by his mother. "You are in so much trouble, young man." Cassie noticed that Greta didn't growl when she was yelling.

"I'm sorry, Eggs. What was that?"

"Just tell him to get here as soon as possible. Okay Cassie?"

Cassie was having difficulty focusing on her phone call with Eggs. Greta and her son were getting even louder in the parking lot. She did her best to block out the noise and said good-bye into her cell. "Thanks again for dinner. Call me later today." Cassie closed her cell phone and walked back into the dining room. Her eggs were waiting for her return.

Morris looked up from his pancakes. It was obvious to Morris that the phone call had been about him. He didn't like the part he could hear. He figured the part he couldn't hear was even worse. "Is everything okay?"

Cassie wasn't sure. "I think you better finish up those pancakes and get over to the station house."

Morris took a large bite of pancake drenched in syrup. "Will you come with me to see the detective?"

"I think you have to do this on your own, Morris. Besides, there's something I need to check out."

Morris was hopeful. "Something that's gonna help me with the detective?"

"I don't see how. Did you watch the Council meeting last night?" Cassie didn't wait for Morris to answer. "This is gonna sound stupid, but . . . does Santa Claus usually wear gloves?"

A Veritable Universe of Christmas Trees

Cassie looked across the table at Morris, wiping the maple syrup from his plate with the last bite of pancake. "Go on, Morris. Go talk to Detective Bebedict."

Morris tried to prolong the last bite of breakfast all morning.

"Go on, Morris. I'll settle up the bill."

Morris, reluctantly, rose to leave.

"Just tell him the truth, Morris, no matter how bad it sounds. If there's one thing I've learned, it's not to lie to the police. Now get out of here."

Morris walked slowly to the door. He looked back at Cassie as though he would never see her again.

Cassie looked around the restaurant, eager to pay her bill and leave, but Greta had not yet returned. She waved down the hostess and paid for breakfast.

In the parking lot, climbing into her Mustang, Cassie noticed the quiet. Greta and her son had taken their argument elsewhere. She popped a Christmas CD in the player—Ella singing some great old songs as only Ella could sing them—and pointed her car toward the mall. Cassie wasn't sure what she was looking for, didn't know why Santa's gloves were tugging at the edge of her consciousness; she only knew she needed to find out.

It was a chilly December day. There was no snow in the forecast, but Cassie could feel it in the air. Ella was dreaming of a white Christmas. Suddenly, Cassie was too. Christmas was a bittersweet time for Cassie, dreaming of the "should have been" Christmases with her late husband. This year, the holiday season had been neither bitter nor sweet. She had hardly even thought about Rob. The holiday season started with an annoying story assignment that had somehow morphed into a double murder. Despite it all, on a back road in the Pine Barrens, surrounded by a veritable universe of Christmas trees, Ella was singing about a white Christmas.

Cassie pulled her Mustang off the road and cried. She cried for Rob and for herself. She cried for Morris. She even cried for Teddy Maciborski and Louis Feldman. Ella sang and Cassie cried.

And then her cell phone rang.

"Hi Cassie. It's me."

"Morris! Where are you? How did things go with Detective Bebedict?" Cassie pulled out a tissue and wiped her eyes.

"I haven't gone to the police station yet."

"Morris, what . . ."

"Cassie, listen to me. I figured out where I know the busboy from."

"You're just avoiding, Morris. Forget about the busboy and go see the detective."

"No, Cassie, I think this could be important."

Cassie didn't have the energy to argue. Perhaps if she let Morris finish . . . "Okay. Morris, I'm listening. How do you know the busboy?"

Morris saw the scene so clearly, he couldn't understand why he didn't remember this sooner. "The first time I went to the pawnshop, the busboy was there."

"In the pawnshop?" asked Cassie. "Are you sure?"

"I'm sure, Cassie. Louie told me the boy was there making a delivery for his father."

Cassie said nothing.

"Cassie, did you hear me?"

Still, she said nothing.

"Are you there Cassie?"

There were no fingerprints on the knife. "Listen to me, Morris. Go find Detective Bebedict. Tell him to meet me at the mall. Tell him I know who the killer is!"

A Free Man has Choices

Since the death of his father, Little Mack had been sleeping poorly, plagued by disquieting dreams, images so startling they nearly hurtled him from bed. He wasn't sure which was worse, the dreams, or the lying in bed awake in the middle of the night, bathed in a pool of cold sweat. The youngest of four boys, Augie's brothers were all dead before Little Mack turned twenty. He was so young when his sainted mother passed on, he only remembered her from family photos. And now, his father was gone. Little Mack was the last of a once proud family. During all his waking moments, Little Mack was suffocating in his solitude. Sleep was worse. Little Mack's sleep teemed with deceased Maciborskis. Little Mack needed no expert to interpret his dreams. It was clear. It was a simple matter of honor. And Little Mack had put it off too long already. The dreams would end when he fulfilled his obligations.

That morning, Little Mack looked in the mirror, ashamed that he had even allowed his grooming to slip in just two weeks. He retrieved his father's straight razor and stropped the blade until it sparkled. He opened the ancient tin of shaving soap, mixing up a creamy lather that could otherwise be found only in a few select barbershops in New York. He soaked his face in water so unbearably hot, he wanted desperately to scream, but not a sound escaped. He looked in the mirror and was a teenage boy again, his father standing at his side, showing him how to use the straight razor. "Safety razors are for girls," Big Mack always said.

Little Mack looked in the mirror, pleased with the results. "Safety razors are for girls," he echoed proudly. He was in no hurry. Little Mack selected a freshly starched white shirt with a spread collar, his jet-black suit, and a red silk tie. His shoes were shined, but not to the Maciborski standard. Little Mack found the cloth and brush and worked the leather until his shoes looked like black glass.

The Lincoln Town Car was dirty. Little Mack briefly considered washing the Lincoln, but he knew it was impractical this morning. The inside of the car, thankfully, was spotless.

He made one stop, en route, for an espresso and the morning paper. He read the front page and skimmed the business news. He checked the sports section for injury reports and compared the lines on Sunday's games. He tipped the kid in Starbucks more than the cost of the espresso. He could put this off no longer. It was time.

Cassie hung up her cell phone. Her Christmas cry would have to wait. She was counting on Morris to send Detective Bebedict to the mall, but she was not going to wait for him. Cassie pulled her Mustang onto the road and, without regard for the posted speed limit, made haste to the Mall of New Jersey.

With just two shopping days left until Christmas, the parking lot had more cars than pavement. There were cars parked in every legal spot, in the fire lanes, on the pedestrian walkways. Cars were simply abandoned on the exit and entrance ramps. Cassie found a vacant spot of dirt nearly half a mile from the doors and counted herself one of the lucky ones. She locked the Mustang and made her way through the car maze that filled the space between her and the mall itself.

Inside was even worse, the mall filled to overflowing with holiday shoppers and all of them were sprinting through the mall. There was no time for these shoppers to relax. No way to enjoy the experience. Just run from store to store, grabbing items from the half-empty bins. No thinking, no comparing, no considering, just grab and go shopping. Merry Christmas, indeed.

Cassie made her way through the mall, careful to avoid blocking the path of rampaging shoppers, arriving safely at the food court. Her customary spot at the edge of the food court was occupied. In fact, every table, every chair in the food court was occupied. Shoppers walked around with their food, circling the food court, looking for a seat, eating even as they walked, antsy to finish and get back into the fray. Cassie found a spot where she might stand at the railing, leaning against a pillar, with a clear view of the vestibule below and Santa's Workshop.

Santa's Workshop made the rest of the mall seem like a leisurely stroll in the park. Children were everywhere, on line and off, swarming around the North Pole, climbing on the giant candy canes, eager to deliver their last minute Christmas lists. Elves worked overtime on crowd control as parents surrendered even the pretense of responsible adult supervision.

And amidst it all, in the middle of this frenzy of holiday activity, sat Santa Claus, the eye of the holiday storm.

To Cassie's practiced eye, he seemed to be having fun. Santa was bouncing kids on his large red knees. He was listening to their urgent requests and laughing at their jokes. When a little girl nearly peed in his lap, Santa merely smiled and sent her to the ladies room in the company of Mrs. Claus. When she returned, Santa made sure the youngster was ushered to the very front of the line.

Cassie wondered if she could be wrong.

Oliver walked out of the station house into freedom's bright sunlight. He did not shade his eyes, blinking after his lengthy incarceration. One night in lock-up had changed him, or so Oliver believed. He had spent the night imagining what he would do if he ever escaped incarceration, but now that freedom was at hand, Oliver didn't know what to do first. He stopped at the convenience store for a cup of orange pekoe tea with lemon and a Hostess Twinkie, his first meal as a free man. It was, he told himself, the best Twinkie he had ever tasted. The cream was creamier; the cake cakier. He savored the Twinkie, silently thanking Hostess for packaging Twinkies in pairs, for the twin Twinkie that waited patiently in its wrapper, for Twinkie number two, as Oliver savored Twinkie number one.

He sipped his tea with lemon and considered the universe of options that were available to a free man. He thought about spending the chilly December day on the beach, strolling on the nearly empty boardwalk, but it occurred to him that he was thinking too small. He could drive to the airport, hop on a plane and before the day was over he could be walking on a beach in Malibu. A free man has choices. Why not, thought Oliver. Why not spend Christmas in California?

Oliver stopped home just long enough to change into his brown uniform and drive to the Mall of New Jersey. He was going to be late for work. He only hoped that his supervisor would understand.

Morris knew that Cassie was right; he was avoiding talking to the detective. He didn't tell her that he had been sitting in the Buick, just down the street from the station house for nearly twenty minutes when he called about the busboy. He'd seen the busboy in the pawnshop. He wasn't sure why that was important, but it had to mean something. Everything meant something. And apparently it meant everything to Cassie. Morris hoped it meant as much to the detective. He walked up the street, climbing the steps into the station house and asked to speak to Detective Bebedict.

The clerk at the front desk, buzzed the detective. "He'll be right out."

"Morris," growled Detective Bebedict, "it's about damn time." He looked at Morris fidgeting in the front lobby. "Let's go back to my desk and talk."

Morris didn't wait. "I have a message . . ." he blurted, but the detective waved him off. "In back, Morris. We'll talk in back."

Detective Bebedict led Morris down the hall to the detective's squad room. He pointed to an old wooden folding chair next to the detective's desk. "Sit."

Morris sat, afraid to talk, afraid not to talk.

Detective Bebedict began. "A few questions have come up about your relationship with the deceased."

Any other time, Morris would have wondered which deceased the detective was referring to. This time, he barely noticed. "I'll be happy to answer any questions, Detective, but there's something I need to tell you right away."

The Detective was pleased. Even the unspoken threat of an arrest was enough to get Morris to volunteer new information. This one, he told himself, was even easier than Oliver. "Okay. Morris. What is it you need to tell me?"

Morris looked the detective squarely in the eye. "I saw the busboy at the pawnshop."

"Huh? What are you talking about, Morris?"

Why doesn't the detective understand? "The kid at the Eggery . . . the new busboy."

Detective Bebedict wondered where this was going. "Okay, you saw the busboy at the pawnshop. Why is that so important?"

Morris wasn't sure. "I don't know, except when I told Cassie about the busboy, she told me she knew who the killer was."

"What?" The detective growled. "Who?"

"Cassie said to tell you to meet her at the mall. She's on her way there now."

Detective Bebedict was on his feet, grabbing his coat off the back of his chair. "You're free to go, Morris."

Morris was still sitting on the wooden folding chair as the detective headed out the squad room door. He called to the detective. "Maybe you'll need help. Do you want me to go with you to the mall?"

From down the hall, Morris heard the detective as he raced for the door. "Go home, Morris."

High Noon

Watching from above, dozens of small boys and girls were climbing all over Santa's Workshop. Cassie was surprised to see that St. Nick was taking pleasure in the performance of his holiday duties. *I guess anyone can get the Christmas spirit,* Cassie discovered, *even Santa Claus.* Cassie found herself rooting for Tommy V., hoping that he was not an armed felon and crazed killer, but only a down on his luck department store Santa. She hoped he was not the Macks' partner, the inside man ripping off unsuspecting shoppers and worse.

Cassie kept one eye on Santa's Workshop and one eye on the mall's center hallway where it stretched down to the outer doors. She hoped to spot Eggs as soon as he arrived.

The first thing she noticed were the shoes. Despite the clatter of shoppers eating in the food court, the rustle of shopping bags, and the Christmas music piped through-out the mall, Cassie imagined she could hear each footfall as Little Mack strode down the hallway, each step rich with polish and purpose.

Cassie watched as he walked through the mall, in, but not of, the holiday traffic. He stood perfectly still as he rode the escalator down one level, the escalator depositing him just on the fringe of Santa's Workshop. Without appearing to muscle anyone out of his way, Little Mack glided through the crowd and suddenly was standing at Santa's side, patting the slight bulge in his suit jacket (right where Cassie imagined a shoulder holster would be located) and whispering in his ear.

Looking down on the scene from her spot at the railing, Cassie could see the alarm in Santa's eyes. She watched as Santa put up the rope at the front of the line, the one with the sign that said, "back in fifteen minutes." She saw the elves start to argue with Santa. An elf even tried to unhook the rope, but Little Mack reached out with one hand and the argument stopped. Little Mack put an arm around Santa and maneuvered through the crowd.

No one dared to tell Little Mack that Santa wasn't scheduled for a break yet. Then one clear voice spoke up for the children. "Hold it right there!"

The crowd of children waiting to see Santa moved aside. In his brown mall of New Jersey security guard uniform, Oliver Berryhill stood at the edge of Santa's Workshop. He screwed up his courage and locked eyes with Little Mack. "Santa's not going anywhere just now."

Cassie looked at her watch. It was noon. High noon.

Little Mack stood his ground; a grim laugh escaped his tight lips. "Well, well. Mr. Local Hero."

Oliver looked at his nemesis, three hundred pounds of granite encased in a fine Italian suit. "Not a hero," he said, "just doing my job." Oliver hoped he didn't sound foolish.

Little Mack wondered when the rent-a-cop had grown a backbone. "I'm impressed." If he'd been wearing a hat, Little Mack would have tipped it. "But not enough to alter my plans. Santa and I will be leaving now." Little Mack turned his back on Oliver, moving slowly but steadily toward the exit, nudging a silent Santa to follow along.

"Hold it right there," Oliver said, in a quiet, calm voice.

Little Mack was surprised by Oliver's resolve. He stopped and looked at the security guard. He unbuttoned his suit jacket, revealing the shoulder holster. "You don't have the firepower to stop me, Berryhill."

"He may not, but—grr—I do." At the bottom of the escalator, Greta took a pistol from her purse, waving it at Little Mack. "Don't—grr—take another step."

Santa had been strangely silent during the exchange between Oliver Berryhill and Augie Maciborski, but the unexpected and oh so familiar growl unloosed his tongue. "Holy crap, Greta. What are you doing?"

Little Mack looked at Greta, but directed his question to Santa. "You know her?"

"That's Greta. My ex."

"Will she use that thing?"

"Yeah. I think she might." Tommy V. grinned. "I'm just not sure which one of us is the target."

Little Mack reached inside his coat, unholstering his Smith and Wesson 686P. "Put your gun down, lady, or say good-bye to Santa Claus."

Greta's laugh was throaty and phlegmatic, from too many cigarettes and just as many disappointments. "I killed your father, Maciborski. Don't think I won't shoot you, too."

The Detective's Advice

Eggs raced for his car and jumped in, firing up the ignition. Compulsively he checked all the gauges. His car was overdue for service and was running that way. Still, everything looked good. The engine sounded good. There was just enough gas left in the tank. Eggs tried without success to reach Cassie by phone. If she was already there, her phone would never find a cell inside the mall so there was no cause for worry when she didn't pick up. He could make it to the mall in fifteen minutes, ten if he turned on the siren.

Eggs reviewed the case in his head as he sped to the mall. It had been a strange few weeks since he was first called to the mall to investigate the very large, very dead man in the bathroom, dead of a very real knife wound to the throat. He had doubted Oliver's story right from the first. The notion that Oliver confronted him in the bathroom about stolen property, that Big Mack pulled a knife on him, that he stumbled and fell, slashing his own throat. It was obvious to the detective that Oliver's first story was an elaborate lie. The detective was not surprised when Oliver finally recanted. His second version of the incident, that Oliver simply walked in on an already dead Big Mack, well it did fit the detective's assessment of Oliver Berryhill, but it led the detective nowhere. And then there was the second murder, Louie Feldman, dead in the break room, of a gunshot. Oliver had been hanging around the break room, too. And now, Cassie wanted Eggs to meet her at the mall. Cassie knew who the killer was. Eggs didn't understand where the busboy fit in, but it must have something to do with Oliver. Eggs wanted to smack himself for letting his captain pull rank. Oliver should still be in lock-up. It was only a couple more miles to the mall. Eggs pressed down on the gas pedal.

And the car decelerated, gliding slowly to a stop, out of gas, nearly two miles short of its destination. Eggs had spent two decades on the job and now, of all times, to have made a rookie mistake. He cursed loudly and repeatedly as he sprinted along on the shoulder of the roadway, the Mall of New Jersey visible now up ahead, maddeningly close, and, at the same time, still so far away.

Morris sat alongside the detective's just-vacated desk, alone in the squad room, wondering what he should do. The detective's suggestion had been clear. "Go home," the detective had told him, and Morris knew it was sound advice. He would go home and wait for a phone call telling him this nightmare was finally over. He would go home and wait and then he would go about the task of trying to get his life, and his finances, back in order. Maybe, Morris considered, he could even figure out a way to get back into the magazine business. The key thing, for the moment, was just to follow the detective's advice.

Morris walked out of the station house, past the clerk at the front desk, down the steps to the street, down the street to his car. The Buick was waiting for him, just where he'd left it, at the expired parking meter. A ticket was tucked under the driver's side windshield wiper. Morris tossed the ticket in the glove compartment, turned on the radio, and drove home.

He pulled into the driveway at the money pit he affectionately called home. A four-bedroom colonial was far more house than he needed. Untangling the complicated mortgages, second mortgages, assorted loans and liens would be difficult, but Morris realized, it was time for him to get out from under this financial disaster. He was tired of playing the victim, tired of waiting around for others to fix the mess that had become his life. "Go home," the detective had said. Morris backed his car out of the driveway and drove off.

It didn't take long before Morris could see the Mall of New Jersey in the distance. He was surprised to see someone running on the shoulder of the road. It was not a good spot for running, the road narrow, the shoulder poorly graded, the kind of road where you might easily twist an ankle. Not a runner himself, Morris knew this only as second-hand information, but it made sense. Still, there was someone running on the shoulder. Morris looked again and began honking his horn, leaning on the horn really. He pulled up alongside the runner and offered him a ride the rest of the way to the mall.

"I thought I told you to go home," Eggs said. "Thanks for not taking my advice."

When Morris pulled his Buick into the crowded parking lot, Eggs asked him to drop him off at the door. "I'd ask you to wait out here, but I guess you wouldn't listen."

Morris smiled. "Go on in. I'll find a place to leave the car."

"Don't—grr—think I won't shoot you too."

Watching from her spot above Santa's Workshop, Cassie could see that events were spinning out of control. She felt dizzy and for just a moment, thought she might fall from the railing. She stiffened at the sound of her favorite waitress turned stone-cold killer. This was not what Cassie meant when she told Morris she had solved the case. It was then that Cassie spotted Eggs. He must have come in through a different entrance because he was already on the lower level, working his way quietly through the mall, approaching Santa's Workshop from the rear.

Little Mack pointed his Smith and Wesson at Greta. "Are you sure you wanna do this lady?"

"Wait a minute, please," Tommy V. was begging now. "Greta, don't. Little Mack, you don't wanna do this. C'mon man, there's gotta be another way to settle this."

"It's a matter of honor, Tommy," Little Mack said, talking to himself as much as to Santa. "She killed my father."

"No she didn't."

"Shut up—grr—Tommy."

"Don't do this Greta."

"I said shut up. I killed his father. I'll kill him if I have to." Greta pointed her pistol at her ex-husband, preparing to fire. "And if you—grr—don't shut up, I'm willing to kill you too."

"Mom, don't!"

In a mall filled with thousands of holiday shoppers, it seemed as though no one said a word. The only sounds Cassie heard, watching from her spot at the railing was the Christmas music coming through the speakers, *Grandma got run over by a reindeer*, and the sound of her heart pounding in her chest. Things happened all at once, but later, when Cassie described the scene, she said it was as if everyone was moving in slow motion.

Halfway down the escalator, running down the steps, Tommy Junior dove for his mother. At the same moment, from behind Santa's Workshop, Detective Bebedict dove for Little Mack. Two shots rang out. Tommy Junior pushed his mother to the floor, but not before she took a bullet to her shoulder, blood arcing through the air as she fell to the floor, screaming in pain. Santa, ducking for cover, collided with the detective as he lunged for Little Mack. Eggs saw the hole in his jeans and knew he'd been hit. He struggled to his feet and grabbed for Little Mack, who was running now, in his finely tailored suit and his polished Italian loafers. Splattered now with Detective Bebedict's blood, he ran for the exit.

A Minor Aggravation

Morris circled in the parking lot, slowly despairing of ever finding a spot to leave his Buick. The lot was sinking under the weight of parked cars. Finally, a parking space opened up so far from the mall itself that Morris found himself looking for a tram to the entrance. Of course, there was no tram at the Mall of New Jersey. Morris began the long walk through the parking lot. Ten minutes later, he reached the first row of cars, those few lucky cars that had taken up residence just a few feet from the front door. Morris wondered how early these shoppers must have arrived to claim the precious spots. And there, in the very first spot, closer even than the handicapped parking spaces, Morris recognized Little Mack's Lincoln Town Car.

He wondered what mischief brought Little Mack to the mall. Morris found himself growing angry at the sight of the Town Car. It's not like the Macks were the cause of Morris's financial troubles. Morris understood they were just the beneficiaries of his fiscal mismanagement. But there was something about the Town Car, sitting there in the very first spot, while Morris's aging Buick was parked in another zip code that seemed to symbolize all that was wrong with Morris's life.

He knew it was petty and juvenile, but he wanted to exact revenge on the Town Car. But how? Morris searched in his pocket for the mini corkscrew that hung on his key chain. He looked around. The lot was filled with cars but largely absent of people. He kneeled down by the driver's side wheel, the Town Car hiding him from the view of shoppers going in and out the mall entrance. The corkscrew was not especially sharp, but after several tries, Morris managed to puncture the tire. Morris grinned at the stupidity of the gesture. He pictured Little Mack changing the tire in the parking lot.

Morris peeked over the car. No one was looking in his direction. He should move and move quickly. And then Morris had a truly inspired idea. Remembering his own experience, Morris realized that two flat tires would be so much more aggravating than one. Two flats could not be fixed with one spare. Morris ducked down behind the car, frog walking his way to the rear tire.

Morris stabbed at the second tire, and took one more peek across the rear of the car. At just that moment, the mall doors burst open and Little Mack careened into the sunlight, bumping into an elderly shopper as she was heading into the mall.

When Little Mack attempted to brush past the old lady, she grabbed him by the sleeve of his hand-tailored jacket. "Hold on there young man. Didn't your mother teach you any manners?"

Little Mack tried to pull away, mumbling something that neither of them fully understood. Rae Harbrough held fast to Little Mack's sleeve.

"I know you," she said. "Your father was that . . . that criminal . . . the one who stole my cashmere scarf."

Peeking over the car, Morris saw the panicked look plastered on Little Mack's face. Staying low to the ground, Morris worked his way back, deeper into the parking lot, away from the Town Car and its temporarily detained owner.

Little Mack said nothing to the little old lady with the sharp tongue and the iron grip.

"It's no wonder you never learned your P's and Q's." Rae Harbrough launched into a lecture on common courtesy.

"Listen, lady. I got no time for this crap." He pulled out his wallet and peeled two one-hundred dollar bills from the billfold. "Here. This makes us even." Little Mack yanked his arm free and ran for his car.

Rae Harbrough watched Little Mack flee from his lesson in manners. She shook her head in dismay. "I blame it on television."

Little Mack jumped in the driver's seat, cramming the key in the ignition, nearly out of control now, grinding the gears and slamming the car in reverse. That's when he realized the Town Car had two flat tires.

Hiding behind a step van, parked some four aisles back, Morris watched the disabled Town Car and laughed. It was just a little thing, just two flat tires, a minor aggravation really in the life of Little Mack, nothing more, but it was enough. Morris felt better. He had gotten even with Little Mack.

While Morris watched, four police cars came screaming into the parking lot, surrounding the limping Lincoln Town Car.

An Uncomfortable, Hospital-Issue Plastic Chair

The nurse let Cassie into the detective's room with a firm reminder. "Detective Bebedict lost a lot of blood."

Cassie looked at Eggs, lying in the hospital bed, scowling at the nurse, and had to chuckle. "You had us all worried."

"I'm fine," Eggs growled. He dropped his voice, embarrassed. "Thanks."

"You will be," Cassie gently chided the detective, "when you start listening to the nurse."

Cassie sat quietly in an uncomfortable, hospital-issue, plastic chair alongside the bed. This man had become important to her. She felt no need for conversation.

But Eggs wanted to talk. "I must have passed out just about the time back-up descended on the mall."

Cassie remembered the moment, watching from above, that she saw the detective go down. That was when she first realized how fond she was of him. "Loss of blood can do that to you."

Eggs growled, but softer now, nearly a purr. "My captain told me you were a big help."

"Well, I had a clear view of everything from upstairs."

"Lots of people watched from the food court, but you were the one who solved the case."

Cassie felt her face turning red. "I always accepted your theory of the crime, that this was about a deal gone bad between Big Mack and his inside guy at the mall. If you couldn't make the case against Oliver, I figured it had to be someone else who was working at the mall."

Cassie looked at Eggs and smiled. "What do I know? I thought it was Tommy V."

"Yeah, the captain told me. You figured there were no prints on the knife because the killer was wearing gloves. And then Morris remembered seeing the kid at Louie's. So it made sense. And in a way, you had it right.

Santa was the inside guy at the mall, passing stolen property to the Macks. But he wasn't the killer."

Eggs struggled to complete the couple of sentences. Cassie could tell that he was getting tired. "Get some rest. We can talk more later on."

Eggs smiled, too weak to growl. "I'm okay. I wanna hear this."

"Are you sure?"

"I'm sure."

Cassie thought back to the scene in the mall. "When Greta showed up claiming to be the killer, I was stunned. Why would she want to kill either Big Mack or Louie? Besides, I was pretty sure, we'd find out that she was waiting tables at the Eggery when the murders happened. It didn't make any sense."

Cassie continued. "Why would the woman lie about the murders? Certainly not to protect her ex-husband. You know, watching from above, the aerial view, I had the sense that I was watching a family drama unfolding below me. That's when it became obvious. Why would a woman confess to a crime she didn't commit? Who would a mother protect, even at the cost of her own life?"

Eggs mumbled, "Her son."

Cassie saw pain in the detective's eyes. She wondered if he was due for more meds. "Do you want me to continue?"

Eggs nodded, weakly.

"Tommy V. was the inside guy passing stuff to Big Mack. But neither of them worked alone. Big and Little Mack were a team. So were Tommy and Tommy Junior."

Cassie continued. "Suddenly it all made sense. Greta and her son got into a big argument that morning at the restaurant. I assumed it was about the busboy job. Greta told me more than once that she was worried about her son, worried that he was capable of making a really big mistake. I don't think she understood yet how bad things were. Tommy V. was just a small-time crook, too lazy for anything other than small-time cons. But Tommy Junior was a growing boy. He had bigger appetites."

She looked down at Eggs, asleep in the hospital bed. "Merry Christmas, Detective."

One eye opened. "My friends call me Eggs."

One Last Thing

Cassie kicked off her shoes, poured herself a Tullamore Dew, and prepared to write her story. She checked her phone machine for messages.

"Hi Cassie. It's Chey. I got a call from my mother. She said there was a shoot-out at the mall. She told me how she apprehended Little Mack when he attempted to make his getaway. And get this, Cassie. She said, and I quote here, she said, 'Oh and your friend Cassie, she may have had a bit part in this as well.' And then she said, 'Be careful, dear. Cassie seems to have fallen in with a bad crowd.' How great is that? Moms. Anyway, I'm proud of you. And one last thing. Merry Christmas."

Cassie freshened her drink and raised her glass. "Merry Christmas."

About the Author

Jeff Markowitz is the author of the Cassie O'Malley Mysteries, humorous mysteries set deep in the New Jersey Pine Barrens. Jeff holds a Bachelor's degree in psychology from Princeton University and graduate degrees in special education and human services. For more than thirty years, Jeff has developed services that enhance quality of life. Recently he discovered that he also has something of a flair for killing people.

Jeff is an active member of the Mystery Writers of America. He loves to write early in the morning. "You can usually find me at my computer at 5:30 in the morning," he says, "plotting someone's murder."

Jeff's previous books include *Who is Killing Doah's Deer?* and *A Minor Case of Murder*.

Curious about other Crossroad Press books?
Stop by our site:
http://store.crossroadpress.com
We offer quality writing
in digital, audio, and print formats.

Enter the code FIRSTBOOK
to get 20% off your first order from our store!
Stop by today!

www.ingramcontent.com/pod-product-compliance
Lightning Source LLC
Chambersburg PA
CBHW060434180626

46817CB00007B/2803